# DREAM TREKKER

D1601523

# DREAM TREKKER

## Jacob Janey

ISBN - 9798531155689
Cover design by: Don Allen
Printed in the United States of America

*For Thomas*

*And now these three remain: faith, hope and love.*
*But the greatest of these is love.*
*1 Corinthians 13:13*

# ⊃ 1 ⊂

Ab eyed her sleeping tormentor. The plump, balding old woman before her wasn't anything she could have imagined. The astral creature Ab had been battling for the last decade was a sleek, slender dynamo, but the physical body her spirt inhabited was anything but. Sickly and frail, the dream trekker lay before her vulnerable and weak. Ab paused to reflect on past clashes with her nemesis.

A seasoned and deadly adversary, Lily Lassiter, had been a thorn in Ab's side since she was old enough to daydream. Older and more experienced, Lily loved to terrorize the young Abigail's slumber. Ab had been a lucid dreamer all her life, but like most astral travelers, she started as a young novice with no guidance. A perfect mark for a sadistic astral predator.

But Abigail was resilient. Enduring those painful years and dodging numerous heartless nightmares, Ab's ability grew until she was an even match for the older trekker. The school of hard knocks had honed Ab's skills, but hadn't tarnished her attitude. Before long, the two women were locked in an epic struggle. But now, looking down on the enemy she had once feared then pursued for so long left her unmoved. Instead of satisfaction, she felt only pity.

Having misdirected Lily's astral person and located her physical form, Ab knew she could do anything she wanted to even the score. She could repeat the maneuver at will. Anytime, anywhere. Lily was at her mercy. A moment of vengeance swept past Abigail as she grappled with her anger.

What good would revenge serve? It would make her just as petty and evil as the bully that slept before her. Holding to the moral high ground, Ab produced a small black dreamcatcher from her pocket, her signature calling card. Normally she would place the memento nearby so when an enemy awoke, they would know she had visited, but now she held the talisman above Lily's face then dropped it forcefully.

As it slipped from her fingers, the dreamcatcher's black feathers began to spin in the air as it materialized into physical form. It was a skill only a master dream trekker could perform. The talisman bounced off Lily's nose and lips, coming to rest on her throat. The motion instantly heaved the woman back from the astral plane. As her spirit hurtled back into her body, her eyes shot open in alarm as she took in the gravity of the situation. Fully aware and cognizant of her vulnerability, the chase was over, it was her final warning. Ab lingered a spectral moment to witness the comprehension and fear blotch Lily's aged face, then turned, and vaporized into the astral wind.

Calle set the hardcover down and her thoughts turned inward. It was uncanny how informative the animé creation was. Every time Calle read another Ab Pistola tale, she learned something about herself. The fictional heroine possessed so many of the same abilities as she did. For the umpteenth time, she wondered if the character was based on a real person. If so, could she locate the person? Would it be a good idea?

Afterall, Ab was a master in all things astral, while Calle was just a novice. Where Ab would skim with easy confidence from one situation to the next, Calle would bumble and stumble around, rarely getting to where she intended to go. Ab was the essence of control, conversely, Calle's dreams were haphazard shots in the dark. Would the physical person attached to the powerful Ab Pistola be tolerant of an upstart like Calle Roslyn? Or would she crush her underfoot like roadkill on the freeway?

Ethan warned Calle about drawing undue attention to herself on the astral plane. Discretion seemed like the best course. Better to observe than to be observed.

Calle came across the legend of Ab Pistola by chance. She had been working as a substitute teacher at the high school when one of her students showed her a comic version of the famous heroine. Calle felt an immediate kinship with the character and she'd been fascinated by her ever since.

It had been part of a tumultuous few days that became a turning point in Calle's life. During her tenure as a substitute, Calle rejoined the living. She had become a recluse after the loss of her husband. The accident was so horrific, it left Calle emotionally scarred and battling PTSD. With the encouragement of her devoted friend Lucy, she took the job just hoping to get her life back on track. Little did she know that with that little push, her life would not only get back on track, it would almost fly off the rails.

Calle shuffled from the couch to fetch a refill of her

coffee. As she mixed a drip of cream into her cup, her cat sidled lovingly between her ankles. His radar must have alerted him to one of his favorite treats and he wasted no time letting her know he deserved a few drops of cream himself.

"Morning Beeler. Couldn't resist the temptation?" Calle smiled into his sapphire eyes. Her invitation was met with cheery meowl and a flick of his black tail. His kitty motor revved up a few rpm's as she set the saucer on the floor in front of him.

"How do you do that?", Calle asked as he continued to purr and drink at the same time. "Even circus magicians have to breathe when they drink."

If Beely heard her, he wasn't listening. He just continued his magic trick as she moved from the kitchen and out to the back patio.

Her back yard was her oasis, her Shangri La. It was a serene garden, beautifully animated with natural drama. Not that she spent much time cultivating the space, rather she just kept the soil moist and let the warm New Mexico sunshine do the rest.

She slipped into her favorite lawn recliner and let her mind wander. It had been quite a while since she talked to Ethan. When they met several months ago, he had become a mainstay in her dreams, but now his visits were few and far in between. It was troubling because she didn't know how to find him. She wondered if something was wrong. Maybe she said or did something of which she was unaware. It would be nice to ring him up on the phone or maybe drop by his house for a social call, but it wasn't that easy.

Ethan was an astral entity. He lived inside Calle's head. Well, in her dreams actually. Cell phones don't get decent service there.

She was a lucid dreamer and recently her dreams had moved out of body. That meant she could astrally project her spirit from her physical self and roam the universe at will. That was where she met Ethan, in a dream.

It all sounds very exciting, but in reality, it is extremely difficult to control one's dreams. In fact, for Calle, there's no telling what would happen or where she'd end up. On the other hand, Ethan was a practiced and efficient dream trekker. He was her teacher in all things astral. He was also her friend and lover, so his lengthy absence had her worried and confused.

One thing that gave her comfort was the fact that Barrow was still stopping by her garden every day. Barrow was a magnificent Steller's blue jay. He was unusual in the fact that he had a symbiotic relationship with Ethan. They could share experiences. It was a magic Calle didn't understand, but had grown accustom to.

She often thought of Barrow as Ethan's spy. It was true, he was, but in a good way. He had proven his friendship and his loyalty was much appreciated. Calle was hoping to see him this morning, but so far, he was a no-show just like his astral cohort.

Calle watched as a wolf spider inched his way along the edge of a nearby planter. He stealthily maneuvered off the flower pot and into the shadow of a stand of purple iris. Satisfied with his strategic position, he turned his multifaceted gaze toward Calle as he waited in ambush for an unsuspecting meal to wander along.

Her curious observation was interrupted when her cell phone began to chirp. For a split second, she hoped the astral world had just activated a new cell tower, but it was not to be. Instead, the caller ID revealed that the call was from her best friend.

"Hey Luce, what's up?"

"Just had some down time here at my Tio's, thought I'd check in," Lucy replied.

"Good, what's going on at the gallery?"

"Sam is on her way to meet my uncle. They're planning a showing or something, I'm just here to formally introduce them."

"Sounds like an excuse for romance," Calle teased. "You've got to tell me how they hit it off."

"I think so too, I'll let you know how it goes. Sam is really excited. I guess waiting all this time for my uncle to come back from Mexico has piqued her interest."

"Well, it's been, what? A month?"

"A little over six weeks."

"That's a long time for a woman's imagination to simmer."

"I know, but I think my uncle is nervous too. He keeps changing clothes and won't sit still."

"That's a good sign. Now they're even. They're a perfect match, keep an eye on them, they'll need a chaperone." Calle joked.

"I will, uh oh, I think she's here. Gotta go."

Samantha Cloaker was an older, new friend Calle and Lucy had made during Calle's short tenure as a sub a few weeks prior. She was an accomplished artist and a self-described Wiccan. Lucy was sure she was a witch, but it didn't really matter because the women had formed a strong friendship and shared a mutual high regard for one another.

Elias Lucero was Lucy's uncle and a respected

gallery owner in downtown Santa Fe. Lucy had facilitated their meeting a few weeks before, but it was delayed due to Elias' trip to Mexico. Despite not ever meeting face to face, the two had developed a healthy relationship over the phone. Their rendezvous was long overdue and everyone who knew about it was racked with anticipation.

Calle usually didn't care for gossip. It could be malicious, but sometimes the news was too juicy to keep to herself. Chiding herself as she scrolled through her contact list, Calle dialed up the remaining member of their circle of friends.

"Hey Fiona, what are you up to?"

"Pretty busy this morning. I've got freshman initiation at Tech next week," Fiona replied. "What's going on?"

"Just seeing what you were doing," Calle fudged. "Did you hear about Samantha and Elias?"

"Yeah, Samantha said she was going to finally lay eyes on the man today, her words, not mine."

"Yep, Lucy just called to tell me she had just arrived. Looks like love is in the air," Calle joked.

"I know Samantha is downplaying it all, trying to act like it's all business, but I can tell she's psyched."

"I can too. Hey, do you need any help getting ready for college? Is there anything I can do?"

"Not really, my parents are all over it. Besides, I'm only going one hundred fifty miles down the interstate. It's not like I'm going to an Ivy League school across the country."

"I know it's selfish, but I'm glad you chose to stay in New Mexico," Calle said.

"Thanks, I'm kinda glad too, but hey, I need to meet

my dad in a few minutes, so I have to go."

"Right on, I'll talk to you later. Oh, you know Samantha is throwing a birthday party for you, right?"

"That's the plan. I'm looking forward to it. You going?"

"Wouldn't miss it for the world."

As Calle rang off, she thought about her friend. Fiona had just graduated high school at the top of her class. She was as close to a mathematical genius as Calle could imagine. Her SAT scores were off the charts and though she was accepted by a number of universities back east, New Mexico Tech offered her a full scholarship. NM Tech, though small, was on par with schools like Stanford and MIT, but the real reason Fiona choose the school was because it was her father's alma mater.

Calle and Fiona had formed an unusual and unexpected bond a few weeks ago. Fiona was a student in a class that Calle had substitute taught. Their kindred attraction led them to a deeper friendship. It was through Fiona that Calle and Lucy met Samantha. Though they differed in age and inclination, the four women hit it off splendidly and had become a tight knit group. Together they made an unlikely clique of scholar, dreamer, mystic, and streetwise beauty.

# ☽ 2 ☾

Tendrils of a misty breeze filtered through the slightly open window. Early morning freshness caressed Calle's bare foot as it protruded from under her grandmother's handstitched quilt. The sensation sent a tingle of gratitude up her leg and into her sleepy spirit as she pulled her limb back into the warmth of her cocoon. It was the small blessings in life that make it all worthwhile. That was the last thought she had before she fell back asleep.

The dream snuck up on her like a playful lover longing for more. It was ticklish as it toyed with her imagination. She played along peek-a-booing like one does with a baby. She loved the innocence dreams could recreate, but as an experienced dream trekker, Calle could only linger there a short while before she took control.

Her instinct was to fly. That's where she felt most comfortable. She effortlessly began to soar over the spectral landscape in search of her mentor.

Ethan had been on her mind a lot lately. He told her that he would be easy to find, but she knew he could shield himself from uninvited astral visitors. He had done it before, but Calle was sure if she kept trying, she would be able to locate him.

She opened her mind to everything and nothing,

all at the same time. The key was to keep her desire smoldering in the background while her mind wandered the universe. Eventually, the two would cross paths. It was a skill that required exceptional mental focus. She had been working on it, but hadn't quite achieved mastery. If done properly, it could lead her to wherever she wanted to go. More often though, it led her to places she didn't expect.

A whimper touched her ear. Then another. Calle's concentration faltered as the vast expanse of the universe collapsed into a moment.

She eased herself down a narrow hallway. It was cluttered with worn children's shoes and unwashed laundry. Calle followed the barely audible weeping of a child. One that didn't want to be found. How she knew this, she couldn't explain, but that didn't stop her from recognizing the truth.

When she entered the small bedroom, a feeble light shone from under the tattered twin mattress atop a makeshift frame of milkcrates and pressboard.

"Hello," she ventured in her most assuring voice. The light went out.

Even in the dark, Calle could see everything. The scattered clothing, the stained paper cups, the dinosaur poster askew above the bed, it was all plain to her. She was a lucid dreamer, she could control her dreams, but she soon realized she was visiting the child's dream. They were in it together.

It was a touchy subject for Calle. Her ethics pushed against her compassion. Dreams were personal, a private exposure of one's true self. Her special abilities sometimes put her in a precarious position. She didn't want to intrude on another's dream, but the fear that radiated from under the bed was more than she could stomach.

She pulled back the blanket that had been draped over the edge of the bed. She knelt down on the floor to look into the desperate hiding place.

Her gaze met the petrified eyes of a little boy. His face was wrought with fear. Tiny hands dropped the flashlight as he put his arms up to protect himself. Calle's heart melted.

"It's okay honey, I won't hurt you," she cooed. He squashed himself further into the corner under the bed. "I can help you," she consoled.

He lowered his hands to look directly in her face. His tension eased a bit as he pondered the situation. Calle could tell she was the last thing he expected to come under the bed with him. He clicked the flashlight back on and she could see his dirty features. It was the face of neglect and abuse. She reached out her hand to reassure the child when a drunken roar exploded from the doorway.

"Spencer, come out of there right now!" an angry male voice demanded. "You didn't do your chores again." The statement was followed by a sarcastic snigger. "You're in for it now, get out here this minute!"

Spencer grabbed Calle by the shoulder and pulled her close, "It's my uncle."

She could smell the child's body odor perfumed by a hint of urine. The boy began to tremble with dread. His terror pushed Calle past her limit.

With the dexterity of a whim, Calle materialized directly in front of the drunken bully standing behind her. Her disgust was palpable as her anger erupted. With nary a thought, she confronted the filthy creature in the doorway.

"Leave the child alone," she threatened.

The unkempt and surprised man laughed, "What are you going to do about it? You're just a silly girl."

He drew his hand back to slap her out of the way, but before he could deliver the blow, Calle transformed into a miniature Tyrannosaurus Rex. His eyes bulged as he froze in terror.

Calle moved within inches of his face and before he could react, she nipped off the end of his nose.

Spencer's uncle screamed as Calle chased him down the hall. She pursued him only for a short distance before he dissolved into nothing. His disappearance left Calle standing back in the bedroom. As Spencer spied from the shadows beneath the bed, Calle returned to her normal shape.

"Is he gone?"

When he realized he was safe, the child flung back the blanket and emerged. "You did it, you're my hero!" Spencer wailed as he engulfed her in a bearhug. The relief washing over him in a flood of tears broke Calle's heart.

"I will always be here for you," she promised. "If he ever comes back, be brave and think of me. You don't have to be frightened of him anymore."

"I will, thank you Dinosaur Lady," he said as he climbed onto his bed and closed his eyes.

Calle kissed the dimple on his dirty, smiling cheek as she slipped from his nightmare.

Her mind cantered as she returned to flight. Her original purpose side-tracked; all she could think about was how she changed Spencer's dream. She had never done anything like that before. She sailed aimlessly through the ether, lost in thought until her dream trek faded back over the threshold into consciousness. She awoke with a powerful feeling of self-righteous accomplishment.

Before Calle could dry her freshly shampooed hair, a familiar 'Jing Jing' beckoned from the bedroom. She hurried to find her cell phone as she mentally prepared to talk to her new boss.

Alby Montoya owned Kokopelli Catering. A seasoned restauranter and an accomplished chef, Alby abandoned his position at an upscale Los Angeles eatery to return to his home town and start his own business. His fledgling catering company was off to a shaky start due to, in his words, 'the sorry work ethic of the locals'. Part of the problem wasn't so much the workers as it was the inconsistent number of catering gigs he could procure. Consequently, the best workers gravitated to steadier jobs.

That's why he liked Calle so much. She was reliable and professional. In the past six weeks, he had come to count on her to manage most of his business while he moonlighted for big bucks in Denver. Calle didn't mind, but for her, the job was only temporary. She didn't want fulltime employment.

Muttering to herself about the early hour, she located the phone, but to her surprise it wasn't Alby. It was the call she had been dreading, it was her boyfriend.

"Morning Matthew."

"Good morning, Sunshine," he replied. His voice way too perky. Calle took it as a bad omen. "Just wanted to call and let you know I'm leaving this morning."

"So, you're off to Montana with your dad?" Calle played along, finger combing a tangle from her hair.

"Yeah, we're going to Kalispell for two weeks."

"Then, you're off to the Air Force," Calle finished. No sense beating around the bush.

"Yep, I'll miss you."

"I'll miss you too, be safe," she added dryly.

"Calle?" An awkward silence hovered.

"Have fun Matthew, but I gotta go, I'm late for work," she interjected quickly, bringing the conversation to an abrupt end.

"Okay, bye."

"Bye."

Calle knew this moment was coming, but she didn't realize how heavy it would be once it actually arrived. He had been completely honest when he told her of his plans a couple months ago, but she didn't want to live a military lifestyle. She had accepted the fact that their relationship was destined for the friend zone, but instead of distancing herself from him, they had become intimate. He was planning their future, while she was trying to find an easy way out.

Matthew was a good man and fun to be around, but Calle liked where her life was now and could not commit to a marriage to the military. Not to mention the fact she was in love with another man in her dreams.

She hadn't come to a conclusion as to the morality of the situation or had she any source of guidance on the subject. It was as Lucy had described. *In a league all by itself.* So, she was winging it, following her heart, trying not to hurt anyone or get hurt. Little did she realize how complicated her life would become sleeping in bed with one man while having sex in her dreams with another. Ethan didn't care, but Matthew would never understand. Maybe she was being a little selfish, but why did love have to be so damn confusing?

Kokopelli Catering was tucked underneath what was once Safeway Grocery in downtown Santa Fe, New Mexico. There's no telling how many businesses had come and gone at the ancient location, but the retrofitted loading dock was now a fledgling catering company.

When in use, the aromas that wafted from the utilitarian facade onto the narrow street below confused and tantalized passersby. It was those scrumptious odors that greeted Calle as she hopped out of her truck in front of the two large garage doors atop the raised loading platform.

Alby was perched on the dock finishing off a taco and fiddling with his phone as the early morning sunshine began to creep up the walkway.

"There's been a change of plans," he said as he pocketed his phone.

"Well, good morning to you too," Calle smiled.

"Sorry, good morning, I was just texting Teresa," he continued. "I've got to go to Denver, so you'll have to meet with the Pérez family."

Alby grew up working at his grandmother's café and when she retired and closed her business, he took her menu and his ambition to the big city. By adjusting the old traditional New Mexican recipes, he presented something uniquely delicious to the upper echelon of society. Before long, he had climbed to the top of his profession and had become the darling chef in town.

After a few years in the spotlight, he began to long for home. Santa Fe had grown into a must-see bucket list item with the rich and with its thriving art scene and genuine old-world charm, the tourism business was booming. Alby was convinced he could do well on his own back in his hometown.

His business model was simple, cater to the wealthy. It was a good plan and he had a knack for dealing with sophisticated clientele. But he had underestimated the number of wealthy people that actually lived in Santa Fe. Many owned expensive homes there, but few stayed there year around. Without a steady stream of rich patrons, his business was spotty. When it was going, it was fantastic, but when it lulled, it was dead in the water.

Consequently, Alby had to moonlight around the country to supplement his income and drum up business. That in itself had become a fulltime job. Enter Calle Roslyn.

"You're going to have to meet with her," Alby said. The pavilion is all set up and I've spoken with her about the arrangements. I told her you could handle the catering and that I would be in constant contact with you."

"She was alright with that?"

"She said she trusts my judgement."

"Okay, so I'm meeting with Teresa?"

"Yeah, Teresa Pérez. She's running the Sister Cities International convention. She's a sweetheart, you'll love working with her," Alby assured. "All you have to do today is to meet with her, familiarize yourself with the layout, and get the schedule for the month. We'll have to take it one day at a time, but I'll be back in a few days. It'll be a piece of cake for you."

Calle hadn't planned to assume so much responsibility at Kokopelli, but Alby had charmed and coaxed her in to the position. She had originally started as a part time waitron, but on that first day when her coworkers didn't show and she ran the entire event by herself, Alby knew he couldn't do without her. Ever since, he had been relying on her more and more. But today, giving her full charge of such a big event with such a valuable client was a surprise to say the least.

The gig, which turned out to be a month-long series of minor events culminating with a major art exhibition, was to be held at the posh Pérez Hacienda. It was located past the end of upper Canyon Road, the Two-Mile Reservoir, and the Audubon Society. Bordering the National Forest, the hacienda predated them all. The Pérez family was directly descended from Spanish settlers and was a recipient of an original Royal Spanish land grant.

Following the inheritance protocol of European aristocracy, the property was willed only to one member of the family thus keeping it intact over the last few hundred years. Over the decades, while other families divvied their land into smaller and smaller tracts to each heir and each inheritance diminished by every generation, the Pérez property remained whole. Consequently, those families' legacies evaporated into history as the Pérez family's influence continued to endure.

Armed with the access code for the large bronzed security gate, Calle idled onto the Pérez property for the first time. The two lane, paved driveway wound thoughtfully through a beautifully manicured lawn and under an expansive cottonwood and aspen canopy. It ended in a circular parking area in front of the main house. The mansion, built in traditional New Mexico style, was the size of a small hotel.

She was met by a smartly dressed valet who directed her to a side alley that led to employee parking located behind the central building. Walking across the parking lot to the employee entrance, Calle marveled at the opulence of the place. It reminded her of the time she attended a fancy dinner at the governor's mansion back in Ohio. She had no idea such a place existed in Santa Fe.

As she stepped on to the portico, an attractive middle-aged Hispanic woman pulled up in a side-by-side all-terrain work vehicle. As Calle paused to let another worker pushing a dolly stacked with cases of wine come through the door, the woman sidled up behind her to wait alongside. When Calle entered the building and found herself at a loss as to where to go, she paused to get her bearings.

"Can I help you?"

Calle turned to face the woman who had followed her in. "Yes, you can, thank you. I'm looking for Teresa Pérez. Can you tell me where she might be?"

"You're in luck," the woman smiled. "I know right where she is. Follow me."

"Oh great, thank you," Calle said as she fell in step with the woman as they veered through another side door. "Beautiful place," she added.

"It sure is, I just love it here."

"Have you worked here long?"

"Sometimes it seems like forever," the woman lamented with cheerful sarcastic fatigue as they entered an office area.

As they passed a desk laden with papers, a younger woman, clad in flannel, holding a clipboard said, "Your mother is waiting for you in the foyer."

"Thanks, I know," Calle's guide answered as they entered the closed office door. "I'm guessing you're the caterer," she asserted over her shoulder as she grabbed a folder from atop a file cabinet.

"Well, yes I am."

"You are exactly as Alby described you," the woman smiled. "I'm Teresa Pérez, welcome to my home."

"Thank you." Taken aback, Calle added, "I'm Calle."

"Sorry for not introducing myself right away, but sometimes by being anonymous, I can get a better read on people."

"No problem," Calle replied, masking her suspicion.

"Okay, splendid," Teresa said as she picked up a neatly wrapped package with a bright pink bow on top. "Let's go meet my mother."

The pair shuffled through the inner workings of the mansion toward the foyer. Passing the kitchen, laundry, and an extensive pantry Teresa jostled their way amidst a throng of workers. The Pérez Hacienda was a large, busy operation.

"We are a registered national landmark and we host several events annually. We also entertain numerous foreign dignitaries on a regular basis. There aren't many venues in the Southwest that can do what we do," Teresa informed as she purposely strode forth.

"And you live here too?"

"Yes, as the proprietor of the estate, I live on the property as does my mother and son, Michael. It's part of my heritage. There's been a Pérez living on this land for over three hundred years."

"Wow, that is a long time," Calle said, hustling to keep pace.

"It sure is. Sometimes it's a bit much, but I try to stay on top of it," she said as they sidetracked through an open patio area. "Excuse me for a moment."

They stopped by a maid's service cart parked at the entrance of one of the bungalow suites and Teresa went to the door calling in Spanish to someone inside.

A short, rotund, middle aged Latino woman wearing a maid's uniform met her at the door. Teresa gave her a hug and presented the woman with the gift she had carried from her office. The two exchanged a short dialogue, then parted, both wearing smiles.

Teresa returned to Calle and said, "Sorry about that. It's Lucinda's birthday and I didn't know if I'd see her again before she left for the day."

"That's okay," Calle replied, marveling at the complexity of her client. She was smooth, Calle had to give her that, but she was tricky.

"Shall we?" Teresa suggested as she gestured up a flagstone path that led back to the main house.

# ☉ 3 ☾

Calle followed Teresa to the main foyer like a tourist on vacation. Teresa informed her that the family no longer resided in the mansion, but in a smaller home hidden away from the public. The mansion was now used as a museum of sorts and in much the way many modern resorts function. High end tourists, business fetes, and special interest groups were typical patrons of the facility nowadays.

On the way, they walked down a long corridor lined with family portraits and past rooms maintained in period decor. The family tree was displayed horizontally and chronologically along the wall, so each step down the hall took the viewer a generation forward in time. Occasionally, Teresa would stop in front of a portrait to point out the person's significance in the family's history. There were several very powerful figures along the way including her father, Ignacio and one of Emilia Pérez, the wife of Ernesto, the original land grant recipient. The image of the staid old woman, the oldest painting in the collection, dated from the early 1700's.

Calle had never seen such a lengthy private linage arranged in such detail before. At least a hundred Pérez family members' portraits were framed and on display. It was the smaller pictures of the less important members that caught Calle's attention, many who had died premature deaths or whose lives were cut short. It seemed every generation endured some human tragedy or another. Teresa pointed out that she was no exception and showed Calle a picture of her late sister who had died when she was in her youth. Calle found it touching that those who led less significant lives were honored alongside the most influential.

Stepping into the main reception area from the service side of things was impressive. But most of the splendor was obscured by the hustle and bustle of busy employees tending to the needs of the clientele. Calle could just imagine how spectacular it would be for first time visitors entering from the grand main entrance.

Teresa maneuvered through the crowd like Moses parting the Red Sea. Calle followed her past the front desk and the concierge, into a large alcove where an older woman sat alone reading the newspaper. The woman leered over rim of her glasses and the top of the page as the women approached.

"Good morning mother," Teresa said cordially. "This is Calle, she's going to be managing the catering for the Sister Cities convention."

Calle smiled at the ancient woman whose facial features were sculpted into a perpetual scowl.

"Calle, this is my mother, Gloria."

"It's nice to meet you," Calle smiled.

The woman's lipstick crinkled as she nodded her head slightly and raised one eye brow then set the paper on a nearby table. Teresa's mother was as thin as a stick figure whose head had grown too large for her body. Maybe her body had grown too small for her head, whatever the case, it sat perilously at an angle atop her bent spine.

Where Teresa was pleasant and engaging, her mother was the complete opposite. Dressed in a flowery summer dress made for a younger woman and shoes too large for her feet, Gloria's fashion statement was as garish as her attitude. Calle stepped back when Teresa helped her mother stand. Once upright, Gloria seemed rather spry as they began to walk toward the exit.

"I thought we were going to breakfast," Gloria snapped, her sharp voice not matching her age.

"We are, but I have to get Calle situated first. Have you seen Otis?" Teresa asked.

The old woman sighed in exasperation then spun to a stop. With unmasked condescension, she scanned the room, then with a gnarled finger, pointed in the direction from which they had come. Teresa looked over the crowd to man approaching at a brisk pace.

"Good morning," he hailed as he joined the conversation and as Teresa's mother wandered out the front door.

"Otis, this is Calle. She'll be in charge of the catering in the pavilion."

"Oh, good," Otis smiled as he removed his ball cap and extended his hand. His dark brown eyes gleamed past tanned, weathered cheeks from under his balding cranium. He was thin, but his strong calloused handshake told Calle he was a man who had worked hard all his life.

She returned his greeting then Teresa began to speak again.

"Otis, please take Calle out back and show her around. I've got to take my mother into town, but I'll be back later." Handing Calle her business card, Teresa continued, "Feel free to contact me anytime about anything. We'll talk later about the agenda and the details of the upcoming events."

"Super, sounds like a plan."

"You're in good hands," Teresa assured as she shuffled after her mother then added over her shoulder, "Otis knows as much about this place as I do."

Otis led Calle back through the building to the employee entrance. He was less talkative than Teresa, but much more down to earth. Calle felt at ease as he described his role as the head of maintenance at the mansion.

As they boarded the side-by-side ATV Teresa had arrived on, Calle asked, "So, how long have you been working here?"

"Oh, it's been at least thirty years now, I guess. Give or take."

"I bet you've seen some changes in your day," Calle joked.

"Sure have, I remember when this property was considered out of town," Otis said. "If it weren't for the Audubon Society and the National Forest, we'd probably be surrounded by houses now," he continued.

"It must have been wonderful then,"

"It was, it truly was," Otis replied whimsically as he momentarily took a mental side trip down memory lane. Calle sensed there was more to his statement than just his appreciation of the once pristine nature of the area.

Calle wondered if she would experience stirring moments like those when she got older. She hoped so.

"I need to stop by my cabin for a minute before we go

24

to the pavilion, would you mind?"

"No not at all. The other members of my crew won't be arriving for another couple hours anyway."

Motoring along the cart path, Calle was impressed with the expanse of the estate. There were bungalows tucked in and around the greenery and a few guests sunning themselves beside the swimming pool. Several of the maintenance crew were busy trimming or watering plants around the pavilion, which stood like a large canvas spaceship in the center of the lawn. Calle and Otis zipped right on by into a thickly forested part of the property, off the pavement, and up a pine needled dirt road.

Otis' cabin was situated like a cracker box wedged between three enormous ponderosa pine trees. Its angled staircase led to a lengthy boardwalk that wrapped around the house like the slats on the deck of a sailing ship. It was just large enough to be small. It had to be; it was twenty feet off the ground.

Calle stood in the doorway of the tree house and surveyed its contents. You can tell a lot about a person by the way they live. When Otis disappeared behind a maze of boxes and his call for her to join him in the kitchen echoed like a whisper in a cavern, she knew he was a hoarder.

Slowly she crept along the labyrinth of stuff. There was everything from old magazines and outdated repair manuals to predigital electronics. Various clothing items that hung in neat rows faced off with dusty hats, fishing rods, and guitar cases stacked atop a huge Marshall amplifier. And in the unlikely case of an unexpected intruder, whimsical knick-knack figurines and X-men action figures were stationed around the room like sentinels poised for ambush.

Gingerly, Calle stepped into the kitchen, which was surprisingly neat, open, and spacious. Apparently, Otis kept this room functional for the purpose it was intended.

"Coffee?" he smiled as he inserted a k-cup into his fancy Keurig brewing machine.

"Sure," Calle responded in awe of his lifestyle.

"Have a seat," he gestured to the kitchen table.

From the open window, they had a spectacular view of a meadow that stretched behind the tree house. The sun was filtering through the pines and onto the grass like a photoshopped postcard. Chipmunks foraged through pinecones on the forest floor while the cool mountain breeze carried the chatter of several quarreling nuthatches to their ears. It wouldn't have been a surprise to see Snow White or at least a dwarf or two to saunter on by.

"Beautiful place you have here."

"Yeah, I wouldn't want to live anywhere else."

Otis settled into a chair across the table from Calle and the two began to talk about the catering job. It was all pretty straight forward and soon the conversation moved lightly into more personal territory.

He told her he hadn't always lived in the tree house and that he started as a gardener many years ago. As a young man, he had been hired by Teresa's father and worked for him until he died. Then he continued working for his wife, Gloria until she retired, and now, Teresa was his boss.

"At first it was hard to work for Teresa," Otis explained. "We sort of grew up together. We were friends first," he said as his attention turned inward for just a second.

Calle sensed a tinge of regret in his demeanor and interjected, "But I bet it couldn't have been worse than working for her mother."

"Gloria? Yeah, she's tough, but she wasn't always so sour," Otis laughed. "Don't worry about her. Her bark is worse than her bite."

"I don't think she likes me."

"No biggie, she doesn't like anyone anymore," Otis joked.

"Okay, good to know," Calle said as she absentmindedly fiddled with an opened Ancestry.com envelope laying on the table.

"Did you sign up for DNA testing?" she asked, changing the topic.

"That? Yeah, I did. I didn't learn anything I didn't already know though. I got it for a Christmas present, so I signed up."

"Cool, I've thought about it, but I never did anything about it."

"They say you can find long lost relatives and learn about your heritage. That's true and I did, but it wasn't anything spectacular. They keep sending me emails with updates and hints about my family tree, but I ignore them. I don't need to see another picture of my grandfather's name on a census sheet or another relative's name on a ship manifest. I've seen enough. I don't think anything miraculous will come from it."

"It's expensive too, isn't it?"

"I don't really know, mine was a gift and I haven't been back on their site in a quite a while, so they sent me this," he said, gesturing to the letter.

"Right on."

"If you're interested, here's a gift card they sent me," he said as he pulled the card from the Ancestry envelope. "If you use this code, you can sign up for free. You can have it if you want."

"Really?'

"Yeah, I don't need it. I know who all my relatives are," Otis smiled as he stood and placed his cup in the sink."

"Alright, thank you."

"No problem. Well, are you ready to check out the property?"

"Sure, let's go," Calle answered as she placed the gift card in her back pocket and followed Otis back outside.

"Well, you've seen the pavilion, so I'll give you a quick tour of the rest of the place," Otis said as he gunned the engine launching the ATV up the path under the trees.

As they passed a small apple orchard, Otis said, "Some of those trees are over a hundred years old. I don't think they grow any better apples, but they sure look scary at night."

Calle smiled at his joke as she scanned the ancient trees. As bent and snarled as they were, Calle guessed he was probably right.

They continued along briskly for a minute then Otis eased back on the throttle as they approached the stables. He leaned into a sharp turn up a narrow rocky path and said, "Hang on, it's going to get rough for a while."

As the gravel spit under the tires, a lanky stable hand leading a saddled black horse waved to them and Otis returned the gesture. They jolted and bumped uphill for several hundred yards before the trail opened into a small dirt lot enclosed by a riot of tall lilacs in full bloom.

"There you go," Otis grinned. "We're on foot from here."

Calle hopped out of the vehicle and joined Otis as they began hiking along a level path. The trail paralleled the lilacs for a several yards before it split away up a rocky incline. It was patrolled by a legion of honey bees.

"How big is the estate anyway?" she asked as she swatted her way through the industrious insects.

"That's a great way to get stung," Otis laughed. "Just relax, they will ignore you. If you flail at them, they will protect themselves. Be calm and they will be too."

Calle nervously heeded his advice and the bees went back to work on the lilacs.

"This part of the Hacienda is two hundred sixty-seven acres, but there's another eight hundred acres up in the forest," Otis said, returning to her question.

"I had no idea it was so large," Calle said as she checked to make sure no bees were following them up the trail. Amused by her paranoia, Otis grinned at her and continued speaking.

"Yeah, that's why the stables are out here. If you take any of these trails off this main one, you will go to the upper property. We use them for horseback rides. There's a cabin up there too."

"Wow, how cool," Calle said as she began to relax again.

"We don't have time for that today, but maybe sometime I'll take you up there. Do you ride?"

"Sort of, but not all that well."

"No problem, we've got some really even-tempered

horses. You'd be okay."

"Alright then, let's see how it goes. Where are we going now?"

"There's a natural spring up here and the family cemetery," he said as they walked under arched scrub oak trees that covered the path like an arbored cathedral ceiling.

"This place is amazing," Calle marveled.

"It is. Teresa thought you should see some of the highlights of the property so you would have a real reference point as you schmooze the guests."

"Ah, I wondered why I was getting the VIP tour."

"Yeah, there's nothing like a genuine description from someone who's actually been there and seen the place. Word of mouth is the best advertising with these people."

"Well, I'll have nothing but good things to say to them, that's for sure," Calle laughed as they approached a grotto cleft into the side of a cliff surrounded by a pile of boulders.

A steady trickle of water streamed from the rocks to form a small crystal, clear rivulet that meandered down the hill away from the footpath. As they got closer to the grotto, Calle could see it was more of shrine. There were prayer candles and rosaries placed neatly inside a large alcove sculpted by river rock. The whole structure resonated with a holy reverence.

"This looks like a special place," Calle ventured.

"Yeah, it is. Legend has it that the water from this spring is blessed. It has healing powers."

"No kidding?"

"That's the legend," Otis replied. "We don't talk about that aspect of it too much. It might inspire a hoard of well-meaning trespassers."

"I can just imagine."

"Come on a little further," Otis suggested as he continued along the path.

Up and over a slight rise, they passed under a wrought iron gate with rusty cherubs welded into the corners. A few yards further, they entered a meadow surrounded by glades of aspen that shimmered a slivery green in the wind. In the middle, under the cool sunshine, a pleasant scent of honeysuckle rode the breeze through a timeworn cemetery.

The path was well trod, but most of the graveyard was overgrown with numerous headstones arranged in uneven rows. Teetering upright and with many of them growing moss or lichen, they lanced from the soil like the unflossed teeth of a buried giant.

Some were nestled back against a hill under the shade of the trees while others loafed openly in the grass, basking in the sunshine. A few were large, gaudy monuments but most were simple granite markers laid flat on the ground.

"This is the family cemetery. There's a lot of history here," Otis said as he walked off the main path.

"Are all these Pérez family members?" Calle asked as she spun a slow arc to take in the entirety of the place.

"Most are, but not all. There are some important friends and employees too."

Calle dallied to read some of the inscriptions. Most were plain with only birth and death dates. But some donned humorous quips or offered a last word of advice from the deceased, as if they could share wisdom from beyond the grave.

She was impressed by some of the very old dates,

but her curiosity was only superficial. It was difficult to be moved too deeply by dead people she knew nothing about.

She looked across the headstones to find Otis kneeling at a grave near a stone wall. He was lost in prayer, so she approached quietly. When she got close, he placed a bright red carnation on the simple marker, then pushed himself to his feet.

Calle didn't mean to intrude and felt bad when she saw tears in Otis' eyes. He tried to hide them as he replaced his hat on his head, but she noticed nonetheless. He looked away as he passed her, then turned back to ask, "You ready?"

The question was aimed at her, but she felt sure he was actually talking to himself.

"Yeah, I'm good," she replied, sending a smile of comfort his way. He acknowledged with a half-smile of his own then turned to walk back to the main path. Before Calle fell in step behind him, she glanced at the nondescript grave that meant so much to Otis. The fresh flower lay austerely on top of a few dried stems and leaves left by previous mourners. The grim arrangement obscured the epitaph on the headstone, but there was no doubt that whomever laid dead in the tomb, their memory was still very much alive.

# ☉ 4 ☾

The walk from the cemetery went without conversation. Though Calle was curious about the grave, she respected Otis' privacy and remained silent. The somber mood was broken when about half way back to the where the ATV was parked, Otis suddenly stopped and raised his hand to signal she do the same. He raised his finger to his lips to indicate for her to be quiet and still.

Otis then motioned for her to follow him behind a stand of pine trees out of view of the trail. They stood like spies waiting in ambush until a dark, rangy woman in cargo shorts with a long black braid and hiking boots up to her knees emerged from the forest and onto the trail about twenty yards behind them. She carried a long thin walking stick, a small lavender backpack, and three plastic water bottles tied to her belt. She warily stepped into the middle of the trail to survey her surroundings. With a look of relief, she turned to stride up toward the cemetery.

"Jamaica Spinner, you stop right there!" Otis cried out as he bounded from hiding.

The compact woman almost jumped out of her skin as she skidded to a halt. Calle shadowed Otis as he strode toward the woman who now had turned to face her assailants.

"Otis, you sneaky old crow! You should know better than to scare an old woman like that," Jamaica hollered.

"And you should know not to trespass here anymore," Otis replied grimly as he closed the distance between them.

As they drew closer, Jamaica didn't appear all that old, but she did have grey streaks in her hair and a few wrinkles on her leathery face. However old the husky, bronzed woman was, Calle could tell she was is great physical shape.

"And you should know that I have every right to that sacred water. My ancestors were using that spring long before you got here."

"I'm not going to argue with you Jamaica," Otis interrupted. "The judge ruled against you and that's that. You're going to have to leave."

"If you think you can bully an old woman like me, you're mistaken. I won't be denied my birthright."

"I'm only doing my job. If you won't leave on your own, I'll have you arrested again."

The woman's eyes blazed with contempt as she glared at Otis.

"You win this time Otis, but your time is coming. Mark my words, your time is coming!" Jamaica spat as she turned on her heel to stomp off the trail and back into the forest.

They stood watching her until she couldn't be seen or heard any longer, then Otis turned back down the trail.

"Sorry you had to see that," he said.

"She seemed pretty upset."

"Yeah, she is, but she's all bluster. She's threatened

me a hundred times before. Her and about a half dozen other trespassers too. It used to be just her and her cronies and it wasn't all that bad, but since someone posted the location of the spring on the internet, the crazies have been coming out of the wood work. Teresa had to take legal action otherwise this place would have been overrun."

"Seems like there could be some compromise," Calle suggested.

"You would think so, but most people that come here have no respect for the place. Graffiti, trash, animal and human waste, it's disgusting. I understand where Jamaica is coming from, but this land has belonged to the Pérez family for a long time. I don't have any choice; I have to be consistent with everyone. Until they can work it out, it's better that no one is allowed in at all."

Calle could see Otis' point, but felt for Jamaica.

About a half hour later, they stepped out of the ATV in the shade of the giant pavilion. There were two mansion employees setting up long folding tables and unloading chairs from a flatbed trailer. Otis escorted Calle around the area pointing out the portable serving stations and the egress to and from the small stage.

"There's power outlets here, here, and over by the back stage steps," he pointed out. "Feel free to use them as you see fit. That goes for the serving stations and the buffet table too."

Calle continued to follow Otis as he rounded a beautiful fountain fashioned to function as a waterfall. The only permanent structure under the pavilion, it sat away from the stage and adjacent to an adobe outbuilding that was surrounded by a lush flower garden. Aided by a large feeder hanging nearby, the garden was abuzz with hummingbirds.

"Over here is the main breaker and a fire extinguisher, in case of an emergency," Otis said as he entered the small building. "You can use this kitchen if you need to prepare anything onsite," he continued as he flicked on the light.

To Calle's delight, the kitchen was a fully functional commercial set up. There was a large grill, two industrial deep fryers, an ample broiler, and tons of refrigeration and freezer space. The back wall was stocked with enough plates, cups, and dinnerware to service a small army. Past that, the room opened up into a dish washing station and a pantry loaded with condiments, pots, and pans. Near the rear exit, a narrow, but adequate employee breakroom was furnished with a table and a few dining-room chairs. With a thoughtful walk-through design, it would be a cinch to stage a large presentation from the facility.

"This is marvelous!" Calle observed. "It would be a lot better to work from here than our catering truck. Can we use this space exclusively for the duration of our contract?"

"Absolutely, in fact, we would prefer you use it instead of your truck. Also, we would like for you to use one of our utility carts to transport supplies from your vehicles to and from the pavilion. We try to minimize full size vehicles on the property anywhere around the guests. So, please leave your truck in the employee parking lot and I'll get a cart ready for you to use."

"Great idea, that's what we'll do," Calle replied enthusiastically. "Everything looks good."

"One thing though, there's a clogged sewer line, but

the plumber is coming later to fix it. So, don't use the toilet here today. You can use the restrooms in the main building. It should be fixed by tomorrow."

"No problem, what about internet service?"

"Yeah, there's a booster antenna across the lawn, so there shouldn't be a problem," Otis said. "Cell service is spotty up here in the mountains so most folks rely on the Wi-Fi. Here's the passcode and my contact number," he said as he pulled a card from his wallet and handed it to her.

"Perfect, thank you."

"Also, we use two-way radios for the staff and management. I'll go charge one up for you and bring it by later. Are you going to be here for long today?"

"A couple more hours, I'm waiting for my crew to show up. They should be arriving any minute now."

"Okay, I'll be back in a few minutes. When is your first day with guests?"

"We have a small event Thursday evening. It will be a good practice for when the larger groups start arriving later this week."

"Sounds like you have it all well in hand," Otis said as he moved toward the door. "Oh, and watch out for El Gordo," he added with a grin.

"El Gordo?"

Stopping with his hand on the door jamb, he faced Calle and chuckled, "He's a rogue chipmunk, sort of our mascot really. Fat as a pumpkin because he raids any food or drink left out. You probably won't see him though; he doesn't like people in general. If you do, just shoo him away, he's cute and harmless. He shouldn't bother you."

"Okay, good to know."

Otis sped off on the ATV and left Calle to wander the area on her own. She had to adjust her plans now that she knew the kitchen was available to her to use exclusively. It would make the event go so much smoother working from the onsite kitchen rather than shlepping everything back and forth every day from the shop. She couldn't believe her luck; it was a godsend.

She had just located the ice machine when an athletic, young red-haired woman wearing standard black and white serving attire tapped lightly on the door. Meekly leaning her head through the opening, the pretty freckle faced girl intoned, "Ms. Roslyn? Good morning... Calle?"

Surprised, Calle turned to face the woman.

"Hey, Verna, good morning to you too," she replied. "Is Ezra here?"

"He will be here in a minute, he stopped by the restroom."

Verna Llyod and Ezra Lincoln were college students Calle had hired a couple weeks prior. They both attended St. John's College and were the perfect part time help. Experienced and friendly, they were both at ease working in a crowd. Though hailing from opposite coasts, Verna from California and Ezra from Georgia, they shared a strong work ethic. Calle knew she was very lucky to have such reliable help knowing the struggles Alby had at keeping good employees.

As the two women walked back under the pavilion, a slim young version of Nat King Cole sauntered up to join them. He also was wearing standard waitron clothing and a pencil thin neck tie with a dazzling smile radiating from his handsome face. His suave movie star impression was dashed when he hailed the women with a voice that hadn't quite matured.

"Hey guys! What a beautiful venue, don't you think?" he began in a smooth southern lilt but his voice cracked on the word 'beautiful'.

"Good morning, Ezra," Calle stifled a giggle and Verna smirked to herself. Despite his faux pa, Ezra's smile remained bright and confident as they seated themselves around the nearest table.

Calle explained the layout and the change of plans for the upcoming events. She gave them a list of items that would need to be transferred to the job site from the shop, then directed them as to how to set up for the next event. As their meeting was coming to an end, in obvious bewilderment, Verna looked past Calle and Ezra, pointed, then asked, "What is that?"

The trio turned to watch in amazement as a person draped in what looked like an Apollo 13 space suit carrying a smoking watering can in one hand and a large burlap bag in the other approached the tent. When the alien creature was only a few feet away, it stopped to set the sack and fuming can on a table, then removed its helmet.

From under what they could now see was actually a finely netted headpiece, a laughing bright-eyed young man called out, "You guys look like you've seen a monster, are you alright?"

"We thought we were being abducted by aliens," Verna quick witted with a grin.

Obviously amused, the young man replied, "Nothing like that, it's my bee keeping suit."

"Aha, that makes sense." Verna's eyes a twinkle.

"My name is Michael, I guess you guys are the caterers," he said as he wiped the sweat from his brow.

"Yes, we are," Calle answered. "Would you like a glass of water?"

Michael accepted her offer then set his bee helmet aside then joined them at the table.

"So, you're the local beekeeper?"

"Yeah, I suppose, we have a few active hives around the property. They keep the flowers and trees pollinated and we make honey for sale in the gift shop. We got a new queen and I was setting up a new colony near the orchard."

"How cool. So, do you go all over town managing your bees or just here?" Verna asked.

"Oh no, I only keep bees here, among other things. I live here. I'm Teresa's son."

"Ah, now I see the resemblance," Calle said, then introduced herself and her crew.

They sat in light hearted conversation for a few minutes before Calle had to get her employees back on task.

"Sorry we can't sit and chat longer, but we've got a lot of work to do today," she said.

"No problem, I understand."

As they shuffled back to work, Verna flirted through thinly veiled seriousness, "Will you be keeping bees here all week?"

"Not every day, but I'll be around," Michael replied cheerfully. Amused by Verna's overture, he smiled her way as he picked up his bee hat, smoke can, and bag. "Nice meeting you," he bade as he retreated toward the main building.

Verna smiled in return and kept sneaking glances his way until he disappeared inside the mansion.

"Don't get any ideas girlfriend, he's mine," Ezra

interrupted Verna's daydream.

"As if. Can't you see he's not gay," Verna replied with a grimace.

"Not yet," Ezra teased.

"Okay, okay guys," Calle laughed. "So, the owner's son is dreamy, but we have a job to do. Focus," she reminded with mock urgency.

Buoyantly, the Kokopelli crew returned to work. It wasn't long until the kitchen and dining area were prepared and everyone was familiar with the plan. Inwardly thankful for having such a fun and cooperative crew, Callie sent her two lovestruck employees home for the afternoon. They would meet again Thursday morning to do the final prep for their first presentation.

After they left, Callie sat down for a late lunch. Between bites of her burrito, she worked on some menu ideas she had for one of the bigger events scheduled for the following week. Then she felt it.

A thin vision of an argument clouded her thoughts. It wasn't herself arguing, but two men at a distance. There was something eerie about the exchange, a foreboding, maybe a warning. She didn't know how to perceive what she had just envisioned. Usually, her déjà vu was clearer and focused on herself, but this was something different.

Her experience told her to remain calm and wait for the premonition to unfold. She had come to trust her intuition unconditionally. It had saved her life not once, but twice in the last few months. So, waiting a few minutes was not an issue.

After ten or fifteen minutes, nothing happened. Not a sign of any argument or even the slightest appearance of any men that could argue. It was unsettling. Usually, her visions would manifest themselves within a few seconds. This was totally new to her. A twinge of doubt began to nibble in the back of her mind as she wondered if maybe she was losing her ability.

A moment later, a large man wearing muddy jeans and a sweat stained tee-shirt clomped under the pavilion behind Calle.

As she turned to face him, he called out sternly, "Have you seen Otis?"

"Not recently," she replied.

"Figures," he grunted.

"Can I help you?"

"Not unless you know how to snake a drain," he said abruptly.

"Sorry?" Calle intoned, a little surprised by his rudeness.

"Well, if you see Otis, tell him I need to talk to him," the man continued. "I'm Herman from Young's Plumbing," he added sharply as he turned to leave.

"Okay, will do," she said. "Is there anything wrong?"

He halted as if she had stabbed in the back. As he dramatically turned around to face her, she wished she could have snatched the question out of the air before he heard it.

"Only if you think getting threatened by a lawyer is a problem," Herman seethed through a vicious glare.

"Oh no, sorry, it's none of my business," Calle replied, opening her palms to him in surrender. "If I see Otis, I'll let him know you're looking for him."

"You do that," Herman said flatly as he turned to exit the way from which he had arrived.

Calle went back to her lunch and wondered if she

should call Otis. He hadn't returned with her radio yet and she was reluctant to get involved with the agitated plumber any further. She decided to let Otis and Herman work out their problems on their own.

Just as she was finishing her lunch, she heard footsteps traipsing under the pavilion behind her. Hoping it wasn't the angry plumber returning, she crinkled the burrito wrapper in her hand as she turned to face the person.

There stood a tanned young man clad in shorts, a polo shirt, and sun glasses holding a package in one hand and a computer scanner in the other.

"I have a delivery for the kitchen," he said with professional bluster. "But they told me to bring it here."

"Okay," Calle said as she dropped her trash into a nearby bin.

"Sign here," he said with a sly grin.

Though she couldn't see his eyes through his glasses, Calle could feel his gaze go up and down her body. It wasn't like she hadn't endured that behavior before, but it still made her feel uneasy.

"So, you work here?" he asked as he gave her the package.

*Duh, stupid and pervy, oh great.*

Opting for the professional high road, she replied cordially, "I work for the catering company."

"I'm Rob Aragon," he stated overconfidently and then went onto talk about himself. Calle listened patiently as the man rambled on.

It was though she were back in college again listening to the same tired, old pick-up lines. Rob continued talking as she walked over to a serving station and put the package on the counter. She had

had about enough and turned back to tell him so, when from over his shoulder she saw Otis and Herman in a heated argument across the lawn beside a freshly dug hole in the grass. Inwardly, she was pleased to see her déjà vu was still reliable, but tired of the delivery man.

Rob's bravado was losing steam because Calle's attention was elsewhere. He turned to see what she was looking at and at once said, "I hope he gets his butt kicked."

She turned her eyes back to him.

"Who?"

"The supervisor. He's a jerk. I hope that guy beats him up."

"Why would you say that?"

"He's always harassing me when I come here. I hate him."

Calle was surprised by Rob's ire. Gone was the happy-go-lucky persona he had been using and in its place was what she supposed was the real personality of Rob Aragon. She wasn't surprised, but wondered what could have possibly happened to make him so vindictive?

The argument across the yard ended with Herman kicking dirt into the hole and Otis walking away in their direction. That was all Rob needed to regain a minutia of his pseudo professionalism.

"I gotta go," he breathed nervously then hurried from under the pavilion.

Otis approached Calle with a serious but composed stride. She was amazed at how calm he was considering what she had just witnessed.

"Hey, I got your radio," he said.

"Oh good, I see you found Herman," she replied. "He

was looking for you."

"Yeah, I know. I hope he gets that sewer snaked today," he said. "I see you've met our delivery person," he continued sarcastically.

"He doesn't seem to like you much."

"I'm not surprised. I caught him smoking dope back behind the corral with one of our stable hands last week and sleeping in his truck a month ago."

"Uh oh, not good."

"No, it's not. I called his boss and left a message, but it didn't seem to make much of a difference. I guess it's hard to find reliable help these days."

He sounded just like Alby.

"Everything going okay here?" Otis asked, changing the subject and gesturing to the tables behind her.

"Perfect, we're going to be ready come Thursday."

"Alright, that's good to know. I'll talk to you later."

"Thanks for the radio, see you tomorrow."

As she watched Otis' slim figure retreating toward the main building, she wondered about her déjà vu premonition. It had finally come true, but the timing was off. She couldn't put her finger on why exactly, so she dismissed the feeling of foreboding she had felt earlier. Sometimes it was just best to let things go, let the universe do its own thing. With a shrug of her shoulders, she moved the package to the kitchen, finished up her work, and then headed for home.

# ⊙ 5 ☾

On the way home, Calle stopped by Kaune's neighborhood market. Anytime she was downtown, she liked to drop in. Located caddy-corner from the State Capital, or the Round House as it was referred to locally, the mom-and-pop grocery store always had something interesting and different. Usually, she would wander the aisles admiring the variety, but today she knew what she wanted before she walked in the door. Piñon bread and a quart of Southwest Corn Chowder would ease her craving and save her from leftovers for dinner at home.

As she walked out with her well-earned treat, her phone began to ring. Of course, it would, her hands were full. She hustled to place her groceries inside her truck, then answered the call. It was her boss.

"Hey, I'm at the airport and had some down time. I thought I'd check in," Alby said. How's everything?"

Calle told him all about the onsite kitchen and the great setup. She reassured him everything was going well and not to worry.

"Well, there's been another glitch. We lost our bartender, know of anyone?"

"Not off the top of my head," she replied.

"Give Raymond a call and see if he can fill in, if not, you'll have to do double duty."

*Oh great.*

"I gotta run, they're starting to board. Let me know what you figure out."

It was times like these Calle wished she hadn't told Alby about her bartending license. He just assumed it would be no problem for her to do two jobs at once. Of course, he would only pay her for one. Calle had come to find out that many small business owners abused temporary help like that.

She got her education, so to speak, by working numerous temporary and part time jobs after she lost her husband a couple years ago in a horrible automobile accident. She wasn't in need of the money so much as she was in need of something to do. Perhaps, if the right job came up, she might stay longer, but for now, temporary and part time was all she wanted.

At first, it was just something to do, but as it turned out, it was therapeutic for her. Moving from job to job introduced her to new places and new people. She liked that, always something fresh. The accident had left her depressed and plagued by PTSD. So, for a while, it was all she could do just to struggle from day to day. By and by, she began to reclaim her life, but it was her last stint as a substitute teacher that really brought her out of her shell and renewed her confidence.

So now, the loss of their bartender was inconvenient, but it wouldn't be insurmountable. Alby's 'call Raymond' suggestion was code for 'you're on your own'. Raymond was as inept as he was difficult and not worth the effort. She would just have to hire another person, either a bartender or another server. Confident she could work it out, she tucked that dilemma to the back of her worry list, hopped in her truck, and headed out.

When she pulled up to her driveway, she stopped to check her mail. She was one of the few remaining residents in the area that still had the old-fashioned mailbox on the post, by the street, with the flag. The post office said they were working on installing new secure boxes for her neighborhood, but so far it was poco-poco, no need to hurry, true Santa Fe style. She had gotten used to Santa Fe as the land of mañana, where the philosophy was, 'why do today what can be put off until tomorrow?'. But still, it was frustrating waiting for something that should have been taken care of a long time ago.

Consequently, she didn't use her mailbox often. Usually, about once a month, she would clean out the coupon ads and envelopes addressed to 'current resident' that were crammed inside. Although once last year, to her surprise, she got an invitation to a neighborhood barbeque. Otherwise, the box was essentially just an icon, but it was a pretty icon with flowers and a bluebird painted on the side.

What piqued her curiosity was that the flag was up. She didn't have any outgoing mail and it wasn't up when she left that morning for work, so someone must have stopped by. Maybe there was invitation to a horseshoe pitch or yard sale, that would be fun.

With high hopes she opened the postbox. Her anticipation was squashed when the tail of a dead rat flopped through the opening. Shock quickly turned to disgust.

Cursing to herself about the awful prank, she fetched a pair of leather work gloves from her truck to remove the dead animal from the box. Holding the rat by his long tail, it looked like it had been gift wrapped. A bright green ribbon was tied tightly around its neck with a small red envelope attached. Gingerly, she placed the carcass on her tailgate and cut open the envelope.

She unfolded the enclosed note and with trepidation read the message. Crudely scrawled script creased the page with the words, *Hex marks the spot!* Underneath the ominous inscription, doodled in the same scribble as if to punctuate the curse, winked a contorted smiley face.

"You won't believe what I found in my mailbox," Calle huffed into her cellphone as she shlepped back across the road onto her property. She held the device to her ear as she walked down her driveway, kicking a pine cone across the gravel with every other step.

"A dead rat!" she exclaimed. "With a note saying I've been hexed."

After a moment of listening, she replied, "Yeah, I threw it in the slough across the road, but I kept the note and ribbon."

She put the phone on speaker just in time to hear Lucy suggest, "Good, you should tell Sam about it."

"You think so? It's probably just a prank. My neighbor says there's been some kids up to mischief in the neighborhood lately. Maybe it's them."

"Sam knows a lot about witchcraft. If it is a curse, she'll know what to do."

"Yeah, I suppose."

"Anyway, I'm glad you called, but for another reason," Lucy said.

"Mmm, okay."

"I need your advice, but not over the phone. Want to

meet for lunch tomorrow?"

"Sure, I'm working up at the Pérez mansion. Want to meet there, they have a great restaurant, my treat?"

"Sounds good, I'll see you then."

"Luce, is everything alright?"

"Right as rain, don't worry. It's not anything crazy, well, not too much. At least not for you anyway."

"Luce," Calle intoned forcefully.

"See you tomorrow," Lucy deflected with too much cheer and hung up.

Calle stared at the phone a second and then placed it in her pocket. She had been dismissed. It must be something important if Lucy needed to talk in person and what did she mean by 'at least not for you?'

Mildly pre-occupied with the call, Calle admired Beely crouched, sniffing the planked top of the old table on her front porch. He truly was a magnificent animal with his sleek black coat and sapphire eyes. She couldn't ask for a better welcome home.

When she reached the step, she called out, "Hey Beeler, how about a treat?"

She stretched out to scratch him behind the ears, but as she stepped on the porch, an unnoticed spider web cobbed across the entry stuck to her face.

"Son of a monkey!" she swore as she swatted the fibers from her eyelashes. Her sudden motion must have spooked her cat because he jumped to his feet and began to hiss. The fur on his back stood on end as he paced the tabletop away from her.

"Oh, kitty, I didn't mean to scare you. It was only a spider's web," she laughed, pulling more web from her face and hair. But her cat only became more agitated as he glared past her.

She turned to see what had caught his attention, but there was just an empty driveway. Beely hopped to the ground in front of her and began to growl a guttural warning to something only he could perceive. He was puffed to almost twice his normal size when he shot across the yard and up a huge cottonwood tree. He sprinted full speed to the end of a long branch and without slowing, he launched himself into the sky as if attacking something, his sharp claws flailing madly in the air as he fell to the ground.

He landed on his feet, but kept his focus on the trail leading to the river. He began to stalk a zig zag pattern away from Calle. As he reached the edge of the glade, a sweet gust of wind hit Calle in the back and breezed through her hair and past her cat. The soft blue glow that passed over her was so subtle and swift, she wasn't sure if it was real, but the goosebumps tickling her arms convinced her otherwise. When the draft whipped by Beely, he bolted into a full run down the trail after it.

Stunned, Calle jogged a few steps after Beely, but he and the gust had already sped away. Flicking the last of the cobweb from her fingertips, she stood at the edge of the yard and looked back over her shoulder then down the trail in utter disbelief. What in the world had just happened?

Before she could formulate a decent guess, her phone began to chirp again. It was her neighbor, Dale Wicker. He was calling to alert her that he had been the latest victim of theft in the neighborhood and that she should keep an eye out. She told him about the dead rat in the mailbox and after discussing it, they decided the incidents were probably unrelated, but to be careful anyway. She assured him that she would be alright with Beely to protect her, but Dale was unconvinced. The conversation was short and to the point, but his concern left her a little rattled.

Calle put her phone in her pocket and just to ease her mind, she took a walk around her property. Other than the dead rat in her mailbox, everything else looked good, it all appeared normal. She wondered if maybe Beely had spotted the robbers when he ran down the river path. That would explain his peculiar behavior. She strolled a few yards down the path, but all seemed serene. Not a trace of her cat or any sign of intrusion. Satisfied there was nothing to worry about, she went into her house.

After an abbreviated yoga routine and a quick shower, Calle slipped on a Smokey the Bear t-shirt and a pair of cut-offs and moseyed out back to her own private oasis of peace. She set her phone and tablet next to her smoking tin and after a few puffs, she let the rhythm of nature wash her cares away.

She flipped open her tablet and went to the Ancestry.com website. After a few minutes studying what the site had to offer, she decided to try out her gift card. In another few minutes, she was signed up and her test kit was on its way.

What would she discover about herself? Her ethnic heritage for sure, but maybe she was related to a long-lost uncle with oodles of cash. Or a descendant of George Washington or someone famous. Yeah, that's the spirit.

Her sarcastic side kicked in when she thought more likely she'd wind up related to a needy no-load, who once found where she lived, wouldn't leave her alone. Whatever the case, it would be fun to find out. And the knowledge of any predisposed illness in her bloodline would be useful if nothing else.

She loaded her pipe again and tried blowing smoke rings as she pondered the possibilities of her heritage. Her rings were thin and wispy, unlike the magic creations Bilbo and Gandalf sent flying about. Though her efforts always came up short, she loved to fantasize herself sitting with them in one of her favorite scenes from all of literature.

She was nudged out of her pipedream as a beautiful Steller's blue jay landed on her sleeve.

"Barrow!" she cried in recognition.

The bird hopped off her shoulder and on to the table nearby. He stood cocking his head back and forth in a curious way staring at her with emerald eyes. She returned his gaze at a loss as to how to communicate more effectively.

Barrow had become a trusted ally and was the symbiont of Ethan, her mentor in the realm of dreams. The blue jay's appearance made Calle hopeful she would see Ethan soon. But he had become reclusive and she was beginning to wonder what was going on with her astral companion.

As she started to ask Barrow about Ethan, the bird leapt into flight and sailed to the top of a towering cottonwood. She watched as he fiddled with something tied at the top of the tree. Momentarily, he glided back to her and laid a keyring with two keys in front of her. It wasn't the first time he had given her something. Several weeks ago, when she first met him, he gave her a beautiful dreamcatcher that still hung on her bedpost.

She picked up the keyring and looked to him for an explanation.

"What are these for?" she questioned as if he could answer.

His brilliant scrutiny revealed nothing. She would have to figure that one out on her own.

"Okay, I guess these are important," she said.

Barrow confirmed her suggestion with a soft coo.

Calle sat contemplating the situation as Barrow preened his tail feathers. Though they were only inches apart, there was a Grand Canyon between them as far as the ability to communicate. The moment dragged a little longer, then with a sharp chirp, Barrow winged away up over her house.

She eyed the keyring closer. They were both short and one was a skeleton key. The other was definitely for a padlock of some sort. Otherwise, there wasn't anything remarkable about either of them.

She putzed around her garden until the peaceful afternoon began to fade. Picking up the keys and her electronic devices, she headed inside for the rest of the evening. Beely was still missing in action, but that wasn't unusual, he was on his own schedule.

The keys would have to be stored in a safe place, so she took them to where she hid all her most valuable items, in plain sight, in a wicker basket, on the top of her dresser. The catch-all was loaded with all kinds of treasures ranging from marbles and jewelry to a needle used for inflating footballs. The most precious item it contained was the pendant Matthew had given her before he signed up for the military.

The pendant was special for a couple reasons. One it was a gift, and two, it was a magical item that connected her with her Guardian Angel.

Isla, Calle's angel, reminded her of the hermit on a

Led Zeppelin album she had seen as a teenager. Except Isla was a beautiful young blonde woman holding a book and a lantern that shone a pale blue light enameled into a pendant, not a sinister old bearded recluse on the cover of a rock-n- roll record.

Unlike the hermit, Isla was also very real. Not that Calle had ever spoken with her or seen her outside the pendant, but when she accepted Calle as her charge, she sent a star into the heavens to remind Calle of their bond. It was quite dramatic, but so far, that was the extent of their relationship.

Calle was proud of her protector, but had never revealed her to anyone. Until something significant happened, she would keep the secret to herself. Not that she wouldn't share the truth with her friends, if necessary, but because she already felt weird enough.

She had her whole life. Being a lucid dreamer and having powerful déjà vu since she was a child, Calle had always been different. It had affected all her relationships in one way or another and she became tired of trying to explain things few people could understand, let alone accept as real. Then after the accident that killed her husband, she developed PTSD and that was just more icing on top of the cake.

And if that wasn't enough, something else monumental was changing in her life. Her lucid dreams were morphing into astral adventures. She was now actively venturing into the astral realm quite regularly. It was very exciting, but also very isolating. Honestly, who does that stuff for real?

So, now Calle lived a double life where she kept a large part of herself hidden. It was too bizarre for the average person to comprehend and she was done trying to defend the truth. It only left her feeling that much different and alone. Sometimes, she felt like a stranger in her own hometown. So, for her own peace of mind, Isla, her amazing angelic friend, would have to remain a secret for now.

Dropping the keyring into the basket, she picked up her pendant expecting to see her angel gazing over the peaceful, distant horizon as usual. But instead, a brewing thunderstorm blackened the face of the pendant and Isla was nowhere in sight. Bewildered, she watched as a foreboding capillary of lightning crackled across the miniature sky.

Something was not right. Calle replaced the pendant in the basket and went outside to check the weather in her world. The sky was clear and bright, nothing like the typhoon looming in the pendant. The hair on the back of her neck began to bristle as she made another lap around her property. Nothing was amiss, but that didn't settle Calle's nerves.

The stormy change in the pendant felt like an omen. Calle dialed up Samantha and left a message. Samantha was a world class painter and openly Wiccan, but those who knew her well, knew she was a witch. A good witch and thankfully, a close friend. Lucy was right, if anyone could give her useful advice, it would be Samantha. Now all she could do was wait.

Sitting on the edge of her bed, Calle brushed her hair into a loose ponytail. Worn out from a long day, she tried reading a little to ease her tumultuous thoughts. The sentences ran together as she reread the same paragraph again and again. She was just about to give up when her phone dinged to life again.

She looked at the caller ID. It was her boyfriend. The physical one.

"Matthew, how are you? I didn't expect to hear from you today," she answered, grateful for the distraction.

"We had a good day on the lake. Dad caught a four-pound trout on a fly rod. It was really cool," Matthew's voice trilled with excitement. "Montana is awesome! How's Santa Fe?"

"Work is good, we lost our bartender, so I'll have to do double duty," she said, intentionally avoiding the topic of the rat, her neighbor, and the pendant. As she spoke, her guilt began to fester. She still hadn't mustered up the courage to tell him about the mystical side of her life. She felt deceitful and promised herself again that one day, when the time was right, she would be completely honest with him about her clairvoyance. But so far, that day had never presented itself and quite honestly, she was afraid it never would.

"Why don't you call Phillip? He's a licensed bartender," Matthew suggested.

"Mr. Peanut?"

"Yeah, he would be perfect for part time."

Phillip Jenks was Matthew's new aircraft fanatic friend. Calle suspected Phillip was partially to blame for Matthew's enlistment in the military. He was an ex-Navy pilot and they had hit it off the moment Calle introduced them. He was also an accomplished magician and juggler on top of being a very nice guy. Calle liked to tease him by calling him 'Mr. Peanut' because the first few times she saw him he was always wearing a tuxedo.

"Okay, maybe I will. Thanks."

"Alright sweetheart, I gotta' go, I'll call you soon."

Calle ended the call feeling like a hypocrite. How long would she kick this can down the road? If she couldn't be honest with Matthew, there was no future for them as a couple. Unable to formulate an easy way out, she went to the restroom and after a quick check of her doors and windows, she snuggled back into bed and turned out the lights.

She was way too keyed up to sleep, so she tried to relax using a meditation technique she was working on to expand her astral abilities. She exhaled and released the tension that had been building up inside her. Starting with her toes then mentally working her way to the top of her head, she began to methodically relax her entire body, piece by piece.

So far, she was only able to access the astral plane while dreaming. When she was successful, she would be in a lucid dream but starting to wake up, asleep and awake at the same time. In that fragile moment, if she could balance on the edge of consciousness and unconsciousness, she could go out of body.

But that was the tricky part, simultaneously trying to maintain that balance while attempting to control the overwhelming fear of separating one's spirit from one's body. Death was the only natural way that separation occurred and one's innate will to survive made the delicate balancing act excruciating. It was virtually impossible to do both at once, but she seemed to have a knack for it, so she felt confident, with time and self-discipline, she could master it through meditation.

The meditation technique, hopefully, would bypass sleeping altogether. If she was right, it would allow her to enter a transcendental state while meditating. If she could master the skill, she would be able to come and go from the astral world at will instead of the hit and miss method she currently relied on. But it was exceedingly difficult and required exceptional mental focus.

Usually, her efforts put her to sleep, but sleeping was no guarantee of astral access either. Then again, as tired as she was, a restful sleep wouldn't be that bad of a trade-off, so, in this case, it was a win-win situation. If she succeeded, she would have accomplished a difficult goal, if she didn't, she would fall asleep, get some rest and maybe go out of body. Either way was good.

Dealing with PTSD on a daily basis had honed her relaxation skills and once relaxed, she began the second phase of her meditation. The idea was to deliberately move from thought to thought as quickly and as smoothly as possible, trying not to dwell on any one thought for too long. It was natural to fixate on a thought and mull in to death, but that only generated a stagnant, counterproductive clog in her thinking. A fluid, unrestricted thought stream was key. If she could establish a rhythm, it would naturally accelerate. Then she would feel the mild electric vibration surround her spirit, much like the sensation she got when she was on the cusp of being awake and asleep at the same time.

Lying there in the darkness, she could feel her cadence gain momentum. She knew the technique was like surfing the edge of a razor blade at high speed. As she thought about how accurate, but dangerous that analogy was, she began to fixate on the idea. That simple hesitation caused her to lose her balance. As it had happened before, the excitement of learning even the slightest tidbit of something new was too much to ignore. Her unbridled curiosity tripped her up again.

She fell right past the slim window of opportunity and into a deep sleep.

As her slumber eased into the shallows, she regained her bearings like a stunt pilot recovering from a blackout midflight. Slipping effortlessly from autopilot, she took control of her dream. Her failed attempt at transcendental meditation was of little concern now, something she could rehash when she was awake. Right now, she was in her element. Lucid dreaming was second nature to her and her blossoming ability to move out of body only made her that much more secure.

She flew aimlessly for a short while, then remembered her need to talk to Ethan. She set her mind on searching him out. The exact mechanics of how she moved from a lucid dream to astral projection was still a mystery, but she knew it started with a strong desire. From there, the transformation was so smooth and seamless, Calle couldn't tell the difference. For her, it had become one and the same. All she could figure was that a lifetime of lucid dreaming must have prepared her for traversing the astral plane.

She began to pick up signals right away. It was like swimming underwater blindfolded, feeling for warm or cool currents in search of the heat source. The cues were subtle, but easily misinterpreted. Keeping her sense of direction loose, she meandered in pursuit of Ethan's spiritual scent. Like an astral bloodhound following a faint trail through a morass of distraction, she patiently maintained her focus and plodded onward.

Her search led over the ocean to a secluded cove along a pristine white beach of an isolated island.

Anchored near the shore, floated a sailboat and on the deck with feet dangling over the side, sat Ethan. His tanned face gleamed as she approached.

"Sweet Leaf! You found me," he greeted cheerfully.

"It wasn't as easy as I thought it would be," she replied as she sidled up beside him to slip her toes in the warm, clear water.

"Nothing worthwhile ever is," he said as his gaze left her face and moved out over the horizon.

She could already feel his warmth seeping into her spirit. As she admired his handsome elfin profile, the memory of their spiritual love making began to simmer from deep inside. It was totally unexpected and it distracted her momentarily.

"Is someone following you?" His question shook her from her erotic musings.

"What? Following me?"

"Yeah, you," he laughed.

"No, I'm all by myself," she grinned in return.

"Mmm, okay," his words said, but his eyes didn't quite agree.

"So, where have you been? I've been trying to find you for a couple weeks. Is everything okay?"

He looked away from her and back into the distance, his reply stuck in his throat.

His uncertainty surprised her. He was always so sure of himself and his momentary lack of confidence alarmed her. She sensed vulnerability and pressed.

"What is it?"

He turned back to face her. When their gaze met, he knew he would never be able to deceive her and really didn't want to try. They were too close, shared too much, their essences had mingled. And though he didn't want to have this conversation, he had to be truthful.

"I'm ill," he admitted as if he had let her down.

"What do you mean?"

"I've been too preoccupied and medicated to concentrate," he said.

"That's why I couldn't find you?"

"Yes, that and the fact I've been concerned about my future. I've been selfish. I apologize."

"Are you going to be alright?"

"Oh course, it's not that big of a deal," he downplayed, unable to look her in the eye. "Are you sure you're not being followed?" he said changing the subject and directing her attention to a swirling black fog gathering in the distance.

Calle turned to see the fog pitch and shudder as a light blue mist constricted its progress. Where the two met, chain lightning boiled violently causing a drippy lavender rain to coalesce into the sea. She thought the colors would have been beautiful if they didn't look so much like blood clouding the lagoon.

"Is that your creation?" Ethan asked.

"No, is it yours?" Calle replied as she looked to him for guidance.

"That is something very powerful," he said as the tempest slowly ebbed their direction. "I don't think we should stay here."

"Okay."

"I don't think it's interested in me; I think it has followed you."

"Me? Why?"

"I don't know, but it should be avoided until we can figure out what it is."

"What do we do?" she asked uneasily.

"Do what you've always done to handle a nightmare, I'll follow and try to misdirect it. Maybe I can discover it's nature."

"When will we meet again?"

"I'll seek you out. In the meantime, be vigilant. Something very strange is afoot."

Eying Ethan, she levitated from the deck, worry splashed across on her face.

He smiled to ease her angst. "Everything will be alright," he reassured as he stood. "Off you go Sweetleaf," he said then kissed her tenderly on the lips.

She lingered long enough to admire his lovely features as if for the last time, then with solemn determination, she dissolved into the ether.

Her evasive maneuvers came easily to her. As a child, she learned right away how to avoid bad dreams. It was one of the first skills she developed as a novice lucid dreamer. Consequently, she had never had a nightmare.

As she moved from scene to scene, place to place, and moment to moment, she became more attuned to the astral plane. It was so much like a dream; she was amazed by the similarity. Her thoughts became commands, her whims a reality. Eventually, she aimed her projection back to her body.

As her alarm clock began to chime, she had already reunited with herself. She awoke one eye at a time.

Her mind was whirling a mile a minute as she stumbled to the restroom. She couldn't get her head around why someone would be interested in her on the astral plane or want to follow her for that matter. Maybe, months ago, when she was depressed, she angered someone or did something foolish in a dream. She couldn't remember. Ethan told her she had been reckless, but that was over a year ago, why wait until now? It didn't make sense.

Maybe it was Spencer's uncle Howard. He probably wasn't too keen that she had bit his nose off and scared the crap out of him. Could he be seeking revenge?

The storm had gathered so quickly, she never really got to visit with Ethan. Then she realized she hadn't asked him about the keys Barrow had delivered either. Nor had she learned the extent of his illness.

Her misgiving began to rise as she worried about his safety. What did he mean by 'discover its nature'? That phrasing made her think he didn't know what they had witnessed and put himself in harm's way to protect her. She remembered the look they shared after his kiss. His emerald gaze was intimate and unconditional, his words encouraging, but she knew him like she knew herself. He was uncertain.

# ☽ 6 ☾

The nutty aroma of freshly brewed coffee filled the kitchen with an unavoidable goodness. Deliberately, like a baker working dough, it kneaded the worry slowly from her thoughts. When the warmth of that first sip touched her lips, she knew Ethan would be alright. Just because he was unsure, didn't mean he wasn't capable and resourceful. He was an experienced dream trekker and was wise beyond his years. He would figure out what was going on, she had no doubt.

"Well, well, if it isn't my feline hero," Calle giggled as Beely sauntered into the kitchen and bumped between her legs. "Where did you get off to yesterday?"

His kitty motor kicked in as she picked him up for quick kiss and cuddle. Beely loved to be loved, but he wasn't one to be held for long, so a few seconds was all he could handle. Like only cats are able, he turned to liquid and Calle released him. He poured out of her arms onto the tile, then padded off to see what was for breakfast while she got ready for work.

Later at the mansion, sitting beneath the filtered shade next to the pavilion, Calle admired the flecks of sunlight that trickled through the swaying leaves of the trees to dance warmly on the grass. She had just finished texting Phillip about the bartending job and was nibbling on a strawberry when Teresa bustled up and sat down.

"Good morning," she heaved through a long sigh.

"Busy morning?" Calle asked.

"You don't know the half of it," Teresa said as she unloaded her radio and a pile of paper work onto the table. "Got any coffee going?" she asked as she headed toward the urn.

With cup in hand, Teresa returned to her seat and visibly relaxed. "It looks like you're just about settled in," she said as she gave the pavilion the once over.

"Yeah, just a few details to iron out before tomorrow."

"Great, at least one thing is going smoothly this morning."

"Oh, things off to a bad start?"

"I wouldn't say bad, but a little challenging would be a good way to put it." Teresa rolled her eyes.

Calle nodded in support as Teresa began to talk.

"The mansion keeps me running all the time, but it's my mother who drives me nuts. Does that ever happen to you?"

"Mmm mm," Calle agreed, as a vision of her free-spirited hippie, dippy mother flitted across her mind. "I can sympathize."

"She's eighty-seven and she has a boyfriend," she said sarcastically as she scratched quote marks in the air with her fingertips. "Whatever that means. I have no idea how he puts up with her, maybe only visiting once or twice a year helps."

"She sounds pretty spry for her age," Calle grinned politely, thinking of the rude woman she had met yesterday.

"That's one way to describe it. More like spoiled and

demanding," Teresa said. "I guess I should be happy he's here since it gives me a break."

"There you go, that's the spirit," Calle encouraged.

"Oh, damn it, here they come now."

Calle followed Teresa's gaze to see the couple in question approach. Odd wasn't an adequate description for the mismatched pair of human beings crammed into the seat of the listing golf cart. As the vehicle coasted to a stop near the pavilion, Calle could see Gloria's boyfriend was as mammoth as she was frail.

"Hello mother," Teresa called out, concealing her previous irritation with the woman.

"We just stopped by to get something to drink," Gloria declared as her companion extracted himself from the confines of the cart.

Not exactly fat, but not exactly fit, the man was big. He was large enough that his belly spun the steering wheel when he got out of the cart. He slogged under the pavilion as Calle stood to assist him with a beverage.

"Calle, this is Fen, my mother's gentleman friend," Teresa introduced, unable to utter the word boyfriend.

"Nice to meet you," Fen said with a nicotine stained midwestern accent.

"My pleasure," Calle replied as she opened the fridge and grabbed a bottle of water. "Water, okay?"

"That's fine," he said. "One is enough, thank you."

As the bottle exchanged hands, she noticed that one of his fingers was about the size of her wrist and his nails were finely manicured and clear coated. Surprised, she took a moment to look closer at his face.

Despite his girth, he was somewhat handsome. He was at least thirty years younger than Teresa's mother with a few wrinkles on his forehead and around his mouth. His light blue eyes cast a scaly condescension as sweat beaded from under his precise haircut. He clearly thought very highly of himself.

Calle's first impression was that of excessive money. She had seen it before and wasn't all that impressed. He was store bought and pampered from his tailored clothing to his shiny designer watch. He probably had never done hard day's work in his entire life.

As the couple spun away under the trees, Teresa caught Calle's eye as she rejoined her at the table.

"I know what you're thinking," Teresa smiled.

"What do you mean?"

"They make a strange couple, no?"

"I didn't say anything," Calle smirked.

"You didn't have to."

"Well, since you mentioned it, what's the deal with your mother and her friend?" Calle laughed.

"It's a long story, but he used to work for my father many years ago. After Papa died, they became friends and have been ever since."

"I guess it's nice they have each other. It's better than being lonely, I suppose."

"Yeah, but he's so different from my father. I've never really understood the attraction. He's so huge and she's so picky about everything."

Calle thought about one of her girlfriends from college who would put up with the worst guys just because the sex was good. She almost made a joke about it, but caught herself before she embarrassed herself. She briefly wondered what the couple could possibly have in common. Maybe it was sex, but that thought made her shudder and decide it was none of her business.

Instead, she said tactfully, "The heart wants what it wants. You may never know what they see in each other. At least they're happy."

"That's true, but happy? I don't think that's in my mother's vocabulary. I can't ever remember her being happy, even when my father was alive. She's always been angry about something or another. I think her attitude drove my father to infidelity."

"That's not good, but not all people want to be happy. They're only content when there's a problem. To them, if things are going well, there has to be something wrong. If there's not an issue, they'll create one. My aunt was like that. I wouldn't worry about it."

"I gave up worrying a long time ago. It's something I can't change," she lamented then sighed. "Anyway, that's enough about my mother."

After going over the schedule for next few weeks and plans for the upcoming events, Calle bade Teresa farewell. She was impressed with Teresa's professionalism and her commitment to family and her business. The woman was pleasant and her sarcastic sense of humor was infectious. She would make a good friend, but being so devoted to her job would probably keep her at a distance. Maybe that was why she had never married.

A brief perusal of the kitchen and a quick of check of her to do list for the next day left Calle satisfied everything was off to a good start. Verna and Ezra had stocked the pantry and the line was set. They had done a great job. The rest of the morning would be a breeze and she should be free after lunch to go with Lucy.

There wasn't really much left to do except visit with Otis about logistics for the weekend. The plumbing still wasn't fixed, but they were working on it. Just as she was about to lock up and go look for Otis, she heard a scratching noise coming from the break room. It was slight, but persistent. She tiptoed to peek around the corner to see the fattest chipmunk she had ever seen sitting on his haunches, on the table, munching a crust of dried toast. El Gordo was on a raid.

Cute as a button, he worked his way through the crust, then waddled over to a paper cup half filled with orange juice, tipped it over, and began to lap up the spilt liquid. As if he knew he was being spied on, he sat up abruptly and scanned the area. His cartoon gaze caught Calle's as he sized up his voyeur. Nary a worry crossed his features, he was as curious about her as she was him.

Animals always seemed to like her and she was sure they made a connection, but when the outside door slammed, El Gordo scrambled off the table and under the table. With the magic moment shattered, Calle turned to see who was responsible. Herman Young stomped around the corner with a scowl on his face and mud on his boots.

"Looks like your drain is repaired," he said midstride as he strode past her. "We just need to check for leaks."

"Okay," she said as she stepped aside. She watched him hurry through the building to turn on all the faucets and flush the toilet. He returned to declare everything was working properly then asked where Otis was hiding.

"I don't know," she said as she looked at the muddy disaster he had wreaked on her spotless floor. She couldn't prove it, but she was sure he had done it purposely for spite.

"When you see him, tell him I'm looking for him."

Calle wanted to tell Herman where he could stick his plunger, but decided the best thing to do was to ignore the hateful plumber. It wouldn't have mattered anyway because he had already stormed from the kitchen.

If she had laser vision, there would be a gaping hole in the man's back. Standing in the doorway, she watched as he fumed away, hoping the karma monster would catch up with him. Her hopes must have been heard because like a missile out of the blue, a pinecone ricocheted off Herman's head knocking his hat to the ground.

Stunned, the already angry man became furious. He grabbed his hat and flung the pinecone skyward as he unleashed a string of profanity to the heavens. Calle watched in amusement as he thrust his hat on his head and tramped away rubbing his temple. The pinecone must have landed a serious blow because she saw a streak of blood on Herman's jeans when he wiped his hand on his pants.

The irony of it all was too much for her. She began to chuckle out loud to herself. What were the chances he would get instant karma?

When Barrow landed on a chair next to her, she realized it wasn't karma after all. It was her avenging blue jay friend that had come to her rescue. That made it even more sweet.

"I didn't know you were here," Calle cooed. "That was a good shot!"

Barrow puffed his feathers then tilted his head back and forth in his silly way in acknowledgement of her compliment.

"Here, let me get you some piñon nuts," she laughed as he flew to the table and she went into the kitchen.

Calle was relaxing near the fountain feeding Barrow pine nuts, when a young woman wearing a calico dress and a white bonnet approached. Barrow took one look at the unusual character then leapt into flight.

"I didn't mean to scare away your friend," the woman, who really wasn't much more than a girl, said sweetly.

"It's okay, he comes and goes on his own," Calle replied.

"I know what you mean," the girl responded. "My uncle feeds cardinals out of his hat. Sometimes there's three or four birds at once. I never would have imagined someone else did the same thing. I can't wait to tell him."

Surprised by the ease with which she accepted Barrow's presence, Calle said, "No he's not alone, there's me too."

A quiet second or two passed and Calle sensed a certain shyness from the girl, so she asked, "Can I help you with something?"

"Oh yes, I'm looking for Otis Delve," she said. "They said he'd be out by the tent."

Calle glanced at the giant pavilion then back at the girl. With an inquisitive tilt of her head, she said, "Well, he's not here right now."

Framed by the lush forest and historic structures behind her, the plain girl looked like a Laura Ingalls character right off the stagecoach. There was something vaguely familiar about her and Calle was overcome with curiosity, so she continued, "What did you need to talk to Otis about?"

It was fleeting, but Calle caught a tinge of uncertainty pass the girl's features, but she recovered quickly.

Steeling herself, the girl met Calle's eyes and said almost confidently, "I'm looking for a job."

The girl's inner struggle struck a chord with Calle. It was familiar territory. Taking in her overall appearance, Calle knew how much courage it took to be different. Maybe it was the lacy headdress or her unadulterated innocence, but there was something genuine about the girl. A quality Calle understood and admired.

"Oh?" Calle said, trying to imagine what kind of job Otis could possibly have for her. "What do you know how to do?" she asked.

"I've worked in my aunt's café back home for the past three years," she said with pride.

"So, you're a server. Do you happen to have a bartender's license?"

"No, but I'm twenty-one and have my server's license for alcohol."

"Aha, unless you're good with a shovel, I don't think Otis can use you because he oversees the grounds crew and maintenance, but I certainly could use a server right now," Calle suggested. "What's your name?"

"Lisa Jill Owens, I'm from Pennsylvania."

Just like with Ezra and Verna, Calle went with her intuition, "Well, Lisa Jill from Pennsylvania, what do you say, want to work with me? You can start right now."

"Really?"

"Really."

Her offer caught Lisa Jill off guard and Calle could almost see the wheels spinning inside the young woman's head. After a beat, Lisa Jill decided.

"Okay, what do you need me to do?" she cheerfully accepted.

"First, you can help me clean up the kitchen and then we'll go to Kokopelli downtown to get your paperwork together so you can work tomorrow with the rest of the crew."

A little while later, Calle helped Lisa Jill unload her bicycle from the bed of her truck. The trip to the shop downtown had been uneventful and preparing the paperwork for Jill, as she preferred to be called, went smoothly. The two women bid each other farewell, Jill off to Walmart to buy her black and whites she would need to work for Kokopelli and Calle back to the mansion to meet Lucy for lunch.

Lucy was already waiting in the foyer when Calle hustled in.

"Sorry I'm late," Calle breathed. "I hired a new girl this morning and had to get her squared away for tomorrow."

"No problem, I just got here myself," Lucy replied.

"Great, let's go," Calle motioned toward the dining room and Lucy fell in line.

"So, you hired another server?" Lucy began as they took their seats at a small booth nestled in the rear of the dining room.

"Yeah, I think she's going to work out really well. She's Mennonite, from Pennsylvania."

"Like Amish or something?"

"Sort of, but not as strict. She wears a prayer cap, but otherwise she's pretty much like everyone else."

"Like what Jewish guys wear, that thing on the back of their heads?"

Calle laughed, "No, it's like a bonnet, but smaller,

lacy, and white. It's actually quite cute on her."

"Mmm, okay. To each their own."

As the two perused the menu and chittered small talk, Calle couldn't stand the suspense any longer.

"So, what's up? What's the big secret?"

A look of apprehension crossed Lucy's face as she tried to organize her thoughts. Whatever she had to share was proving difficult for her to verbalize. Calle sat patiently as Lucy gathered herself, but the revelation would have to wait a few more minutes because just then, the waitron arrived to take their orders.

The distraction was enough for Lucy to settle herself. She looked Calle in the eye then began to speak.

"Well, you remember the dream I had about the guitar player in the graveyard?"

"Yeah, the scary one where you couldn't wake up?"

"That's the one."

"Okay, so?"

"Well, he came back," Lucy stated matter-of-factly. "A few times."

"Hmm, is that a good thing or a bad thing?"

"Both, I guess."

"Luce, I can tell this is bothering you, but you're going to have to get to the point. What's going on?"

"I like him. I like him a lot. And he likes me too," Lucy pleaded like a teenager trying to convince her parents to extend her curfew on prom night.

"What do you mean? You're attracted to a man in your dreams?"

Usually, a statement like that would be looked upon as a sure sign of dementia, but since both women knew Calle had a dream lover of her own, neither even batted an eye.

"Yep, I think so."

The two sat staring at each other, Calle bemused, Lucy serious and forlorn.

"Congratulations?" Calle ventured with a grin.

"Not congratulations, geez," Lucy exhaled pure exasperation. "Fat lot of good you are."

"Sorry, I don't know what to say. What do you want me to do?"

"You're the dream expert. Help me."

"Help you do what? I don't understand."

"Calle, he's not like any man I've ever met. I really like him. I think he's my match." Lucy said with certainty. "But there's always this veil between us, I need to get closer, but I don't know how."

That's when Calle realized the nitty-gritty of Lucy's problem. She was in love. Which came as a big surprise because Lucy was a tough egg to crack. Calle had witnessed at least a thousand would-be suitors come and go, but Lucy was never moved. Most times, Calle didn't think she even noticed them, let alone cared. She was just one of those people that radiated a certain charisma that others couldn't resist. Consequently, she was immune to Cupid's poison arrows.

Calle now understood the brevity of the situation. Lucy was alone and adrift in uncharted territory, in love with a man that only came alive when she dreamed, but unable to touch him physically. Calle could sympathize, but was up to her ears with her own dream-capades. What could she possibly do to help?

"Oh my god," Calle whispered.

"I know, right? What am I going to do?"

"I don't know."

"You don't know?! Can't you come into my dream

and teach me what to do?"

"I'm not that good," Calle admitted. "I hardly know where I'm going to end up when I dream. I'm just learning."

"But you have sex with Ethan all the time and talk to dead guys, why can't you help me?" Lucy countered.

"I don't have sex with Ethan all the time. It's not like that," Calle stumbled. "In fact, I haven't seen him in weeks," she defended feebly. "Well, not like that anyway... It's not that easy, it's complicated. Geez."

Lucy leveled an unsympathetic scowl as Calle squirmed with her thoughts.

"Why not give it a try? I'll let you in my dream, then you can show me how it works. Right? It'll be good practice for you," Lucy persisted.

"I don't know, let me think about it," Calle shook her head then wryly rebounded, "Plus, I'm not really into threesomes."

"Shut up, you," Lucy snorted. "Come on, you know what I mean."

"I do, but you know a lot of my dreams aren't even lucid. And when they are, they usually don't go out of body, right?"

"So?"

"So, it might be a while before I can find you and then I probably won't know what to do."

"But you've done amazing things. Remember finding Pokey in the culvert? You saved her life."

"Yeah, I've been lucky. When it works, it's miraculous. I don't know, maybe, I can do it. I am getting better, but what if I botch it and ruin everything?"

"It can't get much worse," Lucy sighed as she leaned

back in her seat.

"What do you mean?" Calle asked, sensing something dire.

They shared a unique sixth sense connection and it began to kick in, but before it took hold, it cracked into shards as the waitress brought their food. It was a welcome interruption. The discussion was going too deep, too fast. As they nibbled their food, they swirled thoughts inside their heads until Calle couldn't remain silent any longer.

"What do you mean, 'It can't get much worse'? What have you done?"

"I've been going to Fairview hoping to see him," Lucy said slightly above a whisper.

"The cemetery? You're going to the cemetery to meet a guy you dream about?"

"Yep. But when you put it like that, it sounds insane." Lucy stilled. "Geez. Am I crazy?"

"Yes."

The look Calle received almost broke her heart, so she galloped the conversation along as quickly as possible.

"Not really, but when you catch up with me, then you'll know you've arrived," Calle joked hoping to alleviate some of Lucy's fear. "It doesn't have to be all that serious. We'll figure something out. If you want, I'll try to help. No guarantees though, okay?"

"Okay," Lucy smiled in relief. "By the way, you're not all that crazy. Well, not that much," she teased.

"You think so?" Calle hedged. "I've got some secrets you wouldn't believe."

"Really? Try me," Lucy challenged. "I told you mine. It's your turn."

The shoe was on the other foot and it was a lot tighter on Calle's toes now that she was the one wearing it.

"Alright," Calle said, instantly wishing she could snatch her words out of Lucy's ears.

When Calle balked, Lucy raised her eyebrows and insisted, "I'm listening."

"Alright already, geez. Okay, Remember the rat in my mailbox?"

"Mmm, mm."

"Well, I think there's more to it than that."

"Did you call Sam?"

"I left a message."

"Good, now what?"

Calle stalled a moment to organize her thinking. She was about to reveal something she'd kept secret, but probably should have shared with Lucy when it had happened.

"I didn't want to tell you right away because I didn't know how to describe it and I wasn't sure about it because nothing has happened so far, until now. I guess I still don't fully understand it. Not an it really, it's a her," Calle sputtered.

Lucy furrowed her brow, took a sip of tea, then looked at her wide-eyed friend, "You're rambling."

"Okay, okay... I have a Guardian Angel," Calle spit out abruptly. She looked around like she expected the sky to fall or guys in white lab coats to arrive.

Lucy raised one eyebrow, blinked an eye roll, then relaxed back into her chair. Relieved, she expected something much more devious.

"That's it? Your big secret is you have a guardian angel? Hello, I'm Catholic, I believe we all have guardian angels. What's the big deal?"

"Mine's a little different," Calle said.

"Why am I not surprised?" Lucy smirked.

"Just listen," Calle assured, then revealed to Lucy about her pendant and went on to describe the evening on the mesa when she named it and the girl on the surface came to life. She told about how the girl shot a star into the sky, flipped directions, and how the blue light in her lantern began to glow from the face of the disc and had ever since.

"Wow."

"I know. Right?"

Calle went on to describe Beely's strange behavior after she found the rat in her mailbox and then finding that Isla was absent from the pendant, replaced by a lightning storm."

"It's creeping me out, I don't know what to think," Calle finished.

"For good reason."

"Wait, there's more," she continued.

"Of course, there is." Lucy shuffled in her seat. "There always is."

"Then last night when I finally found Ethan in my dream, this powerful cyclone appeared on the horizon. He said he thought it was following me, but wasn't sure. When we parted ways, he told me he would figure it out, but for me to be vigilant. So, now I'm worried I might have pissed off someone or something on the astral plane."

"Oh, my goodness. That can't be good." Lucy was astounded, but her inner strength wouldn't let her be intimidated and her loyalty to Calle began to bristle.

"Don't you worry. I've got your back here and Ethan

sounds like he's on top of it over there," she said as she waved her hand in the air behind her head. "Besides, you have a real guardian angel on your side. How cool is that? It should be smooth sailing from here, right?"

# ⊙ 7 ℂ

In her mind, Calle envisioned the sailing ship teetering on the brink of the waterfall from the cover of one of her favorite Kansas records. *The Point of No Return* began to play background to her imagination. Smooth sailing? Yeah, right up until she was plunging headfirst into the abyss beyond the edge of the universe.

Lucy had departed over an hour ago and Calle was still worrying about things she couldn't control. If she wasn't careful, she would trigger another PTSD episode. *Get a grip,* she told herself. Worrying about bridges that might never be crossed wouldn't do anybody any good.

Immersing herself in her work was the only solution and it worked like a charm. Everything was ready for the debut tomorrow, but she still needed to touch base with Otis before opening day. She dialed up his cell, the call went directly to voice mail. She figured he must be out of service range. Switching tactics, she pulled out her two-way radio and tried to contact him. She felt like Rambo calling in an airstrike as she talked into the cammo colored device.

After several attempts with no response, she decided to take a ride over to his treehouse. Maybe, he was on lunch or something. Besides, it was fun tooling around the estate in the service cart.

Like a Mr. Rourke on *Fantasy Island*, she zipped through the lush resort. What a life it would be to go from one world class destination to the next, not a care in the world, all the bills paid and made in the shade. There was no need to hurry, so she took the longer, scenic route. She slowed her pace to savor the carefree feeling and the cool mountain air that tickled her skin as her fantasy played out in her mind's eye. For a girl who liked to dream, it couldn't have been any better.

Still slightly intoxicated by her wonderful daydream, she puttered up to Otis treehouse. Again, she was intrigued by such a far-out place to live. When she was a little girl, she always wanted a tree house. Either her parents couldn't afford it or didn't have the skill to build one so, the answer was always, 'Oh, no honey, you'll fall out and break your leg'. Unlike Ralphie on *A Christmas Story*, she never got the chance to shoot her eye out. *Probably a good thing,* she mused as she ascended the steps.

Still mentally lingering somewhere between her childhood and *Lifestyles of The Rich and Famous*, she used her secret knock on the door. Three quick soft taps ending with a loud final knock rang from under her knuckle. The last rap must have been harder than she thought because the latch clicked and the door began to creak slowly inward. It continued to swing until it was wide open. Calle stood on the threshold as Otis' mountain of warehoused treasure unfolded into view.

"Otis? Anybody home?"

Fearing Otis might not be able to hear her through the piles of stuff, Calle crept into the jumbled maze. Calling for him, she continued throughout the entirety of his house. She was pleased to see the bathroom was free of debris and while there, decided to use the facilities. When she was finished, she checked herself in the mirror. Realizing the mirror was also a medicine cabinet, she popped it open.

A wisp of guilt flashed past as she inspected the contents of the cabinet, but it whizzed by so quickly, she hardly noticed.

Nothing unusual. Band-aids, shaving cream, aspirin, a tube of out-of-date hydrocortisone... Hmm. She didn't know what to expect, but since having pried into his personal space, guilt was starting to make a comeback. She was about close the door on the whole episode, when the shiny lid of a cylindrical jar caught her eye. It sat tucked in behind a tub of petroleum jelly. She tried to spin the label forward, but accidentally knocked it over causing everything in the vicinity to topple off the shelf. She caught the jar before it fell into the sink but missed a bottle of pills that crashed as loud as a cymbal to the countertop.

Embarrassed by the noisy fiasco, she picked up the container of tablets and inspected what was in her hands. In one, she held a jar of hemorrhoid cream and in the other, an expired script of Viagra.

Okay, that was it. Enough was enough, she just had to know and now she did. Whatever Otis had stashed in his medicine cabinet, or his whole house for that matter, was none of her business. Chastising herself, she replaced the items and shook herself back to the right side of her ethics then hustled to the front door.

Standing on the porch, surveying the forest floor from above, she tried the radio again. The result was the same as before and she was thinking a call later from home might be her only option, when a voice from the radio rang out.

"Miss, if you're looking for Otis, try down at the stables."

"Oh, hello?" Calle replied, hoping she was working the device properly. She thought about playing with Walkie-Talkies when she was a kid and remembered how everyone wanted to talk at the same time, so rarely anything got communicated. Keeping that in mind, she decided listening was better than talking.

"Hi," the laughing male voice replied. "Try down at the stables."

She pressed the send button again and said into the speaker, "The stables, okay, thank you. Over." She threw in the 'over' part because somewhere she had heard it before and she thought it was proper radio etiquette.

A moment of silence passed, then "Roger, roger. Ten-Four good buddy," rang out over a background of laughter. "Over."

*Oh, crap.* She knew she had blown it, so much for radio etiquette. Still unsure how to end this type of conversation, she simply said again, "Thank you," and chucked the damn thing into the dash of the cart.

After a wrong turn that led to a hidden spa area, she got back on track to the stables. Her trek seemed longer than when she had ridden with Otis the day before. Maybe because he knew the terrain better or simply because he drove like a maniac, she wasn't sure, but her pace suited her mood just fine and after a leisurely drive, she arrived at the stables.

The stables consisted of a series of corals, a barn, and a tack shop with hay, feed sacks, and various implements tucked in and around the structures. Up close, it was much larger than it looked from the main path. Running her fingertips along the top rail of the biggest coral, she admired the horses milling around inside as she walked toward the barn. There were plenty of animals, but not a person in sight.

As she neared the barn, she heard voices resonate from behind the side of the structure.

"That should do the trick," a heavy male accent intoned.

"Alright, let's get out of here. Meet you at the..." another man responded but his voice was drowned out by the roar of a diesel engine starting up. She hurried to talk to the men before they departed as another truck fired up. Any hope of conversation was dashed as the two trucks rumbled from behind the building.

She recognized the driver of the first truck as Rob Aragon in his delivery van. He was followed closely by another heavily loaded tandem driven by the wrangler she had seen the day before. She tried to flag them down, but both men snubbed her, each casting a stare of distain as they rumbled on by. They left her gasping for air as she hurried away from the bellowing dust cloud.

She purposely disregarded their rudeness as she walked in the direction of a huge stack of alfalfa bales looking for something to wipe the grit from her face. Some people just didn't have any manners. She found a towel over by some bins of oats and horse treats, but it was so filthy, she couldn't use it. So, she used the hem of her shirt to dig the most annoying grit from her eyes and accepted the fact she'd have to live with the rest until she could find someplace to rinse her face.

With the exit of the two men and their noisy vehicles, the stables took on a peaceful air. The aroma of leather and live horses replaced the dust in her nostrils and made her feel like she was in the old west. Many people don't like the smell of livestock, but to Calle, it was a comfort. But then again, she was one of the strange folks that didn't mind the odor of a skunk, as long as it didn't spray her. Go figure.

Rounding a stack of straw bales, she walked back into the sunshine. No sign of Otis. Across the driveway and past a tractor, she made her way to the tack shop.

It was a large wooden pole shack adorned with antiquated saddles, halters, and holey saddle blankets nailed to the facade. A large pile of luck was heaped to the side of the porch in the form of rusty old horseshoes. Good or bad, it could go either way, it just depended on how they were hung. She picked one up and thought maybe she might keep it. That was, of course, if she could find anyone to ask.

With a clank, she tossed the horseshoe back on the pile and stepped up onto the porch. Cupping her hands around her eyes to get a better look, she leaned her face against the glass to peer through the grimy window. It was about as clear as mud. She sidled over to the closed door and grabbed the depression-era door knob and finagled it back and forth until it unlatched. With a shove, the weathered, old wood panel door swung open and she entered.

Walls lined with horseman's paraphernalia and shelves laden with ranching supplies surrounded the main area of the shop. The worn plank floor creaked as she stepped into the middle of the minor expanse. She spun a slow arc surveying the room. Everything from lassoes, saddles, and cinches to spools of barbed wire littered every nook and cranny of the place. It was like a miniature Tractor Supply store frosted with dust.

She followed the battered footpath worn into the slatted floor, around a counter, and into the next room. From the doorway, she could hardly tell it was an office. A cracked and murky window allowed scarcely enough light to illuminate the sparsely furnished space.

Two straight-back wooden chairs sat in front of a squat pine desk that strained beneath mounds of long forgotten paperwork and an enormous ashtray overflowing butts. On the opposite wall, a pretty cowgirl with red boots, straddling a half-moon smiled from a Miller Beer calendar displaying the month of May, 1985. It hung next to a bovine-shaped electric clock whose second hand would tick dutifully up to the nine then drop helplessly back to the six only to repeat its ascent over and over, essentially trapping the room back in time.

Save a single insect furiously trying to buzz a hole in the dingy office window, the building was devoid of life. And the narrow door in the corner that opened into a small utility closet showed no promise of anything different. *So much for Otis*, she thought as she turned to exit the shop.

"Otis, where are you?" a woman's voice chimed in chorus with her thoughts from the tiny doorway behind her. Calle spun to face the spectral entity beckoning the lost groundskeeper. "Otis. Come in, Otis?"

Recognizing the voice as Teresa's, Calle hurried over to the utility room. The slender doorway belied the size of the room. It was narrow, but much deeper than she imagined. She placed her hand on the door frame as she leaned in trying to find the light switch. Finding no way to turn on the lights, she moved another step into the shadows, following Teresa's radio voice scratching from the far corner. Just past a water heater and further into the darkness, a thin cord hanging from above touched Calle's face. She grabbed the cord and gave a tug downward to turn on the single incandescent bulb sticking out of the ceiling.

Light splashed across the utility room and onto the crumpled body of Otis Delve lying next to a dingy toilet as Teresa's discouraged voice beckoned again, "Otis, come in, I hope you're alright."

## ☉ 8 ☾

Otis was anything but alright. He was hatless and unconscious, face-first on the piss-stained linoleum of the shabby, confined space. With a burlap sack in one hand and an epi-pen near the other, he looked like he was trying to escape when he fell. Ignoring the large knot on his forehead and numerous swollen red marks on his face and neck, Calle straddled his body hoping to find a pulse.

It was feint, but steady. Calle grabbed the radio from Otis' belt and alerted Teresa to the emergent situation. As her concern mounted and she described the scene, she felt a savage sting on her throat. Instinctively, she slapped her hand to swat the attacking insect. In her palm lay a dead honeybee. She cast the dead bee aside to massage her injury. On the throbbing welt she felt the bee's detached stinger and pulled it from her skin.

That's when she realized there were more bees buzzing in the room and that the red marks on Otis' face and neck were probably bee stings as well.

"I've called 911, I'm on my way. What's going on there?" Teresa's tone was mounting hysteria. "Is Otis okay?!"

"He's been stung by a bunch of bees, he's unconscious," Calle reported over the radio.

"Oh my God, Otis is allergic to bees, he could die."

Teresa now frantic.

As Calle looked at the scene, it all started to make sense. "There's an epi-pen here, but it's unused. Should I inject him with it?"

"Yes! Yes! Hurry, it might already be too late," Teresa howled.

Calle ripped open the injector pack and stabbed the needle into Otis' thigh. No reaction, he didn't even stir when the needle penetrated deep into his leg. A wave of unease passed over her. Did she administer the shot correctly? Was he actually dead and she didn't really feel a pulse? Should she try to wake him? She knew time was of the essence, but it seemed like it had come to a halt.

"I've given him the injection, but he's not moving. What do I do?" Calle shouted at the radio.

"There's nothing you can do. Wait for the paramedics," Teresa's disembodied advice soured her optimism like a priest delivering last rites.

Calle stood up and stepped back from Otis as several bees buzzed over his body. *What's with all the bees?* Then she noticed the burlap sack in Otis hand. It was the same burlap bag Michael had been carrying when he visited the pavilion in his bee suit the day before. She leaned back down to get a better look at the bag. Inside, she found more dead bees and Otis' hat.

She checked Otis' pulse once more. It was hard to locate, but when she did, it was still steady. Hoping to help Otis, she wanted to linger near him in the cramped space, but the numerous and agitated bees buzzing around gave her the heebie jeebies, figuratively and quite literally. Keeping Otis lifeless form in view, she retreated to the office and stood at the entrance to the utility room. It was a safer place to wait.

Time kicked back into gear when Teresa slammed through the tack room entrance and into the office. The mask of the serious, capable woman was expertly painted across her face, but her smeared mascara and turbulent gaze revealed the internal heartache she was trying to suppress. She fell to her knees beside her friend and grabbed his hand.

Unconcerned by the bees hovering around her face, she cooed in assurance, "Otis. Otis, hang in there, buddy, help is on the way. You're going to be alright." She kissed his knuckles then held his hand in hers and brought them to her breast. Her body slumped into a protective posture over his as she began to whisper a prayer.

Calle watched and waited as Teresa's prayer turned into muted sobs. She was touched by Teresa's obvious concern for Otis and said a prayer of her own for the fallen groundskeeper and his longtime friend and employer.

It felt like ages before the ambulance arrived. Otis was in bad shape. Fearing for the worst, the paramedics carted Otis off to the hospital as the police arrived.

Detective Shawn Ramirez met the women on the porch outside the tack room. He looked to be about twenty going on fifty. Athletic and fit, he filled out his uniform like it was tailor made. His pale silver eyes shone seriousness and authority over high cheek bones as his gaze quickly swept the perimeter. Calle stood about eye level with his badge as he explained the situation.

"The EMT's reported a suspicious situation," his voice was about as comforting as a cattle prod. "I agree.

It looks like Mr. Delve was ambushed with a sack of bees pulled over his head."

Calle and Teresa shared a glance as he continued, "I've called the crime scene unit, but in the meantime, I would like to ask you both a few questions."

He asked Teresa to wait with another officer while he took Calle's statement.

"So, you're the caterer?" the detective started.

"Yes, I work for Kokopelli."

"Full name, Calle Roslyn?"

"Yes detective," she answered stiffly.

Sensing her wariness, he softened his demeanor. "You can call me Shawn."

She eyed him suspiciously, but his smile disarmed her.

"Okay, Shawn," she began nervously, then went on to tell the him how she found Otis and the events leading up to her discovery.

"And you saw two men leaving the stables in trucks just before you found the victim, could you identify them?"

"Yes, one was the delivery driver, Rob Aragon and the other was the wrangler I saw here yesterday."

"Do you know of anyone that might have an issue with Otis?"

"Not really, I've only been here a couple days. Otis is such a nice guy, I can't think of anyone," she replied then had to correct herself. "Actually, the plumber was angry with Otis and stormed off this morning."

Calle described her experience with Herman Young. As she did, she remembered, Otis' confrontation with Jamaica Spinner at the spring the previous afternoon. After going over the details with Shawn, she realized that having a job like Otis', he probably had had a lot of confrontations over the years. Some of those could have produced some serious enemies. Some that may have been waiting for the right moment to serve up a cold dish of revenge.

Any one of a number of people could have attacked Otis. Detective Ramirez had his work cut out for him. But one thing nagged her all the way home and she was convinced that thing was the crux of the investigation. The attacker would had to have known about Otis' allergy to bee stings.

Later, with her senses on edge, she idled into her driveway. Maybe being so keyed up over the situation at work made her suspicious, but she was sure there were new tire tracks in her driveway. Being careful not to drive over them, she parked her truck in the shade under a towering cottonwood.

Closer inspection confirmed what she suspected. A vehicle had been in her driveway. The wide and deep tracks had to be a larger vehicle, probably a pickup. The driver pulled up to the shed, but must not have gotten out. The were no footprints in the soft dirt beside the tire tracks.

Maybe someone was lost and just needed to use her driveway to turn around. She walked back to the pavement where she could see the tracks as they exited her property. The vehicle did not turn around, it had resumed its path back toward town.

She was about to chalk the whole thing up to paranoia when she spotted Beely half way up a tall tree. He was crouched in a stalking position near the end of a large limb. Camouflaged by a branch full of leaves, he looked down to her and gave a low meowl, then returned his gaze to the road.

She leaned her head back and shaded her eyes, "Beeler, what are you doing up there?"

Without a sound, he shot her a serious glance like he was too busy to be bothered, flicked his tail petulantly then resumed his surveillance of the area.

She eyed him curiously, but knew he was going to do whatever he wanted regardless of her attempts to get him down. Cats are independent like that. They own you, not the other way around.

Calle had learned long ago that Beely was an unusual animal, so him being up the tree wasn't a big deal. But his recent behavior combined with the suspicious tire tracks made her rethink the situation. As she was promising herself to be more observant and cautious, a Santa Fe County Sheriff's K-9 unit drove past on the main road, alleviating some of her concern.

She left Beely to his feline pursuits and went inside her house. Dumping her purse and worries on the sofa, she made a quick jaunt to the restroom and then straight to the back patio. She could feel the tension peel away as she sat peacefully in the shade and enjoyed a puff of a new marijuana strain and a cool glass of iced tea.

The first blue tailed lizard of the year snuck from under a bush to bask in the sun. Calle marveled at how a creature so sleek and fast could move so spasmodically and deliberately. He must be on the prowl.

It was moments like these that really got to her. The blatant honesty of the natural world was nourishment for her soul. As simple as it seemed, it was truth in its most basic form, pure and sacred. It was real.

She watched in silence as Mr. Bluetail juddered off in search of dinner, then pulled out her phone and speed dialed her favorite confidante.

"Hey Luce, what's cookin'?"

"Whatever it is, you'd better not eat it if I'm the one doing the cooking," Lucy laughed. "Unless it's a PB&J, then you're okay. What's up?"

"Nada, well, not really."

"There's something, what is it? Did you find another dead guy?" Lucy teased.

"Not dead, but unconscious."

"Oh my god, really? What happened?"

Calle went on to describe how she searched for Otis' at his treehouse and how she found him in the bathroom at the tack shop.

"He was stung by a bunch of bees. It looks to me like someone ambushed him and stuck a burlap sack full of honeybees over his head. I found his hat and a bunch of dead bees inside the bag nearby. I got stung too."

"You're not allergic, are you?"

"No, but Otis is."

She continued to talk about injecting the epi-pen into Otis' leg and how the cops thought there might be some criminal intent.

"I left after giving my statement and the crime scene team arrived."

"So, now what?"

"I guess we just wait and see. When Otis wakes up, we'll find out."

"So, he's going to be alright?"

"I think so. He was alive when they took him to the hospital."

"Sheesh."

"I know, right?" Calle scribbled invisible figure eights on the tabletop with her fingernail. Changing the topic, she continued, "I wanted to tell you, I'm going to try to visit your dreams tonight, so don't be alarmed if I show up."

"Really? How cool," Lucy bristled. "I'll be ready."

"Remember, it may not work tonight, but I'll keep trying. If does ever work, it will most likely be a surprise to both of us, so try to be ready. If that's at all even possible."

"At least you're going to try, that's all that counts."

"Okay, so we're on the same page. Let's see what happens," Calle said as Barrow flitted onto the birdbath. "Hey, my blue jay friend is here, I'll call you later."

The black crown on the magnificent bird's head prickled as he sloshed in the water, took a couple sips, then shook out his wings. He stared at Calle through golden flecked, emerald orbs that on any ordinary blue jay should have been black. But Barrow was far from ordinary.

When Barrow was around, Calle felt a certain nearness to Ethan. She knew they were connected and though reassuring, it was also weird in its own way.

Calle held out her wrist and Barrow sailed to a soft landing on her thumb. She found the irony of Ethan's bird sitting on the very same appendage that in the astral world, she wore a feathery silver ring that he had given her, amusing.

On the astral plane, she sported a ring of fragrance on her thumb and here, at the moment, on the physical plane, sat another magical creature of his upon the very shadow of that ring. It was mind boggling. There was a time not so long ago, she would have never even imagined something so bizarre, but today, it was just another charming fact of her life.

They sat in admiration of each other for a few moments when she moved to stand and said, "Come in, I've got some peanuts for you."

When she reached the door, Barrow nervously jumped into flight. He landed on the back of one of the lawn chairs nearby and cocked his head suspiciously at her. The bird did not want to go inside. No matter how much she wooed him, he would not come near the door.

"Alright, have it your way," she said then fetched a few peanuts and placed them on the table. Barrow eagerly nabbed one and winged up through the trees. "Weirdo," Calle chuckled to herself as she went inside and closed the sliding glass door behind her.

After a hot shower and dinner, she headed for bed. It had been a long day. In the evening, there was nothing she liked better than to curl up in bed with a cozy mystery and join someone else's adventure for a few chapters.

As she passed her dresser, she picked up the pendant that continued to flash a broiling typhoon on its surface. Where was Isla? Without a clue, she chucked the pendant back into the basket next to the mysterious keys Barrow had given her. Her basket of simple treasures was rapidly becoming a basket of mysteries.

As she turned to face her bed, she caught a fleeting glimpse of something moving in her periphery. Surprised, she abruptly spun her head to face the closet, only to see her clothes hanging like they always did. She looked on as Beely jumped off her bed and began to investigate, sniffing the contents of her closet.

"You saw that too?"

He slowed as she joined him at the threshold of the closet and peeped her head inside. It was the same as it always was, nothing out of place, no one there.

"Sheesh, Beeler, we must be losing it," Calle smiled, thinking her sudden reaction must have put him on alert. Dismissing the incident, she picked up her cat and nuzzled him close then set him on the bed. She crawled in after him and the two burrowed under the quilt, relaxing together until slumber overtook them both.

For Calle, falling asleep could mean a number of things. One, she would simply rest soundly then awake refreshed just like any other normal human being. Two, she might do thing number one, but dream fanciful dreams, again, like most everyone else. Three, she could do both one and two, then her dream could go lucid, unlike most everyone else.

Once in a lucid dream, she would be fully aware that she was dreaming and could do anything she wanted. She was in complete control. She could create and manipulate her dream any way she wanted. It was very liberating, but more importantly, when she was lucid, that's when the ever-elusive option number four became possible.

Case number four was where things got very peculiar. It was then that how extraordinary she truly was became evident. She could do what only a handful of people in history had ever been able to do. She would be able to go out of body. Literally. If she desired and things went just right, she could separate her spirit from her physical self and traverse the astral plane. Still tethered to her body, she couldn't completely leave it behind, she would always have to return. At least as long as she was alive. But while lucid and out of body, she could do amazing things.

The astral plane encompasses the real universe as we know it, but it is so vast, it goes way beyond what one can imagine. Movement is not necessarily determined by time and space, it can be, but it's not a requirement. It is efficiently traversed faster than the speed of light or slower than absolute stillness. A strange concept for human beings who have never been absolutely still, but then again, nothing in the real universe has ever been either. Everything has always been in motion since the beginning.

With a whim, she could go and do as she pleased. Wherever, whenever, however. It was heady stuff, something you couldn't pick up in school. It was something few knew about and even fewer talked about.

Becoming both physical and astrally aware simultaneously is an extremely rare occurrence. Everyone is an astral being, a ghost attached to a body living on the physical plane for a while. Most people have an inkling of their spiritual self, but are blind to the fact they are already living the afterlife. When people die, their spirits are released from their physical limitations and become solely astral entities. They leave their bodies behind and speed off beyond physical recognition. But there are a precious few, for whatever reason, have the ability to be physically alive and astrally free at the same time. Calle Roslyn was one of those people.

However, astral traveling is not an exact science and there is not a 'how to' book to guide those who have the gift. As Calle had learned, at least in her case, it was a hit and miss endeavor. A crap shoot at best. So, though she had visited other's dreams, spectrally observed real-life situations in real time, and talked to the dead, she hadn't quite figured out exactly how it all worked. Though she had gained a trove of experience, there was so much more to the iceberg than the tip she understood. In fact, she had more failures than successes dream trekking but she remained determined.

So, when she turned out the lights and snuggled next to Beely, she opened her mind to the possibility of a dream trek. She knew she might not be able to achieve that state at will, but she knew it would come sooner or later. Her plan was to relax and not to try to force it. Embrace her desire, but let the universe do its thing, waiting for it to start on its own. She would be ready when it did. Then she would go in search of answers.

Somewhere after the walk on the plaza then the tennis match, her dream became lucid. Her awareness began to glow like the sun coming over the horizon. She was in her element, but something was different. She could feel the energy that usually accompanied a lucid dream, but she felt confined. She took as much control as she could, but was trapped like a person in a waiting room where the TV was stuck on mute and it only played two channels. She toggled between a scene where as she lay in her bed asleep, Ethan would show her an amulet then read to her, then to a scene where Howard Lewis taunted her with wild faces and crude gestures. She was stuck either trying to hear Ethan's words or being unable to deal with Howard's threats to torture his nephew. Back and forth, she grappled with Ethan's benevolent form and Howard's noseless grimace.

Unable to break the cycle, her anxiety began to mount. Anxiety is the bane of astral control. She knew she was about lose what little she had, but she had learned to expect the unexpected. Though it was disturbing, she was undeterred and kept trying to maintain her focus. She was determined fight her fear as long as she could.

The contents of the dream grew less important. The real conflict became her inner struggle within herself. She fought desperately to stay in the dream as long as possible. Her own mental tenacity was what was at stake and what she hoped to expand. She knew this was a chance to test herself. She also knew it was the key to any future dream trekking success. She struggled valiantly to contain her angst until she could no longer maintain her balance on the edge.

Straining for control and besieged by self-doubt, any hope of helping Lucy had long since evaporated. It was all Calle could do just to balance on the tight rope of the trek. But it didn't last long.

The dream exploded in slow motion as an electric serpentine tendril of sapphire wound a stranglehold around a searing flow of molten lava bubbling only inches from her face. The resulting thunderclap flung her into consciousness with such force she banged her head on the night stand. She could still smell the stench of quenched sulfur as she coughed a dry throated gasp and sat up on the floor next to her bed.

Rubbing the bump on the back of her head, she watched as Beely hurdled the blanket twisted around her legs to sidle up next to her. She pulled him close as he pushed his furry face to her cheek. She sat in his tender care as she tried to process what had just happened. Whatever it was, it was new and it was powerful.

# ☽ 9 ☾

The Kokopelli crew finished the set up for the day as Barrow took the last peanut from Calle's hand. Where he was storing them and how he had beat her to work that day was a mystery. Last time she saw him, he was at home in the large cottonwood by her shed as she rolled out of her driveway earlier that morning. But here he was now, miles away, bigger than Brazil, keeping a close watch on her.

The guests weren't to arrive for another few minutes so the crew gathered around the fountain to wait.

"So, I bet Santa Fe is very different from Pennsylvania," Ezra said as he looked to Jill.

"Yah, there aren't any mountains where I come from, just lots of farm fields."

Verna pointed to her head, "What's the deal with the bonnet?" Her question tinged with mild sarcasm.

The minor snark blew right by Lisa Jill and she answered cheerfully, "It's called a prayer cap. In my religion, women cover their heads in public."

Phillip moved next to Calle as they watched the younger members of their merry little band wade into the deep end about women's rights, religious freedom, and long held tradition.

Ignoring their debate, he said, "Check this out,"

as he pulled a twenty-five-dollar poker chip from his pocket. He let Calle hold the red disc emblazoned with the words *Camel Rock Casino* in the center.

"Thanks!" Calle said quickly with a smile as she pretended to put the token in her pocket.

"Aha, pretty sly, aren't you?" Phillip laughed as she gave the chip back to him. "That's one way to make something disappear, but how about this?" he said as he deftly spun the chip along his fingertips then into his palm. He closed his fingers around the chip then quickly opened his hand to reveal nothing but air.

With one hand on her hip, she stood in minor amazement as he reached to touch her other hand. He rolled that hand into a fist, massaged her closed knuckles, then with a flourish, opened her hand to reveal the poker chip inside her upturned palm.

"What the... How did you do that?" she sputtered.

"Wouldn't you like to know," he laughed. Still smiling, he held her gaze, then closed her fingers around the chip again and massaged her hand once more, then asked her to open her hand.

As she slowly released her grasp that she had intentionally kept tight around the chip, she could already tell the token was gone. Now completely astonished, she held her empty hand between them.

"That's amazing, I wish I could do that," she met his eyes, spinning the compliment and request into a smile.

"Well, that trick is pretty hard for a beginner, but here's a trick you can do. With a little practice of course."

"Of course," she repeated as he took the token and spun it cleverly between his fingers. He then clapped his hands gently, then opened his palms to show they were now empty.

"Okay," she said as he clapped his hands again only to reveal the reappeared poker chip. "Pretty slick, what's the secret?"

"It's a combination of precise dexterity and misdirection. First you have to be able to spin the item smoothly between your fingers. That takes lots of practice, but once you master that skill, you can use it anytime, anywhere. Secondly, remember people like to see what they think they're going see, but they can only truly see what their attention is focused on. Draw their attention, even just for a split-second, away from your move. Then of course, time your move to when their attention is diverted."

"Sounds easy enough."

"So, you say," he laughed as he flipped the token in a high arc to her.

"Ach, geez," she chuckled as she fumbled to catch the chip.

"Good catch," he teased, then reached into his pocket to pull out a silver dollar. "Start practicing like this," he said seriously as he slowly spun the coin around his knuckles in one hand.

She gave a sincere, but clumsy effort and her token fell to the ground. He picked up the token and placed in her hand, then aligned the token in her fingers just so.

"Go slowly, your hand muscles must gain strength and you'll have to grow comfortable with the feel of the trick. Be persistent and concentrate. It will come to you. At first, it will feel foreign, but after a while, it will become second nature to you."

She stared at her rigid fingers as she tried again. His advice was exactly what she had been teaching herself about controlling her dreams. Little did he know, but she already had a head-start honing her ability to concentrate. She slipped easily into a shallow trance like a chess master orchestrating a checkmate.

In her mind, she could see and feel the token rolling precisely around her fingers. As if she could will the trick into being, the token spun from one finger to the next then the next. Before she knew it, the exercise was complete, but just like in her dreams, the second she diverted her focus from what she was doing to how amazing her accomplishment was, she ham-fisted the token into the air and across the lawn.

"Oh, crap!" and "Well done!" were uttered simultaneously.

As she bent to retrieve the token, he said, "Keep working on it, you're off to a good start."

She tried to give the poker chip back to him, but he refused saying, "It's yours now. It can be your good luck charm."

She was about to argue, but just then, Michael and Teresa rounded the edge of the pavilion.

Calle slipped the token into her pocket and as mother and son neared the group, everyone turned to face them. Calle's magic lesson and the social debate were set aside as the catering crew directed their attention to the approaching pair. Concern for Otis and the anticipation of the news about his situation hung like a thick cloud under the huge tent as Teresa began to speak.

She explained that since Otis had no living relatives, she went to the hospital to check on him. As she reported that Otis was in a coma, Calle could see angst hidden under Teresa's presentation. Having witnessed

Teresa's reaction yesterday, she knew Otis' situation wasn't just business for the woman. Teresa and Otis shared a deep connection, of that, Calle was certain.

As Teresa answered questions about the incident, Calle watched her son. It was hard to believe Michael had any reason to ambush Otis, but why was his bee sack at the scene with Otis' hat inside? Unable to find any hint of guilt on the handsome young man's face or in his body language, something did catch her attention. Despite his best efforts, he couldn't disguise his obvious attraction to Jill. He couldn't keep his eyes off her.

He kept sneaking glances her way trying to make eye contact. When she finally noticed him staring, she blushed and tried to ignore him, pretending to be enthralled by Teresa's diatribe. Young people were so goofy.

Calle's mind began to wander back to when her life was once so innocent. It was a magical time, being young and idealistic, but she wouldn't want to be that naïve again.

Just as she was starting to feel wise and mature, she remembered the pain of losing her husband and the deep depression that followed. She thought about her love life now that was split between a real-life pilot in training and her secret astral lover. She might not be as naïve as she once was, but she wasn't any less confused. Goofy, confused, what's the difference? Love is tricky.

Calle's contemplation was interrupted when she noticed that she wasn't the only one interested in Michael's subtle overtures toward Jill. Verna was playing at nonchalance, but Calle caught a whiff of jealousy as Verna passed a glare from Jill to Michael and back. Apparently, love triangles were in season.

Just when Calle thought Michael was going to die of frustration, his mother announced that he would be taking over many of Otis' tasks until further notice. Michael's face turned a bold pink under his dark features as the attention of the group turned toward him. Caught with his mind galloping through La-La land, he was relieved when he realized he didn't have to speak, instead, he waved his hand and half-smiled, happy to return to his musings.

As Teresa was wrapping up the impromptu meeting, guests began to filter into the shade of the pavilion and the Kokopelli crew sprang into action. A resilient Michael made a beeline for Jill, but she politely dismissed his ardor as she carried a water pitcher to an already seated four-top. Before Teresa rounded up Michael to get back to their own duties, she called Calle aside to ask if Ezra could be spared for some time to help Michael. Calle said she would talk to Ezra, but for now, they had to focus on the hungry clientele that had already filled the dining area.

Calle was proud of her crew. They handled the rush like seasoned professionals. Lisa Jill fit right in and proved to be a fast learner and a hard worker. Calle mentioned to Ezra Teresa's proposition and Ezra readily agreed. He would work with Kokopelli during large events and part-time with Michael. He didn't waste a minute to start teasing Verna about the arrangement.

"I told you he was mine," Ezra's taunt chirped on the last syllable.

"Ha, you sound like a scratched record. Besides, he doesn't swing to your side of the fence," Verna volleyed as she looked to Jill.

"That's because he hasn't got to know me yet."

"Oh, yeah, good luck with that. He's got his eye on little miss innocent there," Verna waved a hand toward Jill.

At the mention of her name, Jill turned to pay closer attention to the conversation she had been actively ignoring.

"What about me?"

"Nothing, Verna's just jealous of me getting to work with Michael."

"There's nothing to be jealous about, Michael has a thing for her," Verna motioned again to Jill.

"Sorry to disappoint you, but I have no interest in Michael," Jill said. "I have a beau back home."

"But he's two thousand miles away."

"Maybe so, but he's still there waiting."

"When the cat's away..." Ezra was enjoying himself immensely.

"Why would you come all this way to Santa Fe if you have a boyfriend back home?" Verna pried.

Lisa Jill saw Calle approaching and said, "Table fifteen needs refills and their dishes bussed." Then she grabbed the iced tea pitcher and strode back on the floor without another word.

"She's right guys," Calle pointed to the diners. "Let's go."

Ezra exchanged a mischievous grin for Verna's scowl as they got back to work.

Besides a spilt glass of water on table six, the opening event flew by without incident. If things went as efficiently as they did on first day, the rest of the gig at Pérez Manor would go as smooth as silk, but Calle knew sooner or later something would come up. It always did.

# ☽ 10 ☾

YouTube can be useful and it can be entertaining. It can also be a load of manure. After a couple hours trying to find any legitimate posts about lucid dreaming or out-of-body experiences, Calle sat frustrated. Her efforts to find anyone who was similar to her had gone unrewarded. There were tons of people posting nonsensical encounters with guides and seers, but nothing like what she had seen firsthand on the astral plane. She was convinced most postings were contrived notions sensationalizing a fictional narrative in order to attract followers. In other words, just a heapin', helpin' pile of horse shit.

There was one woman though, who seemed to be sincere. She spoke of spirit guides and a distorted sense of time where astral time and physical time were not always in sync. Calle had noticed the time discrepancy as well. So that was as close to similar as she got. Apparently, the only creature on the planet that was anything like her was her fictional animé hero Ab Pistola. Her and of course, Ethan, whom she had never actually laid eyes on in the physical sense.

But then it occurred to her, why would any genuine astral traveler waste their time on YouTube? Reality is always stranger than fiction. Plus, it's always true.

She folded up her Surface and made her way to

her back yard. The night was closing a sleepy sunset just over the horizon as she loaded a bowl and tried for the umpteenth time to blow a decent smoke ring. A wistful cloud of smoke that resembled a crumpled bicycle rim dissipated into the swaying leaves of the nearest cottonwood. Soon, thousands of seeds from the tree would fall from its branches and coat the ground with wads of cottonlike balls that would roll around like snowflakes out of season. She sat in quiet contemplation and let her thoughts ramble.

A curious mind likes to wander. It enjoys a languid perusal of all things theoretic. Topics don't have to be serious or meaningful, they can just be. They don't require any real attention at all if you don't want to dwell on them.

Sometimes, drifting along a thought stream will spark your imagination and sometimes it can whirlpool you into a bog of unanswered questions. But unlike the murk of swamp water, most questions can be sluffed off into the basket of 'does it really matter?' or 'who cares?' and your whimsical thoughts will continue tumble along blissfully. But some questions demand your attention and won't leave you alone. Like the way warm dog poop accidentally stepped in squishes through your bare toes on the way to the bathroom in the middle of the night. Not necessarily that disgusting, but equally demanding nonetheless. The questions nag and can't be ignored.

One such thought brought Calle's ambling daydream to a screeching halt. Her metaphoric toes had mushed into the quagmire that was Otis Delve.

Why would anyone want to pull a bag of angry honeybees over the head of a nice groundskeeper? Since she was convinced it was no accident, what purpose would an attack like that serve? Was it a prank gone bad or an attempt at murder? It was definitely imaginative, really, most murderers use a gun, right? Maybe it was meant as a warning, but went too far. Suicide attempt? Calle put her pipe down and chuckled to herself. *Yeah, that's it. Geez.*

She closed her eyes and leaned back in her chair. She let the sounds of nature fill her senses, but the image of the burlap bee bag laying near Otis' fallen body and the Epi-pen inches from his hand kept playing over and over in her mind. He must have known he was in peril and tried to inject himself, but was too poisoned by bee venom to do it in time. Maybe he should have called for help on the radio first. It was hard to envision exactly how it all went down, but she was sure it was foul play. Then who was it? And why?

Her mind went immediately to Michael. Afterall, it was his bag and his bees. What reason would he have to attack Otis? He probably knew Otis his whole life and by the way his mother was affected by Otis' condition, he was probably pretty close to him too. But he didn't seem too concerned about the whole thing. Instead, he was clearly more interested in girls, Lisa Jill in particular, but wasn't that normal for a teenager of the male persuasion?

She thought about people who might have a score to settle with Otis. That woman in combat boots who Otis argued with at the spring came to mind. Jamaica was a small, angry woman, but they say dynamite comes in small packages. Since she was so persistent, she was probably more familiar with the layout of the mansion property than one might imagine. It wasn't much of a stretch for Calle to imagine the compact woman stalking the property after hours or sneaking around during the day. She was clearly competent and not afraid of confrontation. She also wasn't scared of the law, otherwise, she wouldn't be such a tenacious trespasser. Besides, Otis threatened her with another arrest if he caught her on Pérez property again. Maybe she'd had enough of Otis and finally tried to put a stop to his harassment. *Hmm...*

What about the plumber? Herman Young was definitely angry enough to do something to Otis. But how would he know to use a bag of bees? Maybe, he just wanted to make it look like an accident. He had disappeared that morning, pissed off and looking for Otis. What if he found him and the bag was nearby and he took advantage of the situation?

Maybe, maybe, maybe. This was all conjecture. Most likely, detective Ramirez already had the situation under control. The crime scene unit probably had enough evidence to solve the case. Calle chucked her musings into the 'it's none of my business anyway' bin and resigned to see where the police investigation led. She would ask about it tomorrow.

Later, standing in front of the stove, Beely sashayed a figure eight between Calle's legs as tears began to fill her eyes.

"What do you want, you little beggar? You don't even like onions." Calle whittled the last slice of onion into the pan. She wiped the sting from her eye with the back of her wrist as she made her way to the sink for a proper handwashing.

"Here you go kitty," she said as she emptied a can of albacore into his dish. Beely spun impatient circles around her ankles, butting his head against her shin, and purring loudly waiting for the last chunk to fall. When it did, he launched himself into his dinner like he hadn't eaten in months.

She barely escaped with a grin. "Hungry? I guess, geez."

Calle settled in with her dinner in front of the TV. She didn't consider herself a chef by any means, but there were a few recipes that she had down pat. The most important part of any good recipe was good ingredients.

She loaded a fluffy homemade tortilla with fajita fixings and took a bite. The savory taste of caramelized onion and peppers tickled her tastebuds as she flipped through the channels. A rerun of *Celebrity Ghost Stories* grabbed her attention. It was about some rock-n-roll bass player that encountered a ghost at his sister's house in Tucson. You never know how much of anything on TV is true, but it looked plausible and it was something she could readily identify with.

Between fajitas, turning her poker chip awkwardly twixt her fingers, she sat staring at the TV screen as her thoughts began to drift. She recalled her last attempt at dream trekking. Why had she felt so confined? She knew what Howard Lewis was trying to do, but what was the significance of Ethan reading to her and what was the amulet all about?

She believed that all dreams meant something. Even if they weren't lucid or went out of body, they still had a connection to our true selves. She also knew that all dreams weren't created equally. They are as diverse and different as every dreamer. For most people, dreams are reflections of their imagination and personal experience, an event on display for them to simply view. But for others, like with Calle, yes, they could be reflective, but they could also be interactive.

It was that interaction she craved. She was getting used to dictating the parameters of her experience and had come to expect a certain mastery over every dream. Certainly, she wasn't in complete control all the time, but not having any power at all when she knew she should have, bothered her. She began to wonder if she had lost some of her skill, maybe regressed or something. Anything was possible, but without any outside guidance, she would have to rely on trial and error.

It was a problem she could only solve when she was lucid and out-of-body. She pondered her abilities again. Sometimes she was in the groove and in complete control and then there were times, like last time, where she would encounter something new, something that challenged her influence.

She wondered if she could keep her promise to Spencer. Could she garner control when he needed her or would she be stuck trying to get it together leaving him alone and vulnerable.

She had to admit she had made a promise she might not be able to keep. Not that she wouldn't try, but because maybe she just wasn't as good as she thought she was that night. Guilt started to splash around her as she consoled herself that she hadn't failed yet, but she knew it was a real possibility.

In her mind's eye, she could see the sneering face of Howard Lewis as he continued the abuse of his nephew, knowing she was helpless to do anything about it. That was not something she could allow.

She made a promise to herself to conquer any obstacle she encountered when it came to control of her astral endeavors. Come Hell or high water, she would gain mastery of her gift no matter how difficult or how alone she might have to be to do it.

Her inner turmoil had sparked her anger and ruined her dinner. She put the leftovers in the fridge and took herself outside to admire the rising moon and the sparkling stars. She eyed her own star twinkling just where it was supposed to be. She thought about Isla and the storm smoldering on the face of the pendant. She wasn't sure what was going on with that, but the soft azure glow of the star above confirmed that her guardian angel was still on duty. The unspoken promise they shared was still strong and all would turn out alright. That thought inspired her, turning her anger to a concrete resolve.

Beely had taken his leave to make his late-night rounds, leaving her to herself as she got ready for bed. Calle wasn't too concerned about his whereabouts because he usually went tomcatting this time of night anyway. He could let himself in through the cat door in the laundry room. A few months ago, she worried about him being alone in the house when she was away, so she had a door installed high up on a shelf above the washing machine. It was camouflaged on the outside and was his secret passage in and out of the house.

Lying under the covers, she scanned the words of a dull section of her book. The author had abandoned the plot to dwell on every detail of a courtyard hidden behind a hedge. Apparently, it was a meaningful place to the author, but it's over defined description left Calle uninterested. After skimming a few paragraphs, she faded off to sleep.

Like she knew what she was doing, she went lucid and out of body almost immediately, but the freedom she expected eluded her. She tried to fly, but she was like a ladybug trapped inside a terrarium, bouncing off the glass ceiling only to fall to the ground.

Standing atop the cubic monolith, there was no way down either. Calle's foot slid in the sand near the edge sending sparkly grains falling endlessly into the black abyss. She fell to her knees then laid on her belly to scootch closer for a better look. Peering cautiously over the edge, escape seemed hopeless.

This confinement was getting old. She knew she was lucid and felt control, but only to the extent she didn't try to leave the vicinity of the monolith. Intuitively she knew astral freedom lie outside the boundary. No matter how far she flew, she was confined to only a few yards above the dunes. She glanced to the heavens to see Ethan waving the amulet and reading aloud words she couldn't hear. Just like in her previous dream, his image was translucent and unapproachable. He wouldn't be any help.

She plopped her butt into the sand to collect her thoughts. She needed a plan. Trapped in her own lucid dream was not anything she had encountered before. She had two choices. One, flit around on the top of the dirt column in frustration until she woke up or two, do something constructive while she waited. She hated to wait, so she went with option number two.

Deliberate confrontation with her invisible constriction hadn't worked and her attempts to overpower the captive energy surrounding her only led to a tightening of the bindings holding her in place. She needed something more subtle. She needed to understand her captor better.

There was no sense prolonging her irritation. She wanted to wake up and come at this from another perspective, but there was the rub. She didn't have a reliable means to exit her dreams when she needed to. Remembering what Ethan advised, she kicked back in the sand and began to meditate. Surprisingly, even in a dream state, the process felt familiar. She relaxed her astral grasp and let her spirit drift.

With her eyes closed, she imagined herself on her yoga mat in front of the sliding glass door in her living room. Finding the rhythm of her heartbeat connected her with her physical self. She was standing on the threshold, one foot on the physical carpet in her front room, the other in the astral sand trap her spirit lay in. For a split second, she was consciously aware of both planes at the same time. That fleeting glimpse of supreme balance was exhilarating, but it didn't last.

She could feel the astral plane begin to fade as she returned wholly to the physical. The transition was instantaneous, but for Calle it moved in slow motion then stopped altogether to teeter on a pin point. Light speed and stillness combined strangely into a knowing, a simple understanding. It was eternity wrapped up in less than a nanosecond. Like the feeling you get when you think you understand that complex math problem, but then realize you don't. You knew you had it for a second, but for the life of you, you can't remember any of it.

Calle eased back into her body like a pickpocket's

hand under a victim's lapel. She was aware of the warmth of Beely snuggled next to her thigh and the caress of her grandmother's quilt on her cheek, but her mind was lagging far behind, sozzled with awareness. She had just tripped over something unimaginable. She replayed the events of her experience over and over in her head hoping to remember every detail. She knew she would forget most of it, but she was desperately clinging to anything to remind her of where she had been and what she had done.

She could remember being trapped on the monolith and her attempt to escape using meditation. She remembered how easy it seemed and how she passed through some kind of barrier. An infinitesimal membrane that separated the physical from the spiritual. An astral placenta where time stood still and place meant nothing. The complexity of the whole thing left her baffled and intrigued. She couldn't remember as much as she had seen, but she could remember the look on Ethan's face as she passed him as he read to her. The cat was out of the bag. He knew that she knew.

# ☽ 11 ☾

Wouldn't you know it? A perfect day to sleep in and she couldn't sleep anymore if her life depended on it. After her dream meditation episode, Calle was wide awake. She kicked off the sheets and started her day.

Lackadaisically going through her morning routine, she pondered what she had learned from her dream. First of all, she had stumbled upon something quite profound. It was a pretty good guess that she had momentarily been conscious on both planes simultaneously. Ethan said that state existed, but was very rare and dangerous because of the conflicting qualities of each plane.

Specifically, an astral being is not affected by some of the deadly constraints of the physical world. That confusion could lead to the death of her physical self. Ethan used her flying for an example of what one's astral self could do, but their physical body could not.

It wasn't hard for Calle to think of a couple other situations too. Poison, fire, and extreme cold to name a few. They would harm her physical body, but they would have no effect on her astral self, except of course to detach her spirit from her body permanently. She had no desire to join the population of the dead just yet, so though intriguing, she would tread lightly when it came to supreme balance.

It occurred to her that all the dangerous differences resulted in the death of her physical body, not her astral entity. Was it possible for her astral self to perish as well? How would that work?

If her astral self died, would she be reincarnated back to the physical plane or was there yet another plane of which she was unaware that she would thrust into? What if an astral death resulted in one's complete undoing, ceasing it to exist entirely? Or, would her spirit decompose into quantum bits of energetic fertilizer to be reconstituted into a new astral creation altogether? She wondered what Ethan would think of that, which brought her to the second thing she had learned from her dream.

It was Ethan himself who was constraining her from going out of body in her dreams. That snake! When she was in that all knowing moment, her most pressing question at the time was answered.

It was everything and nothing as one, another impossible paradox, but it was clear, he was the source of her hindrance. Why was he purposely binding her? She knew it had to do with the amulet and his reading to her, but she couldn't figure out why or remember a single word of what he had read. Her absolute trust in him battled with a rising sense of betrayal. She wasn't sure what to think, but next time, she would be ready. She wasn't sure how, but she would get to the bottom of it.

The last of the steaks and frozen food were stowed in the walk-in freezer. Just a few more minor chores and the rest of the day would be all hers to do as she pleased. The crew had the day off, so it was just Calle prepping for the next event. It wasn't until the following week that the gala kicked off into full swing and the catering crew would be swamped again. The next few days would be short and simple. A little work here and there, but essentially a few days off.

Her mind was galloping merrily through a daydream when reality reminded her to pay attention to what she was doing. The ladder leg settled with a jolt as she stretched out to reattach a string of rope lights that had come loose along the steel rafter of the pavilion.

"Son of a..." she cursed as she quickly grabbed the rafter to steady herself. With her balance regained, she blew a breath of relief then turned to look Barrow eye to eye. He was on the next rafter watching her like she was more entertaining than a high wire act.

"You would have just sat there and watched me fall, wouldn't you?"

He cocked his head curiously as if to say, "What could I have possibly done to help you?"

"I know, I'm just kidding," she grinned.

"Kidding about what?" a voice from below intoned.

"What?"

"Kidding about what?" the man repeated.

Calle spun her head to see who was talking to her. As she did, the ladder lurched, throwing her off balance again. She leaned into its tilt and carefully descended a couple rungs until she was only a few feet from the ground.

"Who were you talking to?" Detective Shawn Ramirez grinned as he helped stabilize the ladder and looked from Calle to Barrow and back.

"Myself," Calle lied as she hopped to the ground. The police officer glanced again at the blue jay as she asked, "What brings you here this morning?"

She wasn't convinced he was satisfied with her answer, but her question moved the conversation forward.

"Coffee," he smiled as he met her gaze. "Do you have any brewed up?"

"No, but it will only take a second to put some on. Have a seat I'll be right back." She motioned to the nearest table as Barrow glided from under the pavilion to a nearby tree branch in the sunshine. She then walked behind a half partition into the wait station to put the coffee on.

From over the short wall, she asked, "So, what's going on with Otis?"

"He's still in a coma," the detective said as he shuffled the corners of a few stacked napkins with his thumb. "It doesn't look good."

"What do you mean?"

"I called the ER this morning, he's not showing the robust reaction to treatment they expected and at his age…"

"Mmm."

"Apparently allergy patients usually respond better, but we'll see."

"Do you have any idea who did this to him?" Calle asked as she handed the detective a warm mug.

"Not yet, but the evidence appears to be circumstantial. We can't prove it wasn't an accident."

"Isn't it clear someone pulled the bag of bees over his head?"

"Not entirely, it's possible he bumped his head

then dropped the bag of bees or perhaps, something completely different happened."

"Didn't you see his hat inside the sack?"

"Yes, but that doesn't mean someone attacked him."

Calle couldn't believe her ears. She quickly replayed the memory of Otis unconscious on the bathroom floor in her mind. She had no doubt he was attacked.

Shawn could see the incredulous look on her face and said, "We're not ruling out foul play, but right now we don't have enough evidence. Until Mr. Delve wakes up and tells us what happened, we're at a standstill."

"You've got to be kidding."

"No ma'am, that's where we're at. But if it makes you feel better, I personally think it's suspicious. That's why I'm here this morning."

"Oh?"

"I am asking you to keep an eye out for the next few days. If you see anything suspicious, call me."

"Why me?"

"Because you're an outsider, you don't have anything invested in the situation. Besides, you are going to be working around all the potential suspects. An unbiased observer could be very helpful for us if this turns into an assault charge or worse, a homicide."

"Okay," she said as the word homicide echoed through her brain. She took his business card. "I'm not sure what I can do, but I'll try."

"I'm not asking that you have to investigate anything or interrogate anyone, just go about your business and if you notice anything unusual, let me know."

"Right."

"I'll be in touch, thank you," he said as he rose to exit

the dining area.

Calle watched his muscular form as he strode through a cloud of hummingbirds and disappeared behind the fountain. She wondered if he was aware that she had been in the middle of the city's last big murder story a couple months ago and if that might have motivated him to ask for her help. She hoped that wasn't the case, but couldn't believe he wasn't aware of it. The memory of rolling around face to face in a burning building, fighting for her life with a crazed killer made her second guess her decision to help now, but she recognized injustice when she saw it and couldn't turn away.

The clink of the coffee mugs in the busser's tub signaled the end of her morning chores. She hung her apron in the pantry and washed her hands as she thought about what the detective had said. He said she didn't have to investigate, but didn't say she couldn't. It was a case of he said, she heard. Obviously, there was something not right about the whole thing and he had asked her to help.

Her stubborn curiosity wouldn't let it be and pushed her out the door and onto the ATV. She would take an innocent drive around the property and if something caught her eye, well, she couldn't help that. She convinced herself that she wasn't really investigating, just looking around. Besides, forgiveness is much easier to obtain than permission. With that thought, she fired up the dusty machine and rumbled off in search of clues.

The stables seemed like the most logical place to start. If the CSI team thought there wasn't enough evidence to warrant further investigation, then they must have overlooked something. Of that, she was sure.

Calle learned from her last reluctant foray into crime investigation that things aren't always as they seem and that professionals don't always discover key evidence. She trusted the local police and knew they did the best they could, but they were overworked and underpaid. They were diligent to a point, but they weren't Scotland Yard and Sherlock Holmes wasn't on the case.

Before she headed up to the stables, she had to stop by her truck to drop off some paperwork and stow her purse. That done, she grabbed her cell and the two-way and spun a U-turn in the parking lot. She was almost off the pavement and onto a service road when she recognized a large figure standing beside a white van emblazoned with the words *Young Plumbing and Heating*. She veered towards the man and idled to a stop near the front bumper of the van.

A splattering of sunshine strained through the shimmering leaves onto Herman Young's face giving him the appearance of an angry troll. He slid the side door shut with the force of a locomotive piston, then turned to Calle with a grunt.

"What do you want?" He lowered a clipboard as his shoulders tensed. His body language screamed irritation. It was all he could do to just to feign civility. Despite his effort, he was not pulling it off very well.

Calle met his bluster head on.

"Good morning," she countered with friendliness. It was taking the high road, but she knew nothing irritated an angry person more than someone being nice. It placed the burden of social grace squarely on the irritated person's shoulders, forcing them to face their hateful attitude. Either they gained control of their emotions or they would have to bear the guilt of poor manners. Maybe she wasn't completely on the high road, more like in the conniving ditch somewhere beside it. It was patronizing, but maybe she could get the plumber to act civil, at least for a few minutes.

He shuffled a glance past her then back to her face. She could see him grapple with himself. Like an open book she read his expressions as they flitted from anger to proper business etiquette to the realization that the woman before him did not deserve his wrath. With a sigh, he leaned against the front fender and started over.

"Good morning. Sorry about that, but this job has got me all keyed up," he admitted with a forced smile.

"That's okay, I get that way sometimes too." She accepted his olive branch. "So, you're finished with your job here?"

"Yeah, I came to hand deliver the final invoice at the office. I couldn't afford for it to get lost again." His sarcasm thick as sludge.

"Oh yeah? Is that a problem around here?"

"It has been with me. Maybe you'll have better luck since you don't have to answer to Otis."

"I hope so, but that shouldn't be a problem any more, at least in the near future." She probed, hoping to stoke a reaction.

"Yeah, why's that?"

"Otis is in the hospital. He's in a coma."

Herman shifted his weight and stared at the gravel. Crushing a dirt clod with his boot, he asked, "What happened?"

"Bee stings. He's allergic."

"Well, isn't that too bad," he said with spiny acerbity.

"You don't seem too concerned."

"I'm not," he raised his head and turned a heated look her way. "In fact, I think it serves him right. Karma is a bitch." His anger began to swell.

"Did you find him yesterday?" she pressed.

"No, I went to his tree house, but he wasn't there. He said he would be, but he wasn't. That weasel."

"Did you try the stables?"

"No, this is a big place, I'm not going to go all over it looking for him. If he didn't want to talk to me, he could have hidden anywhere. I would never have found him. It's better I deal with the front office anyway. I wish I would have done that from the beginning."

"Well, at least that's all behind you now."

"Thank God, once I get my money, I'll never set foot on this property again," he hissed.

A few minutes later, Calle thought about Herman as she buzzed up the service road toward the stables. If he hadn't seen Otis, it would have been impossible for him to attack him. His story made for a good alibi, but his anger and satisfaction at Otis' condition made her question his innocence. He said all the right things, but that didn't necessarily mean they were true. She found it hard to believe he hadn't heard about what had happened. Afterall, it was the talk of everyone at the mansion. Something was off about the angry plumber.

The route she chose to the stables was new to her. A gardener suggested the dirt road as a quicker alternate to the path that ran through the body of the estate and past Otis' treehouse. The narrow lane she was on ran behind the scenes, a more direct connection to the stables from the employee parking lot. She realized this was probably the same road Rob and the wrangler had used yesterday when they left her standing in the dust.

The idea of those two fueled her suspicion. She slowed her ATV thinking she might notice something resembling a clue. What clue that might possibly be, she had no idea, but she idled along like an old woman who, while searching for an address, turns down the radio thinking the silence will help her see better.

The mental picture of herself as that elderly person lulled her into a daydream about her golden years. She was absent mindedly enjoying the fantasy when a sudden jolt of movement, slightly behind her and to her right, yanked her attention back to reality.

A cloud of dust swirled from the path as she slammed on the brakes. A black, maybe dark grey silhouette of something large wisped along the edge of her vision. She turned her body abruptly to track the image with her eyes, but it moved so quickly, it was gone before she could bring it into focus. The only indication that remained was a deep blue tendril of steam that lingered in the air. But that too, evaporated before she could make any sense of it.

The forest hushed except for the sputtering engine of the ATV and she dismounted to take a closer look.

Moving gingerly through the scrub oak, she stepped over to the area where she had seen the apparition. Standing where the steam had disappeared, she found no indication of a footprint nor any sign of disturbed foliage. Nothing to indicate something had been there recently.

Perplexed, she quietly stood in the warm sunshine, her senses on high alert. The pristine forest stared back at her, offering a mute consolation. Then faintly, she caught a whiff of the musky odor of a sweaty mammal and a hint of burnt sulfur, but only for half a breath. Then that too, dissipated, leaving her alone under the stoic judgement of the trees.

Mocked by self-doubt, her imagination began to roil, conjuring the image of a behemoth sasquatch spying from the shadows. She spun a full circle looking for any tree or bush large enough to conceal such a giant creature. The forest was still, but her insides were churning. Her back and neck began to tingle with anticipation as she shuddered the chill from her spine.

Nervously and without looking back, she jumped on the ATV and sped up the path, unconcerned about any clues that might be blowing right by.

As the stables came into view, the unmistakable aroma of working horses was a welcome alternative to the pungent odor rotting in her mind. But she couldn't forget the odor, though brief, it was an unusual stench she hadn't smelt before. Its acrid flavor would be etched in her memory forever.

Not so long ago, she might not have even noticed it at all, but since Ethan had given her the other worldly Ring of Fragrance, her whole life had taken on a new vibrant tint.

The ring she wore on her astral left thumb was meant as a gift to enhance her visits to the astral plane. Since the sense of smell is a rarity for astral beings, the magic ring added a little zest to her astral experience. It also had the unexpected side effect of enhancing her physical olfactory system as well. Consequently, many once mundane physical odors were now palpable.

Sometimes an aroma would be accompanied by a taste or texture. It wasn't a certainty for every odor she encountered, but it certainly had spiced up her sense of smell.

But there was more to it than that. She was beginning to believe the sensation often accompanied anything or any event that had a direct astral connection.

For example, sometimes when she held her pendant, she could smell the pastoral serenity of the scene painted on the porcelain. More than once, she sensed the aroma of roses when she gazed upon her star in the night sky. She had grown to accept that these olfactory sensations indicated the nearness of her guardian angel.

There were other instances too, like when she caught a olfactory suggestion of chocolate wafting from an abandoned building downtown only to discover that eighty years prior, it was a thriving chocolate shop. It was like the essences of both planes were overlapping to coalesce in her nostrils.

But the smell she encountered in the forest wasn't roses or chocolate, it was something else entirely. And it was accompanied an apparition, a fast one at that. Another quandary, for which, she didn't have an answer. It was unnerving, but she had no means to decipher its origin. She would have to give it some thought, but in the meantime, she had an investigation to conduct.

As she approached the barn from a different angle, she could see the truck the wrangler was driving when he rudely sped past the day before. Walking along a huge stack of bales, she plucked a stalk of alfalfa from one and stuck it in her mouth. Another wonderful smell accompanied by another healthy taste. God, she loved the simple things in nature.

Near the end of the hay stack and the edge of the barn, she heard the clang of falling garden tools behind her. Her startle reflex spun her uncontrollably to face the clamor. Besides the curse of unpredictable anxiety, her PTSD had made her hyper sensitive to abrupt and unexpected loud noises. Her exaggerated startle responses were embarrassing when they happened in public, but fortunately, this time she was alone.

She blew a sigh of relief when she realized there wasn't a Rocky Mountain Yeti sneaking up on her. But she was too savvy to believe in coincidence and happenstance. Something must have knocked that shovel and rake over. A level head would serve her well, so she remained still and surveyed the scene for an explanation.

She didn't have to wait long because the explanation tumbled from behind some other nearby implements right into the path behind her. It was a small in size, but huge in circumstance as a chipmunk frantically fought tooth and claw with a hungry stoat for its life. The chip was holding her own, but Calle knew she was no match for the agile and deadly predator.

Hatching a desperate plan, the chip bolted from the fray. At full speed plus twenty percent, the tiny creature barreled directly at Calle with its ferret kin attacker loping in hot pursuit. In a cartoon, it would have been funny, but in reality, it was very serious. She stood in awe as the two usually cute creatures shot between her legs and zipped in tandem up the trunk of a tall pine tree.

She pivoted quickly to watch as the chase careened out and around a long thin branch. Without slowing, the chipmunk reached the end of the branch and made an all or nothing leap into the air. The branch bent with the weight of both animals then sprung like a diving board when the chip launched. It flung the tiny creature head over heels a good thirty feet through the atmosphere and into a fluffy bough of a tall blue spruce nearby.

The stoat, not as desperate, screeched to a halt at the end of the swaying branch and clung for dear life as it watched its prey crash land into the tree nearby. If the chipmunk was dazed or injured, she wasn't waiting around to check. She tumbled down a few branches before righting herself then raced away into the forest canopy.

Calle glanced back at the stoat still hanging on to the end of the gently swaying branch. He quickly regained his composure then met Calle's gaze with bright enthusiasm. He may have lost a meal, but the look he shared spoke volumes. Sure, the kill was necessary for survival, but he was more thrilled by the chase. With a mischievous flick of his ears, he turned to begin his descent to the ground. Completely ignoring her, he merrily loped off into the underbrush looking for more adventure.

Feeling like an extra in a Disney film, Calle marveled at the courage and tenacity of the chipmunk while admiring the finesse of the stoat. She couldn't believe what had just happened right in front of her, in real life, in real time. There was nothing good or bad about it. There was no hero nor villain. The whole episode was simply nature at its finest. There was probably a lesson to learn somewhere in it all, but she was so grateful to have been an eye witness, she didn't even try to figure it out.

Smiling to herself, she turned to where the whole drama had started. The tools were still laying across the road, so Calle went to put them back where they belonged. With a rake in one hand and a shovel in the other, she paused when she heard gravel crunch under footsteps that were coming around the barn behind her.

"Can I help you with something?" an impatient male voice demanded.

Calle leaned the tools next to a pile of similar implements. Rubbing her hands together to knock the dust from her fingers, she turned to face the man.

"Hi, I'm Calle," she said as she extended her hand and walked toward him. It was the same wrangler she had seen the day before.

Her forwardness must have disarmed his attitude. He tipped his hat and met her halfway.

"Ned Luper, nice to meet you ma'am." He shook her hand. "Are you lost? Can I help you with anything?" he drawled with a flirty undertone.

It wasn't her forwardness that was disarming; he was attracted to her. Though he was handsome in his own unkempt cowboy sort of way, she didn't share the sentiment. But since he was feeling frisky, she decided to use it to her advantage.

"I'm not lost. I work for the catering company."

"Oh, yeah, Rob said there was a pretty girl working in the tent."

"There's a couple pretty girls working there," Calle dodged the compliment. *But I'm not one of them.* "You should stop by sometime and visit," she leveraged.

"I think I just might," he grinned. "What are you doing out here?" He dipped his shoulder as he hung a thumb through a belt loop.

"I was the one who found Otis yesterday." Ned's grin flattened. "I was trying to figure out what happened. Did you see anything?"

"Naw, I was working. I didn't even know Otis was out here." His hand went the back of his neck as he scanned the distance behind her.

She thought about the conversation she partially overheard yesterday and pressed.

"I saw you and Rob driving off yesterday and thought maybe you guys might have seen something."

"That was you in the barn?"

He knew that it was, he had looked right at her. "Yes, I was looking for Otis," she played along.

"Well, I don't know if Rob knows anything, but I didn't see a thing."

"Did you happen to see Herman Young yesterday?"

"Herman Young?"

"He's a plumber."

"Oh, him yeah, he was out here in the morning. He was not a happy camper."

"That sounds like him," she said. "What was Rob doing back here?"

"Rob and I are friends. We used to work together."

"Oh, what did you guys used to do?"

The question must have touched a sensitive area because Ned abandoned any flirty ambitions he had been clinging to.

"You sure ask a lot of questions, are you a cop?"

"No, I'm a caterer. I was just wondering what happened."

"Well, then it's really none of your business, is it?" he said sternly.

"Not really, I was just curious."

"Curiosity killed the cat," he interrupted. "Some things are best left alone," he added forcefully as he locked eyes with her to emphasize his point. There was a tense moment then he said, "Well, I got to get back to work, nice meeting you." He nodded his head as he broke the mini-stare down then spun on his heel and walked away.

As she watched him march back around the end of the barn, she wasn't so sure their meeting was all that nice, but she was certain about a few things. Namely, something unscrupulous was going on and someone was trying to cover it up. And Otis was in a coma because he was smack dab in the middle of it.

## ☽ 12 ☾

All hospitals have one thing in common. They are sanitized to the point of sterility that makes them all smell the same. Calle didn't need any assistance from any magic ring to know she had just entered one.

The medicinal aroma instantly conjures deep emotions associated with life changing events. Ranging anywhere from the miracle of child birth to the heartbreak of a loved one dead on arrival, no one who's been a patient or just a visitor is immune. For Calle, the tangy pharmaceutical odor of Christus Saint Vincent Trauma Center hung in her nostrils like medicated death and thrust her back to a dreadful night, not so long ago, when she watched her husband die right there in that very building.

The abrupt shudder that was triggered by that thought was accompanied by a short, sharp yelp, but Calle ignored the stares of the alarmed couple passing by. There was no telling what they thought of the pretty, young woman who, for no apparent reason, recoiled her head and flinched a protective hand to her face with a whimper, trying to avoid an invisible threat. Embarrassment flushed crimson up her neck and across her cheeks. She wanted to shout, *I have Post Traumatic Stress Disorder! I'm not mental!* But that would only make things worse, so instead, she looked away, pretended nothing happened, and marched towards the elevator.

A few seconds alone in the rising cubicle was all she needed to recompose herself. It wasn't the first time she had experienced a powerful startle reflex in public and it probably wouldn't be the last, but at least she didn't have a full-blown panic attack right there in front of God and everybody. As humiliating as it was for her disorder to be on full display, she put it behind her. It was either that or crawl into a hole and hide. Been there, done that. Not an option anymore.

She entered the third-floor patient wing looking for Otis. Walking down the hall, trying not to stare into open rooms was like trying to pass a fresh auto accident on the highway, it was impossible. Morbid curiosity moved her eyes involuntarily from doorway to doorway. Fortunately, most had their privacy curtains drawn around the patient's bed, but a few remained wide open as if to put the vulnerable person on exhibit for anyone to see. Occasionally, her voyeurism was met with the angry scowls of loved ones at the bedside only to hear the zing of curtain rings sliding shut behind her as she moved past.

At last, she found Otis' room at the end of the corridor. His curtain was drawn, so she announced her arrival with a soft, "Excuse me, Otis?" As she said it, she thought, *how stupid, he's in a coma, he can't hear me.*

But a meek female voice replied, "Come in, he's sleeping."

As she stepped behind the curtain and into Otis' room, her attention immediately went to the frail man lying in bed amidst a tangle of electronic leads, an oxygen mask, and an IV tube trailing from his severely contused forearm. Otis looked more dead than alive. His face and neck were bruised and covered with some sort of salve. One eye was swollen shut like he had been punched by Mike Tyson and the top of his head was wrapped with a gauzed bandage, but despite looking like a run-over mummy, he appeared to be resting peacefully.

It was pretty much what Calle expected, but what caught her completely off-guard was the young, teary-eyed Mennonite woman sitting next to the bed, holding his hand. The girl stood, released Otis' hand, and met Calle's gaze, then began crying in earnest. Instinctively, Calle pulled the girl close into a hug and began to console her. The girl mumbled something inaudible as she sobbed into Calle's shoulder, but after a few moments, she began to settle. Calle pulled up a chair next to the bed and the two women sat down next to Otis' bedside. They looked at each other, then at Otis, then back to each other. Calle cleared her throat.

"Lisa Jill, what are you doing here?"

"I wanted to visit Otis," Jill hiccupped.

"I didn't know you knew Otis," Calle said genuinely confused.

"I don't, not really."

Calle sat on the edge of her seat.

"I was hoping to get to know him."

Calle's mind swirled into a dark area. "What do you mean?"

"I found him on the internet."

Calle's heart dropped like a brick into her stomach. "What?!"

Her shock startled Jill and the young woman leaned back, then continued.

"He's my dad. Well, my biological father anyway, I have a dad back home."

"What are you talking about?"

"I found him on Ancestry.com, he's my father."

Relieved somewhat, Calle's thoughts went back to that afternoon she sat at Otis' kitchen table and the conversation they shared about long-lost relatives. Otis said he knew everyone he was related to, but she would bet her bottom dollar that if he wasn't already in a coma, this little tidbit of news would've knocked him into one. She shook her head and herself back to focus on the moment.

"Did he know?"

"No, I tried to email him a number of times, but he never responded. So, I came to Santa Fe to find him."

"Mmm." Calle was surprised again by the strength this seemingly timid woman possessed.

"You came all the way from Pennsylvania. Here. All by yourself, to find your dad?"

"That's right."

"Wow."

"But, wouldn't you know it, before I could introduce myself, he has an accident and goes into a coma."

Calle wasn't willing to debate the accident part of the statement or voice her doubt about the innocence of Otis' nonresponse to Jill's emails, so she sat patiently and listened.

Lisa Jill went on to explain that when she was an infant, she was adopted by a Mennonite family. Then after graduating high school, how she found her biological father through Ancestry.com, and her quest to meet him and possibly reconcile with him. It was quite a story, but the details were cut short by a nurse who informed them that visiting hours were over and they had to leave.

Jill kissed her new found father on the cheek then followed Calle into the hall. Calle couldn't help but admire the character of the young woman. Her determination was clear, but her devotion to a man she never really met and most likely abandoned her as a child, was remarkable. Probably foolish, but her optimism and blind faith still resonated with hope and decency. As the nurse was closing the door, Calle took one last look at Otis and wondered that if the man survived, would he appreciate such a blessing as Lisa Jill?

After dropping Jill and her trusty bicycle off at her friend's house, Calle aimed her Silverado towards La Cieneguilla, her own home just south of Santa Fe. Jill was staying with a local Mennonite family, who offered an extended, open-ended welcome to the young woman. Jill was an anomaly in town all by herself, but a Mennonite family living in Santa Fe, that was something Calle wouldn't have believed unless she had witnessed it with her own eyes. Go figure.

About ten minutes from her driveway, Calle's phone chirped.

New Mexico law says drivers should pull over and stop when talking on the phone, but since she was the only motorist on the scenic backroad, Calle put it on speaker and answered. After a quick hello, Samantha got to the point.

"Yes, I think it's a real curse, I've seen this thing before."

"Oh, goodie," Calle sighed sarcastically.

"Have you seen anyone suspicious hanging around your house or your work? Like maybe an old woman?"

"No, no one like that. There's been a few break-ins around the neighborhood, but they've been thieves. Looks like two or three men, judging by the boot tracks around the crime scenes. At least, that's what my neighbor says."

"Hmm."

As Samantha formulated her thoughts, Calle remembered when they had first met a few weeks before. It was a tense exchange and Calle didn't trust the woman initially. Both women possessed special gifts. Calle was born a lucid dreamer, which now had grown into something much more. And Samantha, on the other hand, was a gifted artist and a witch. She could see auras around people and had an insight to their essence. Samantha's uncanny ability to see Calle clearly, unnerved her. But since fate had thrust them together, they got to know one another better and by opening up honestly with each other, they had become fast friends. Now, Calle trusted Samantha completely.

"I'm working on a medicine bag for you. It will protect you from most dark magic, not all mind you, but most."

"Really? Is it that serious?"

"If it's what I think it is, then yes, it is, but I'm not sure yet. Better safe than sorry."

"Oh, marvelous, what should I do?"

"Be vigilant, keep an eye out for anything unusual and keep me posted if anything else out of the ordinary happens."

"Okay," Calle paused then blurted out, "Well, a guy at work had a sack full of bees pulled over his head and is in a coma because of it."

"What?"

"A guy at my work was attacked by someone with a sack full of honeybees."

"No kidding? Up at the Pérez Mansion? That's bizarre."

"I know, right?"

"Strange indeed, but I don't think that has anything to do with the dead rat in your mail box or the curse someone has put on you, do you?"

"No, I don't either."

Calle used her knee to steer as shifted her cell phone to her other hand.

"How's your cat?"

"Beely? He's fine, why?"

"Has he been acting strange lately?"

"Beely acts strange all the time, what do you mean?"

"You know, strange for him."

Calle thought about telling Samantha about her cat launching off the tree the other day, but dismissed the notion as Beely just being Beely.

"Not really."

"Okay, but remember, Beely is special, he might be able to sense something."

Calle didn't need to be reminded about how special her cat was, he reminded her every day. Since he adopted her a little over a year ago, he was always doing something unusual. From nurturing baby bunnies and playing with tiny sparrows to his over protective attitude toward her, his behavior could be unpredictable at times. He was the alpha male in the family when he felt it necessary, but more often, he was her confidant and shoulder to cry on. As mysterious as a secret agent or as cute as a kitten, he could go from zero to a ferocious wolverine in a second flat if it suited him. What could she say? He was a weird cat and he was completely devoted to her.

"I've got to get some peyote for your medicine bag and when I do, it will be ready. I'll bring it over then."

"Peyote? Where are you going to get peyote?"

"Don't you worry about that. Let's just say it gives me a reason to visit an old boyfriend."

"Ah, I see," Calle said as she idled onto her driveway. "Speaking of boyfriends, How's Elias?"

"Splendid, we drove down to Socorro the other day. Had a fabulous time."

"Business or pleasure?"

"At my age, I always try to include pleasure in everything," Samantha laughed. "Both. We visited a gallery then Fiona took us on a tour of the college."

"How is she doing down there?"

"Very well, she's taking a painting class."

"Good for her. It will give her a break from all those math and physics courses. I don't know how she does it."

"She is amazing. She's convinced time travel holds the key to magic. I don't see the connection, but then again, there's a lot of stuff she understands that I don't have a clue about."

"Amen to that, she probably feels the same way about you." Sitting in her driveway, Calle shifted her truck into park and turned off the engine. She remained in the cab and watched the leaves sparkle in the sunshine as Samantha continued.

"She asked me to tutor her."

"In math?"

"Yeah, right," Samantha joked. "I could give her some pointers on painting, but she's interested in magick. She's thinking of turning Wiccan."

"I'm not surprised. She really looks up to you. What did you say?"

"I agreed, on one condition. She has to go slow and not commit to anything right away. I don't want her to do something so serious on an impulse. She's young and though very bright, she has her whole life ahead of her. No sense making a decision she might one day come to regret."

"I like that thinking. Her parents might not be on board either."

"Precisely. So, we'll take it slow and see where it goes. In the mean-time, she can work weekends and holidays with me or at Elias' gallery, every college kid can use extra money. If nothing else, it gives us time to visit."

"Sounds like a good plan." Gravel ground beneath Calle's Sketchers as she hopped out of her pickup and locked the door. "Well, I'm home now. No sign of anything out of place, but I'll keep you posted if anything happens. When do you think you'll be coming over?"

"Won't be for a couple days. My friend lives on the High Road to Taos. So, I'll drive up there tomorrow. It should be lovely this time of year. I'll come by as soon as I get your medicine bag together," Samantha replied. "You should be okay until then."

"Alright, thanks for everything, be safe." Calle rung off, her thoughts swirling a mile a minute as she crossed the threshold into her casita.

# ☽ 13 ☾

Later that night, Calle didn't hesitate when she realized she was lucid. She didn't try to fly around Ethan's barrier or transport herself anywhere. The simple, spontaneous idea seemed sound. On impulse, she went with it.

Meditating was never easy, and in a dream, it was even harder. She had no delusion about obtaining supreme balance or even escaping the restriction held on her dream. No expectations, only hope. By turning her focus inward, she was thinking outside the box. It was worth a try.

Without a glance his direction, she wove her thoughts in and around herself. She knew he was watching as he read, but she was unconcerned about his attention. Cauterizing herself from his influence, her isolation began to expand. By ignoring him entirely, she soon found freedom. Like a summer breeze through a chain link fence, she reclaimed the liberty of her dream.

With the filter lifted from her perception, the proverbial blinders were removed and she was engulfed by wave after wave of astral climate. It was like she had been buried alive only to feel fresh air on her skin for the first time in ages. It felt wonderful and drew her out of body like the moon coaxing the tide.

Her spirit stretched into the ether and her

consciousness began to settle like tired feet inside a pair of comfortable boots. Not having been out of body for a while, she quelled her enthusiasm to get her bearings. No pressure, it could be anything she desired.

She didn't expect to gain freedom so easily, so she didn't have a plan, but then it dawned on her. What about Spencer?

Without a thought, she was standing on the gabled back porch of a small clapboard house. In the yard she could see Spencer digging in the dirt with a small gardening trowel. An unopened packet of seeds lay in the grass next to him.

"Honey, that's deep enough. If you plant them too deep, they won't feel the warmth of the sun. Then they won't grow." An older woman in a threadbare cotton dress advised as she knelt on the grass a few feet away. Her greying hair was pulled up into a bun under her straw hat and adoration beamed from behind her bifocals as he turned his head her way.

"Like this." She pawed the ground with a crooked stick next to her knee. "See? Then just pop in the seeds and cover them up. And just like that, you'll have flowers all over the place." She smiled and waved the stick like a wizard casting a spell.

"Oh, Grandma, you need to water them first," Spencer giggled.

"Well, I suppose you do, don't you?" she smiled. "You're so smart."

Calle watched as Spencer and his grandmother finished planting their flowers.

"How about a glass of Kool-Aid?"

"Can I make it? I like grape." Spencer sprung to his feet while his grandmother wobbled to hers.

She dusted the dirt from his clothing then grasped his hand and as they were turning back to the house, a deep threatening voice boomed from over the gate.

"Mona, you dried up old prune," Howard Lewis declared then chuckled to himself at what he thought was a clever insult. "Spencer should have been home yesterday!"

The boy and his grandmother stopped stock-still in the yard as the older woman scowled a reply.

"Don't you remember calling last night and telling me you were too busy to come for him?"

"I did no such thing. You're trying to kidnap him," Howard growled.

Spencer's eyes grew wide as he moved behind his grandmother, still holding her hand.

"You're drunk again, aren't you?" Mona defied.

"What I do is none of your business old woman," Howard spat as he flung the gate open and stormed their direction. "I'm taking my nephew home, now!"

"Not this time, I'll call the police."

"So what? They won't do anything, just like last time. Now, get out of my way, I'm taking Spencer." Howard grabbed Mona's arm.

Mona released Spencer's hand. "Run honey, call the police!" she screamed as Howard drew back his other hand to slap her.

Mona cowered to absorb the blow that never came. Leaning away, she peeped open an eye to see Howard's hand restrained by an angry young woman. Howard released Mona, turned, and spat, "What the hell?!"

Then Spencer screeched, "It's the dinosaur lady!"

"It's not hell, but you'll wish it was when I'm done with you," Calle stated as calmly as an executioner.

Panic swept across Howard's face as his bleary eyes registered with whom he was speaking. Mona hurried Spencer off to the house as Calle's free hand latched onto Howard's ear and pulled his face closer to hers.

"I told you to leave the boy alone," she grimly added.

In sheer horror, Howard leapt from Calle's grasp and fell to the grass on his butt. Crawling backward like a crab, he spun to his feet and without looking back, dashed through the gate and out of Spencer's dream.

Calle pivoted toward the porch, but the confrontation must have frightened Mona, because there was no sign of her or Spencer anywhere. Calle stood alone in the fading lawn of Spencer's dream and realized she had stopped the nightmare, but hadn't solved the problem. She needed to find Howard and enter his dreams.

As Spencer's dream dissolved around her, it left a trail. She never noticed that about a dream before, but then again, she had never looked. Calle locked her attention onto its de-fabricating fringes and followed. Like steam wisping down a drain, the dream trickled back into the dreamer. As the last misty drops of Spencer's dream evaporated, Calle found herself in his bedroom hovering over his sleeping body. From there she knew she could probably find Howard asleep somewhere in the house and the exact physical location of their home.

It was the first time she had ever followed a dream. When she had entered Matthew's dream a few weeks prior, she left in the middle of it. And when she exited Spencer's previous dream, she just let it go. This was totally new.

In all her experience as a lucid dreamer, she could

always go anywhere she wanted. She assumed that was true in dream trekking, but now she realized there was more to it than that. There were limitations.

It was apparent that she could only go where her imagination would allow or somewhere she had already been. Going where you want depends entirely upon knowing precisely what you want. And if you are unaware of a place or thing, or you aren't familiar with that something, you don't know what to want, so you can't get there. The astral plane, just like the physical plane, would require a certain amount of exploration. *Hmm.*

She would have to think that little bit of realization over later, but now, she needed to find Howard. Lowering her astral feet to the floor, she went in search of Spencer's uncle. Across the hall and two doors down, she entered his bedroom. It was a mess with the TV playing on mute. And there in the middle of a bare, stained mattress, tangled in dirty sheets, lay Howard Lewis' sleeping carcass.

Now was as good a time as any she supposed. Reaching out mentally, she tried to enter Howard's dreams. Her efforts were met with resistance. Maybe he wasn't dreaming. Maybe he was dead. Shocked by that thought, she watched until he heaved a snort and rolled over.

Okay, he was still alive, so now what? She hesitated, pondering the situation. What would Ab Pistola do? Calle knew the anime hero would simply zip right in and take care of business. Just like that, cool as a cucumber. But what she read in the comics and saw on the internet, did not apply here.

*Hmm.* She looked closer to Howard's facial features

hoping to notice anything she might be able to work with. She didn't see anything outright, but she could sense the essence of a dream. It was similar to the trail Spencer's dream had left, but cocooned around his head and upper torso. She redoubled her effort to penetrate the cloud.

Each time she tried to enter the membrane encasing his dream, Howard dismissed her. Not with words or gestures, but just a simple denial, like her key didn't fit the lock. Nothing personal, just not interested. It felt like a time back in college, when she and a friend tried to enter an exclusive night club in Atlanta, but were denied because they didn't have an invitation or weren't pretty enough.

Maybe that was it. She hadn't been invited. She hadn't been invited because, as she was, she was of no interest to Howard.

She thought of what she had just learned about dream trekking and how you could only go where you had been or where your imagination could lead you. It was a fat chance in hell she could ever imagine what craziness Howard might dream about, but maybe she could get him to ask her in. Get an invitation so to speak. That sounded like a good idea.

New strategy. What would grab Howard's attention and make him invite her in?

Nothing came to mind as she stood over his sleeping body. She gazed around the room looking for anything to give her a clue. The walls were bare except for a Metallica poster and an old picture of Santa Claus with darts sank into his holey face. The Grinch had nothing on Howard Lewis. Calle was at her wits end when she noticed the ad on the tube.

Sexy girls beckoned the viewer to come to the casino. The one wearing stilettos and a cowboy hat, smiled enticingly at the camera, then took a sip of her cocktail. Then suave men joined the girls to escort them to the roulette wheel. The advertisement screamed debauchery; it was lecher's dream come true. Perfect.

With the woman's appearance fresh in her mind, Calle mimed easily into the harlot on the screen. From the high heels to the heaving cleavage, she was utterly transformed. Though she couldn't see herself, she knew she had nailed it. Summoning a cocktail to her hand, she banged on the door to Howard's dream and like a tractor beam, she was pulled in.

Upon entry, she was surprised to arrive standing behind him. He was wearing torn blue jeans with stretch marked love handles protruding beneath a bulging black tee-shirt. He was facing a swampy pond and as ducklings would swim by, he would blast them with a lever action rifle. The surface would erupt into a tower of water, mud, and tiny feathers. Laughing hysterically, a spent shell flew out of the chamber as he cycled in the next round.

"That'll teach you, you little bastard." He hung his face over his shoulder and with a gleam in his eye, he bragged, "Helluva shot right there!"

Unsure what to say, Calle just stood watching as he waited for a response. The whole scene was beyond explanation. But there it was, a half-naked woman in high heels, standing in a swamp, with a beer-bellied thug, shooting ducklings point blank with a high-powered rifle. Good times.

Calle knew dreams didn't always have to make sense, but this was way more than she could have imagined. She was shaken from her rumination when he started moving her direction.

"What's wrong darlin'?" Howard leaned the rifle on a stump, picked a beer out of the cooler, and as he popped it open, walked toward her. "Not havin' fun anymore?"

She stumbled as she tried to take a step back. Stupid shoes. Howard seemed delighted by her vulnerability. His demeanor darkened. "I know what you want." He sloshed a muddy step closer.

He moved much faster than she thought possible. In an instant, his body and lips were on hers and before she could scream, beer spilled down her neck as he pawed at her breast. The chaos of it all stoked his lust. The crazier it got, the better he liked it.

There was no doubt in her mind that he had done this before. He was a rapist, of that, she was certain, but his aggression had caught her off guard. It was his dream and he was in control.

Calle struggled under his weight as he ripped her clothing. Manhandling his grimy fingers under her shirt, he was reeling in ecstasy as she regained her composure. Where there should have been a terrified woman's flesh, Howard found only a handful of mud. She had disappeared.

Not really, she had only transported herself away from him. And as he turned around to face her, she cut the costume routine and morphed back to herself.

"What the hell?" Howard Lewis had never had a dream like this before.

She stood her ground, but didn't know how to continue.

"I know you," he hissed. "You're that dinosaur

bitch!" He spun on his knees.

How he could recognize her came as a surprise. They had met in Spencer's dream, not his. How could that be? Do people's dreams sometimes overlap? Was Howard a dream trekker too? She didn't think so, but maybe everyone is a little clairvoyant in their own way.

She didn't have time to think about it because he lunged for the rifle and leveled it at her chest.

Standing in front of a loaded gun while a madman fondles the trigger is never a good feeling. But a lifetime of lucid dreaming gave Calle the confidence to step forward and squeeze the end of the barrel flat. He pulled the trigger, but nothing happened.

"You're not going to shoot anybody, you're going to listen," she glared as she seized the gun from his shaking hands and tossed it aside. Before it hit the turf, it faded into nothing. If he was a trekker, he was not a very good one, she realized as she took control of his dream.

Fear began to creep from up from his shoulders and across his scraggily bearded face as he grappled with the fact that his twisted fantasy was turning into a full-blown nightmare.

"I don't like having to hurt you, but if you continued to abuse Spencer, you and I are going to have problems." She motioned her fingers back and forth between them. "Understand?"

Howard was too afraid to answer. He stood petrified like a jackrabbit in a spotlight as she stared him down.

Wondering how to drive her point home, she felt the landscape changing around her. It had snuck up on her. It was not of her doing. Something had followed her into Howard's dream.

She lifted her head to the horizon and saw a violent storm churning her direction. At the leading edge of the maelstrom, a menacing tornado flitted in and out of view. It looked surprisingly a lot like the Tasmanian Devil from Looney Tunes, but it wasn't cute. Instead, it seethed with a deadly virulence. Crackling with blue lightning and smoldering like melting rock, it tried to fight free of a larger squall.

It was then, Calle realized the storm was actually two very powerful cyclones locked in battle. One spewing open contempt for her, the other fighting to contain the approaching menace.

A sweaty, sulfuric stench accompanied the wicked unspoken threat that seeped into her spirit.

"You will be mine, dreamer."

The danger coming from the tornado emboldened Howard and he turned to Calle. "You're not so tough now, are you bitch?" he taunted.

Sensing a weak spirit, the tornado turned on Howard Lewis. The entity did not appreciate his interference. His brazen stupidity drew the tornado's appetite for destruction like wind blowing flames up a parched hillside. It gushed a blazing napalm-coated claw from its main torrent in his direction, grasping for easy prey, but Howard, seeing his mistake, had already clamored for safety. Seconds from certain death, Howard's form disappeared from the dream like a popped balloon. Calle could imagine his pulse pounding as he hurtled awake in a cold sweat back in his bedroom.

With Howard gone from the dream, it was all about Calle now. The entity wasted no time going for her. The lightning storm that had ignored the attack on

Howard, swiveled in her defense and kept the menace from reaching her, but only just. As the two typhoons collided, the mighty clash showered electric sparks and bits of lava that stunk of charred, rotted animal flesh all around her.

When she recognized the odor, her skin began to goose pimple. Terror paralyzed her. Then a familiar female voice she had never heard before, pushed the threat aside. It repressed her fear and told her to flee. On instinct, she reacted.

Calle willed herself back to her bedside, bypassing Ethan altogether. For a moment, she was safe, but didn't think she could avoid the conflict for long. Quickly, she glanced around her bedroom and then to Beely who was lying next to her body on the bed. As if sensing her return, he raised his head, his cobalt gaze on high alert. His vigilance welcomed her and bolstered her spirit. With him, here in her home, she knew she had found sanctuary.

She laid her spirit on top of her sleeping body and with every ounce of concentration she could muster, relaxed into her astral meditation routine. As she searched for her biological rhythms and just before she matched them and awoke, a thought occurred to her.

How could she, for one minute, be all powerful and in control, then in the time it takes to flip a coin, be so vulnerable and on the run?

A few moments later, lying quietly against her pillows, stroking Beely's felty ear between her forefinger and thumb, she was lost in deep contemplation. What the hell had just happened? Then the more pressing question asserted itself. Who, or what, in the astral universe would be trying to kill her and why?

# ☽ 14 ☾

In, out, and around again and again. Calle spun her poker chip between her fingers and then shifted hands. A trick is only as good as the hand that holds it. At first, the coin trick was just for fun, but after doing it successfully a few times, she worked at mastery. Though she was right-handed, her left hand seemed to fit the sleight of hand maneuver much better. Much like the two sides of her life.

She had a few minutes to burn before she had to go meet with Lucy, so she sat in her grandmother's rocker, working on her magic trick, and considered the events surrounding her life. Dead rats, bees, comas, and curses. Common everyday things that your average twenty something widow deals with all the time.

She gave up on normal a long time ago. Growing up with acute Déjà vu thrust her way off center and when her dreams moved out of body, well, that just sealed the deal. Her PTSD wasn't helping much either. She was anything but ordinary and probably never would be. That was something she was still learning live with. Okay, so be it, but what was going on with the astral side of her life?

Malicious storm clouds bent on harming her, guiding angelic voices, and her astral lover trying to constrain her. Not to mention her intrusion into other people's dreams, something she swore she would never do again. She searched herself for a common thread, something that would bind the whole mess into a neat, manageable package, but the dots just wouldn't connect.

Most people would say, "Oh, I'll sleep on it.", but for Calle, that would probably only convolute her problems even more. Geez, *such is the fabric of dreams,* she mused to herself as she got up and started her day.

It was supposed to be a day off, but since she was the lead on the catering crew and her boss was missing in action, there were seldom any days she was completely off. She would have to stop by the mansion for a few minutes at some time during the day, but the rest of it was hers to do as she pleased.

And later, that very pleasing little something met her at the door of Lucero's Gallery of Fine Art. Bounding with energy and cuddly cuteness, Polkadot, the spunky Jack Russel terrier puppy and watchdog of Elias' gallery, skittered around her ankles until Calle picked her up for some up-close loving. The happy duty little pup was so excited that she nearly squirmed out of Calle's arms.

"There you go little one," Calle chuckled as she set the puppy down on the terra cotta tile. Pokey's little paws were already churning a mile a minute and when they touched floor, she shot down the hall like a greyhound on the hunt for anything that moved. "I wish I had some of that energy."

"You don't know the half of it." Elias gave Calle a hug as Lucy walked into the entry foyer.

"Good morning, are you ready?"

Lucy nodded then kissed her uncle goodbye.

"Okay, let's go," she turned to Calle.

"Yours or mine?" Lucy asked as their shoes crunched across the graveled parking lot.

"Mine's already warmed up," Calle replied as they shuffled toward her pickup. "Where to first?"

"I'm not all that hungry yet, want to go to Fairview?"

"Sure, it's on Cerrillos?"

"Yeah, at Cordova Road."

As they wound through the crooked streets of downtown, Lucy began to give Calle the skinny about her dreams and the man in them.

"So, it starts out somewhat distant, then it becomes very intimate. He always plays me a love song. It sets the mood and then we sit on the rock wall and start to talk. Well, usually I do most, well, all of the talking, weird right? He's a good listener."

"Mmm Hmm." It was weird because though Lucy was articulate and witty, she was a woman of few words.

"I want to hear his voice. Our relationship is all about feeling, we communicate by touch. He's the most sensual lover, but he doesn't ever say anything. But I understand him completely. Sounds crazy, right?"

"Sounds pretty good to me, a man who listens and satisfies your sexual needs is what *Cosmopolitan* would describe as ideal."

"You make it sound like a porno," Lucy deflated. "It's way more than that."

"All women think that when they are in the throes of lust."

"You suck. You know that?" Lucy grimaced as Calle smiled.

"I know."

"There's a deep connection, I feel it. It's more than

a fantasy, I can tell he loves me. It's impossible to explain."

"I get it. Sometimes, we feel things that are beyond words or common sense," Calle offered in support.

"I know you know. That's why I want you to help me." Lucy's expression turned serious. "I need to know more about him. Who he is, where he comes from, why he chose me... I don't even know his name, geez."

Calle studied her friend. "Do you think you might be getting played?"

"Not a chance, I understand men better than you think."

Calle knew that was a fact. Lucy understood men better than any woman she had ever met. Guys were always swooning over her and trying to get her attention. Though she had slept with a few of them, there was no one who could judge character or see through masculine bullshit better than she could.

"Okay, I believe you," Calle resigned. "I just wanted to make sure."

"It's alright."

"Dreams can be very different than the real world."

"I realize that, that's why I asked you here. Maybe I'm doing something wrong."

Calle thought that might be part of it, but suspected her friend had fallen hard for this guy. Their unusual sixth sense between them was causing Calle's protective nature to bristle. Lucy was out of her element and Calle realized she truly did need help. Calle's trepidation turned to conviction. She would do whatever she could to help her friend.

"Maybe, I don't know, we'll have to see. So, now what?"

"Hmm, well, I was thinking you could check out the place, you know, get a feel for the layout. I'll show you where I like to sit when I visit and where he and I usually get together in my dreams."

"Mmm, okay," Calle raised an eyebrow and grinned. "I don't need to know all the gory details."

"Like I would tell you my secrets," Lucy's mood lightened as they turned through the wrought iron gates of the old cemetery.

"You already have," Calle teased.

"Not those secrets, other secrets," Lucy stumbled. "Oh geez, shut up."

With the awkward part of the morning happily behind them, they wandered the cemetery together. Lucy pointed out specific spots in the graveyard where important things had occurred in her dreams.

"He always appears over here," Lucy said, pointing to a vacant section away from the busy road. "Then he walks toward me and we sit over here." She ambled to a short retaining wall partially covered with ivy.

"It's actually a very pretty place," Calle observed. "And the view," she gestured to the Sangre de Cristo Mountains in the background.

"Yeah, it is." The conversation lulled for a moment. "There's that creepy mausoleum I told you about. The one with the evil presence." Lucy pointed.

"Hmm, it doesn't look all that scary," Calle said as she walked toward the concrete crypt for closer inspection. "It's pretty plain, no inscriptions, just this scar where the name was chipped out. I wonder what that's all about."

"I don't know, but I don't go anywhere near it and it leaves me alone. I'm good with that," Lucy said with a shudder.

"Fair enough," Calle replied. She circled the monument, eyeing it from top to bottom. On the lee side of the crypt, Calle noticed a niche under a decorative marble inlay. She leaned down on one knee and blocked the sun from her eyes with one hand as she peered into the crevice that was about two feet above the foundation. There was a strip of ribbon stuffed into the space. She inserted her other hand inside and as her fingers touched the fabric, a large rat sprung from a hole in the ground at the base of the mausoleum.

Calle screamed in alarm as the rodent scrambled past and around the monument, disappearing down another hole.

"Holy Moses!" she exclaimed as she withdrew from the crypt. Lucy jogged to her side.

"What happened?"

"It was just a rat, he startled me."

"Did he bite you?"

"No, he just ran past me." Calle let out a deep breath.

"I think that's enough for today, don't you?" Lucy cocked an eyebrow.

"Yeah, I guess."

"Told you the crypt was evil."

"It was just a rat," Calle downplayed.

"Yeah, a rat that scared the crap out of you," Lucy jibed. Calle noticed Lucy didn't linger near the crypt for long.

"Yeah, yeah, you hungry yet?" Calle brushed off the dirt from her jeans and joined her friend on the path away from the mausoleum.

"Yeah, lunch sounds good, let's go."

It was Lucy's choice for lunch and since it was such

a splendid summer morning, La Casa Sena was the perfect spot. Just off the plaza and surrounded by shops and vendors, the leafy courtyard dining patio area offered privacy and ambiance right in the middle of the hustle and bustle of downtown. The old building was originally an affluent hacienda at the end of the Santa Fe trail, but now it was one of Santa Fe's most popular stops for locals and tourists alike.

After an hour of appetizers and tacos in the shady oasis, they decided to go up to the Pérez mansion. It wasn't all that far from the plaza and since Calle had a couple loose ends to tie up before her next few days off, they thought it would be a nice way to spend the afternoon.

"I've only been to the restaurant, I would love to see what the rest of it looks like," Lucy gushed. "I hear it's really fancy."

"It is and for the next couple weeks, I've got the run of the place. And an ATV to use while I'm there. I'll show you around, take a little tour. What do you think?"

"I'm in. Sounds like fun."

# ☽ 15 ☾

Lucy lounged, sipping a margarita, and surveying the splendor of her surroundings under the pavilion while Calle chatted with a pastry chef in the kitchen. A curious Barrow flitted from the fountain to the top of a blue spruce nearby, scattering a legion of already jittery hummingbirds. Pérez mansion was as marvelous as it was reputed to be. From the manicured lawns and gardens to the attention to detail it for which it was famous, it was spectacular.

She reclined in the shade and kicked off her sandals to dangle her ankles and feet from under the pavilion in the warm afternoon sunshine. With her Ray-Bans on and her eyes closed, she couldn't imagine that anyone rich or famous could possibly feel any more content than she was at the moment.

"Good afternoon, Gorgeous." The statement rattled her daydream. She hadn't heard his approach. Not moving a muscle, she slid open her eyes to assess the intruder.

"Beautiful day here in the mountains," a slender, but fit, delivery man continued as he set a box on the table next to her and fiddled with his cap. "Is this the first time you've been to Santa Fe?" he asked over-cordially, unable to corral his enthusiasm. His eyes roamed greedily from her rich, midnight black hair to the tips of her naked toes.

He thought she was a guest at the resort and was certain he had never seen a more beautiful woman in his entire life. He also couldn't believe his good luck for in running into her. He leaned his butt against the table and tried to radiate confidence as she turned her naturally photogenic face toward him.

"I've been here before," Lucy replied. She sounded like she could be the girl next door.

His confidence turned to sand in his pockets as her accent resonated as exotic as she looked. He didn't recognize the unique dialect that all Santa Fe locals use, even though he probably had heard it many times before. He had, but just not from anyone as attractive as she. Star struck and shaken, he tried to look into her eyes, but all he saw was the reflection of a blue-collar sap in her sun glasses. He knew right then she was way out of his league. They both did.

Amused, she tried to help. "Is this your first time?" she asked, intentionally leaving the question open for interpretation. Not that much help, but a lot of fun.

"First time?" he stammered. His imagination reeled.

"In Santa Fe."

"Santa Fe? Oh, yeah, I mean no... I live here." The words tumbled out of his mouth like his tongue was super glued to his teeth. He couldn't have sounded more foolish if he tried.

"I do too. My name's Lucy." She extended her hand. "What's yours?"

He readily accepted her greeting. "Rob Aragon, I'm on a delivery."

"I see," she said as she looked at the package on the

table.

"I'm not sure who to give it to. The office said to drop it off at the pavilion. I need a signature." He picked up the package to read the recipient's name aloud. Do you know if a Calle Roslyn is here?"

"Sure, she's the caterer. She's in the kitchen talking to the pastry chef," Lucy nodded her head in the direction of the open kitchen door.

Reluctant to leave Lucy's company right away, Rob bulldozed the conversation onward.

"I've heard about her."

"Oh?"

"Yeah, I met her the other day and my friend Ned spoke with her up at the stables. She's the gal that found the grounds keeper in a coma."

"Oh, really?" Lucy played ignorant.

"Yep, he was stung by a bunch of bees. I guess he was allergic," Rob bragged, proud to be the fountain of knowledge. When Lucy didn't respond, he continued. "Serves him right, he was bossy and too nosy. Nobody liked him."

"Hmm." Lucy knew that being quiet sometimes prompted people to open up and talk way more than they should.

"And that catering woman..." He looked again at the package then to the kitchen door. "She's the same way. I wouldn't be surprised if something happened to her too."

"Is that right?"

"Yeah, she was snooping around up at the tack shop and asking a bunch of questions about things that are none of her business," Rob said with authority, trying to impress the fair maiden sitting in front of him.

About that time, Calle and the pastry chef exited the kitchen, shook hands, and parted ways. The chef turned toward the mansion and Calle started toward Lucy and Rob.

"Calle Roslyn?" Rob asked business like, his personality doing a one-eighty as she approached.

"Yes," she replied tentatively, having recognized him from their previous meetings.

Rob pulled out an electronic clipboard and thrust it Calle's direction and said, "I need you to sign here for this package."

"Okay." Calle signed. "Thank you."

"Thank you," Rob replied using what he thought was a professional tone, giving no indication he had ever met her before. He spun on his heel and as he walked away, flung a farewell with all the charm he could muster at the woman he hoped to impress. "Bye Lucy."

"Bye." Lucy waved. Calle didn't have to ask; she had seen it a thousand times before.

As Rob disappeared around the edge of the tent, Calle went to put the package in the kitchen and locked the door. As she turned the key, she said, "That's my new food processor. It will come in handy at this gig." She jingled the keys into her pocket, took a few steps toward Lucy, then asked with a smirk, "You ready to take a tour?"

"Yeah, let's go." Lucy joined Calle as they hopped on the ATV. "What's with the smarty pants grin?"

"Nothing, just like watching you in action," Calle smiled.

Lucy knew what Calle meant. "For your information, it wasn't what you think."

"Oh really? That wasn't just another goofy ass guy

trying to impress you?" Calle beamed.

"Well, that part, yeah okay. Oh, just shut up," Lucy volleyed playfully through a grin.

Calle laughed out loud as the two spun away from the huge tent. Just as they were getting up to speed, Calle pressed the on the brakes and slowed the ATV to a crawl. She put her finger to her lips and shushed, then pointed to a plump chipmunk sitting on a fallen log spinning a strawberry in his paws under his nose.

"There he is," Calle whispered.

"Who?"

"El Gordo, he's our kitchen pirate."

"He's cute. And fat, that's the fattest chip I've ever seen," Lucy laughed.

"I know, right?"

El Gordo was not as amused with them as they were with him and he tucked the whole strawberry in his jowl, then sped off into the underbrush to enjoy his looted feast in private.

"That was cool," Calle said as they resumed their trek up the hill. Lucy agreed, then sat back to enjoy the ride. After a moment, she spoke up.

"For your information, I was helping you investigate, not that you would appreciate my efforts."

"What?"

"Back at the pavilion, I was helping."

"Okay. Alright, what did you find out?" Calle's amusement turning serious.

"That guy, Rob and his partner up at the tack shop, Ned is his name I think, they don't like you very much. Or Otis either."

"Why? I've never done anything to either of them. I don't even know them."

"They didn't like you wandering around the stables and asking questions." Lucy grabbed a willow leaf midmotion off a tree branch that protruded into the path as they sped up the hill.

"Well, they are acting suspicious. They're up to something, I sure of it. I bet Otis did too."

"I don' trust them, neither should you," Lucy warned as she flicked the now wadded leaf back into the forest.

"Point well taken. That wrangler, Ned, told me to mind my own business. And not in a nice way."

"Maybe you should."

"I haven't done anything to anyone, but I don't like being pushed around by bullies."

"I know, the new and improved Calle," Lucy said ironically, referring to her friend's recent change in attitude.

"I happen to like the new me," Calle said defensively with a humorous undertone.

"I do too," Lucy caught Calle's eye. "Much better than the depressed version. But have you forgotten that the last time you got involved with guys like this, you almost got killed? Just a couple months ago?" She tapped her forehead with her fingertips in a gesture that said, "Duh!"

"I know, but that was different."

"Oh yeah, how so?"

"Someone was murdered then."

Lucy deadpanned a look of skepticism and raised an eyebrow.

"What?" Calle met her scrutiny.

"Well, someone is in a coma now, almost dead," Lucy shook her head.

"There you go, a good reason to get involved." Calle poked the steering wheel with her index finger to emphasize her point. "Plus, Shawn asked me to keep an eye out for suspicious behavior. He thinks there's something going on too."

"Shawn?" Lucy shot Calle a mischievous grin.

"Detective Ramirez, geez."

Lucy knew she had Calle on the ropes. "So, what's up with Shawn? Did he ask you out? Or try to deputize you?"

"You're impossible," Calle laughed. Lucy joined in as the ATV slowed to a stop in front of Otis' treehouse.

"Well, are you going to answer my question?"

"No."

"No, what? No, you're not going to answer or no, he didn't ask you out?"

"No, he didn't ask me out. He's not bad looking though."

"I knew it!"

"No, you don't know anything. There's nothing going on. I only spoke with him a couple of times."

"And now you're on a first name basis with the lead detective, I see," Lucy jibed. Calle chuckled and shook her head in frustrated derision.

"There's no investigation, no dating, he just asked me to report anything suspicious."

"Mmm Mm." Lucy nodded, leaned her elbows on her knees, and pulled her hands under her face. Balancing her chin on her thumbs, she gave Calle a humorous but sarcastic side glance.

Calle tilted her head, raised one eye brow, and changed the subject.

"This is Otis' house, pretty cool, don't you think?"

172

Calle said as she pointed to the unusual structure suspended in the trees.

"Yeah, totally cool, I've never seen a treehouse that someone actually lived in," Lucy replied, accepting the good-natured truce.

The women stood in admiration of Otis' treehouse a few more minutes and after a quick walk-a-round, they resumed the tour of the Pérez property.

The breeze began to whisk the portly morning clouds into stringy cotton candy vapors across the afternoon sky as they lollygagged up the trail toward the stables. They stopped at a fork in the path to make way for a golf cart barreling downhill toward them. Calle pulled a little farther off the main track to avoid the broiling cloud of dust that billowed in its wake.

With their ATV pointing up the hill toward the cemetery, Calle and Lucy watched over their shoulders as Gloria and her boyfriend zipped by, locked in a seriously animated discussion. The couple was so absorbed by their debate, they didn't seem to notice the parked ATV or the bemused women sitting in it.

Highly entertained, Lucy turned to Calle. "What was that?"

"That," Calle waved her hand at the retreating golf cart, "Is true love on wheels," Calle joked cynically.

"Those two? Really?"

"Yep."

"I didn't get a real good look at them, but she's old enough to be his grandmother and he's big enough to swallow her whole."

"I know, right?" Calle laughed.

As the dust cloud began to engulf their ATV, Calle urged their vehicle into motion a few yards up the hill.

Looking down the dirt fogged trail toward the stables, she suggested, "I wanted to show you the tack shop, but I don't want to go through that." She pointed at the dust cloud with a nod of her head. "Let's go up to the spring and the cemetery instead."

"Good idea," Lucy coughed.

As the ATV escaped the gritty haze, Lucy drew a deep breath of fresh air and asked, "Who were those people?"

"I don't know them very well, but that was the owner's mother and her long-lost boyfriend."

"Wow, strange couple."

"That's for sure. It's pretty weird."

"Yeah, I guess," Lucy pondered. "Love will make you do weird things."

"I suppose, but that," Calle thumbed over her shoulder, "I don't get."

"What's not to get?" Lucy asked dubiously. "They're two people in love."

"I know, but..."

"Oh, you mean, they're not normal like, say, someone who has an astral lover or a woman who is infatuated with a man in her dreams? Normal like that?"

"Aha, aren't you the clever one, using the truth on me?" Calle grinned. "Touché, well played."

"Just sayin', love makes you do weird things."

"That it does."

Though the trail was just as rocky and steep as the first time Calle scaled it with Otis, it seemed a lot quicker this time. Calle parked the ATV under the shade of a large scrub oak and the girls hiked across the open area and along the fragrant lilac stand.

Honeybees swarmed a haphazard ariel display, buzzing from one blossom to the next unconcerned about the women trudging through their air space. A particularly fat bee loaded to the gills with pollen orbited Lucy's head and face as if looking for a place to land. Unfazed, Lucy shooed the insect away with a listless wave of her hand.

"Doesn't that scare you?" Calle asked incredulously.

"Not really, they're just curious."

"They make me nervous."

"Why? Even if one stings you, it will only hurt for a minute. And it will mean a death sentence for any bee that does."

"What do you mean?"

"When honeybees sting you, they lose their stinger. It gets stuck in your skin. It has little barbs on it and can't be easily removed. So, a honeybee can only sting you once and when it does, it rips their abdomen apart and kills them. Not right away, but they die soon after. So, they would rather not sting you, if they can avoid it."

"I did not know that."

"So, if you leave them alone, they will return the favor."

"That's kind of what Otis said," Calle said as she stumbled on some loose rocks.

"Wasps, hornets, and bumblebees are whole different story. They can sting repeatedly. It's much worse. And unlike the docile honeybees, they are all attitude."

"Maybe that was why Otis wasn't afraid of these guys."

"Maybe, but if I knew I was allergic to bees, I wouldn't be so cavalier. There's a fine line between bravery and stupidity."

The women's conversation lulled then petered out completely as they toiled up the trail. When they reached the grotto and the spring, Lucy stopped to take in the beauty of the area. Calle followed suit and wiped the sweat from her brow.

"This is an amazing place," Lucy commented in awe of the natural splendor. Calle leaned against a large rock in the shade and watched as Lucy approached the spring and the primitive sanctuary built around it. Calle felt a certain reverence there, but for a devout Catholic woman like Lucy, the sanctity of the place was as powerful as any cathedral.

Uninhibited by her friend's presence, Lucy knelt before the grotto, crossed herself, and began a silent prayer. The sincerity of moment was not lost on Calle. It never was when she was with Lucy. She closed her eyes and sent a silent prayer of her own heavenward, ending hers before anyone could notice. Unlike Lucy, Calle was inhibited and rarely prayed where people could see.

When Lucy was finished, Calle was quietly waiting for her.

The tender moment passed without fanfare and the two explorers resumed their trek to the cemetery. As the rusty archway hove into view, Lucy turned to her companion and joked, "This makes two cemeteries in one day, we may be going for a record."

"I like cemeteries."

"I know, I guess I do too. They make me feel closer to the past. I think of all the things these people said or did, what kind of friends they had, or what their hopes and dreams might have been."

"I feel a certain connection too."

The dialogue lagged as they stopped at the entrance of the graveyard. They stood in silent contemplation of the scene. A slender breeze shimmered the silvery green of the aspen leaves and the sumptuous flavor of honeysuckle filled the air. Barrow sat perched on the head of a rusty cherub eavesdropping on Lucy's next question.

"What do you want done with your body when you die? Buried or cremated?"

"Buried." Calle answered without hesitation.

"Me too. Where would you like to be buried?"

"I don't know. Does it really matter?"

"I think so. It gives those who knew you a place to visit and a connection to your future relatives who might wonder who they are and where they come from."

"Hmm, never thought of it that way." Calle turned her thoughts inward as her feet began to shuffle between the headstones. "I guess I would like to be buried naked beneath an apple tree."

Lucy was curious, but didn't pry. She watched as Calle reflected, then stopped to gaze down at a grave overgrown with buffalo grass. Lucy joined her friend next to the roughly hewn stone lying flat on the earth with the inscription, *Lucia Pérez 1797*, ground into its face. The pair stood beside each other as the wind wisped through their hair, regarding the ancient marker.

After a few moments, Calle continued, "Then every year when the apples are ripe, people can say, 'Calle sure is tasting sweet this year'."

Before Lucy could say, "What a great way for

people to remember you," Barrow fluttered to a landing on Calle's shoulder. His abrupt arrival shattered the sentiment, but woke them from their contemplation to see two old women approaching from the glade beyond the cemetery.

Though there was something vaguely familiar about one of the women, Calle didn't recognize the spindly old hag draped in black with purple lace stranded into her salt and peppered hair. However, there was no mistaking Jamaica Spinner or the double-barreled shotgun she was toting.

The purply haired woman raised a gnarled alabaster finger, pointed it at Calle, and croaked, "There she is."

The hushed accusation vaulted through the serenity of the graveyard like a javelin. Barrow took it as a threat and scrambled into the air in defense of his friends. His attack was met by a blast from Jamaica's shotgun. The agile blue jay barrel-rolled and narrowly avoided the deadly pellets, but the discharge peppered the tree branches above her companion's head.

"God Almighty, you crazy bitch! You almost shot me!" Old Purply screamed as she fell to the ground. "Shoot her, not me!" She again pointed to Calle.

"Shoot her yourself, you old witch!" Jamaica spat as she cracked open the shotgun, ejected the spent shells, and quickly shoved in replacements. With deadly confidence, she approached the startled women. Anxiously, Barrow watched out of range from the top of a towering ponderosa pine.

"You're trespassing!" the cammo clad mad woman declared.

"I work for the Pérez family," Calle shouted back.

"They're trespassing too. I'll give you to the count of three to skedaddle."

"You don't own this land. You don't belong here," Calle returned.

Jamaica cocked both barrels and closed the distance. "This gun says I do. One..."

Lucy grabbed Calles arm. "It's not worth it," she urged.

"Two..."

"You're right," Calle agreed as both women began to hurry away through the tombstones.

Under the gateway arch of the cemetery, Calle turned to see if they were being followed. Jamaica was standing right where she was when they left and the old crone in black had joined her. Jamaica looked triumphant holding her gun aloft, but the glare from her creepy companion blistered pure evil.

Calle knew the wily old woman and her sidekick would be long gone by the time security arrived at the cemetery, but she called them anyway. They told her they had several run-ins with Jamaica and assured her that the old woman was harmless, but they would check it out anyway. Apparently, every time they confronted her, Jamaica played the helpless old woman card, victimized and misunderstood, successfully eliciting sympathy and pity from the officers. Calle had met the woman twice and knew she was anything but helpless. In fact, she was convinced the old bat was capable of just about anything.

Back in the safety of the parking lot, Lucy laughed, "You sure know how to have a good time."

"Sorry about that. I had no idea we would get ambushed by a couple of lunatics."

"No worries, it was fun," Lucy smiled as Calle unlocked her truck.

"Oh yeah, loads of fun. I didn't know Jamaica had an accomplice."

"She seemed to know you. Did you recognize her?" Lucy asked from across the bed of Calle's truck.

"Never seen her before in my life."

Lucy's light hearted demeanor faded as her eyes focused on the dead animal in the bed of the pickup. Calle followed Lucy's gaze to another strangled rat hanging by a blue ribbon from the headache rack of Calle's truck. Their eyes met, then Lucy said, "Just curious, but what color was the ribbon earlier today at the mausoleum at Fairview?"

Calle's tone darkened, "Blue."


That evening, Calle's dreams galloped freely from lucid to out of body. Ethan was nowhere to be found. Surprised to find herself alone in her trek, she reached out for him. Her efforts came up fruitless, she could not find him. She absentmindedly twiddled the ring on her thumb, something wasn't right. He said he hadn't been feeling well. Was it serious? Maybe she could help. A wave of melancholy engulfed her. She missed Ethan. There was so much she needed to share, but there she sat, alone, surrounded by herself. Again.

Self-pity threatened her thinking, but the new and improved Calle would not allow it to take control ever again. Steadfast, she bit back the bitter feeling of hopelessness, but as strong as she had become, she couldn't shake her longing for Ethan. The dark dejection persisted.

Even though he had caged her dreams for a time and

didn't explain himself, her heart ached for him. True, she wanted to give him a piece of her mind, but mostly, she wanted sit and talk with him. Watch his handsome face as he listened to her like no else ever had. Her emotions began to reel. Love does indeed make you do weird things.

Her sour mood drew her to her favorite place to sulk. Sitting atop the southern spire of the cathedral, Calle began to hum *Always and Forever* to herself. Not a natural singer by any means, she let her loneliness drive the tune. The lyrics took on an eerie, black tone that soothed her yearning for her astral soul mate, but no longer sounded anything like the song playing in her head. As her emotion swelled, so did the intensity of the dirge.

There are things that dwell on many planes at once. They are transcendent because they are universal. Good, evil, love, hate. Deep passions that are the essence of all that is. It is not uncommon for them to occur on one plane and make themselves known on another. Calle's lament was so genuine, her sincerity began to spill over to the physical plane.

She did not notice when a young couple admiring the façade of Saint Francis Cathedral was halted by other worldly noises murmuring from the spire above. She continued her song unaware her feelings were manifest for all to hear on the streets below. Neither did she notice nor did she care when a small crowd gathered to record the chaunt with their cell phones.

When she read about the ghost of Saint Francis Cathedral the next morning, she dismissed it as a hoax, another sensational story trying to gain attention on YouTube. There was no ghost, that was a fact. She knew it was so because she had been there.

# ☉ 16 ☾

Just a few more steps. Isn't that what everyone says when they're trying to convince themselves of the merit of their toil. But then after they succeed, there's always more steps that follow. That truth became quite clear as Calle mounted the summit of the jagged outcropping of basalt overlooking the expansive Caja del Rio.

Beely serpentined between her shaky legs, elated to be on top of the escarpment, but for Calle, a shady rest spot was in order.

Looking out across then down the spectacular vista before her, Calle subconsciously counted the many steps back to her casita.

"Geez, don't you ever get tired?" she asked her cat as she plopped her butt on a smooth boulder next to a scraggly piñon pine. Beely's responded by jumping on her lap, rubbing his cheek to hers, then in typical feline fashion, darted off in search of something to stalk.

Back-wristing the sweat from her brow, she said to his retreating backside, "Don't go far, we're leaving as soon as I catch my breath."

A mischievous flick of his tail was all the acknowledgment she got in return.

She cracked open a bottled water, took a sip, and let the clean New Mexico breeze tickle her skin. There is something about sitting and watching the high desert in silence that soothes and invigorates. It reduces one's worries to a manageable size by reminding one how tiny a cog in the universe we really are. Not that we are insignificant by any means, but that we are just a part of something much larger than ourselves. It is humbling and reassuring all at the same time.

It was exactly what Calle needed. A chance to recenter herself, a moment to sort it all out.

She spied a petroglyph of a bird etched into the face of a crag jutting out over a nearby arroyo. The petroglyph itself was unusual because few were of birds, but the fact that there was a petroglyph was not a surprise. In fact, she had past hundreds of them on her hike up the rocky trail. Only a few years prior, the state set the area aside as a protected space due to the prolific Anasazi artwork that decorated the small canyon. Fortunately for Calle, the park was only a mile or so from her house.

As she contemplated the etching high above the game trail, her mind went back in time as she imagined the native artisan. A daredevil balancing on a handmade ladder, banging an obsidian stone against the cliff, in deep concentration trying to bring his vision to life. Why would he risk life and limb for something so unnecessary? Who was he trying to impress?

Calle tried to think of a reason for the artist to take such a risk. Maybe he was motivated by something spiritual. God knows, this area always moved her, possibly it did him too. Perhaps he knew something his friends didn't. Maybe she and the ancient artist weren't all that different after all.

In the past few months, maybe a year, her once

private lucid dreams had morphed into full-blown out-of-body adventures. She used to be like everyone else, not sure if there was something after death or if what you see every day is all there is. Not any longer. For her, there was no doubt about it. Not only was there an afterlife, but there was a lot more, a whole lot more.

But being privy to something so powerful and so true isolated her even further than just being the quirky kid with Déjà vu or the nut job with PTSD. That was one of the reasons Ethan's behavior was so troubling. Not only had she grown to love him, but he was the only person who understood that side of her life, otherwise on the astral plane, she was alone.

Her thoughts went to Ab Pistola. The fictional animé character with astral abilities similar to Calle's, Ab was everything Calle was not. Athletic, rich, calm, cool, and collected in every situation, Ab towered in striking contrast to Calle's struggles with PTSD and self-doubt. Though she was getting stronger, she still had a long way to go if she were to match Ab's confidence and audacity.

However, competing with a pretend character alive only in the media, one she suspected was not so pretend by the way, was not her goal. All she needed was a means to cope. And she knew, that was a million times harder than parading around like a superhero in her dreams. Loneliness in any form can be debilitating and by definition, it required one to deal with it by themselves. A catch-22 she didn't want to get caught up in again.

Her worries about Ethan swirled in her head as she braced herself to face her dilemma the only way she knew how. Calling for Beely, she resumed her hike downhill. Keeping busy was the plan. It wasn't a clinical solution by any means, but it kept her moving and moving was the opposite of stagnation. Sooner or later, she would run into something that would change her outlook. Such as it was, that was the plan.

The clip clop of a horse's hooves stolting from the main trail broke Calle's introspection. She leaned against the H-shaped railroad tie reinforcement at the corner of two barbed wire fences and watched as a lone horseman approached on a chestnut quarter horse. When the rider and his steed got close, the denim clad cowboy called out to her.

"Well, if it isn't Calle Roslyn," he hailed then leaned away to spit a sunflower seed husk from his lips. Turning back to face her, he repositioned the remaining wad of seeds in his jowl with his tongue then continued, "What are you doing way out here?"

Recognition dawned on her as she matched the voice with the person.

"Free country. Ain't so?" she jibed back, shading her eyes to look up at the man.

"I suppose it is," the rider laughed at her spunky retort.

"And what are you doing way out here yourself, Dale Weaver?"

Dale stood up in the stirrups then repositioned himself in the saddle.

"Acorn and I like to go joy riding out this way every now and then, what's your excuse?" the sixty-something cowboy shot back as he reined his pony to a stop a couple yards from her.

Dale was Calle's next-door neighbor, but the term next-door was misleading. Though his place was adjacent to her property, they rarely laid eyes on one another because they both lived on acreages and their houses were a few thousand yards apart. The last time they spoke face to face was earlier that year at the flea market carnival where Dale moonlighted as a story teller. But they had talked only a few days ago on the phone and as they stood chit-chatting, Calle brought the conversation back to the essence of that phone call.

"Did you ever catch up with those thieves that hit your place?"

"No, them sons-of-bitches will probably get away with it. The sheriff says there's nothing he can do," Dale's tone took on a bitter edge. "Any sign of them around your place?"

Calle thought to mention the dead rats, but decided the rats were another problem she didn't want to have to explain right now. Instead, she stuck to the only relevant thing she could think of.

"I saw pickup tracks in my driveway the other day, but nothing was stolen. I don't know if it was thieves casing my place or if it was just someone who was lost."

"Mmm." Dale scratched his stubbly chin. "I hope they leave you alone. Hopefully someone will shoot the bastards," he grumbled as Beely leaped from behind a tall weed up on top of the fence post next to Calle.

The abrupt appearance of the black cat startled Acorn and the mare began to prance backward nervously.

"Whoa girl," Dale consoled in a loud voice as he struggled to gain control of his anxious mount. Acorn reluctantly heeded his command, but never took her eyes off the blue-eyed feline.

"That your cat?"

"Yeah, he's my partner in crime," Calle joked, rubbing Beely behind his ear as his tail flicked mischief.

"Strange animal."

"I've heard that before, but that's the way I like him," Calle asserted.

"I've seen him prowling around my place lately," Dale said. "I hope he's a good mouser. I've also got a squirrel problem, maybe he can help."

"Maybe," Calle answered knowing full well Beely wasn't a killer by nature, unless provoked. Then he could be vicious, her mind went back to an incident with a bobcat a few months prior.

Dale's horse had had enough and couldn't contain her nervous energy. Calle couldn't tell if Acorn just wanted to go home or if Beely worried her. Either way, Dale picked up on it too.

"Well, Acorn wants to get moving, so I'll see you later." He tipped his hat and with the squeak of twisting leather, he spun his horse in a circle before pointing her down the trail. "Call me if you need anything, I'm just a minute away."

"Will do, same goes for you too," Calle shaded her eyes again as Acorn kicked up her heels into a lively canter.

When they arrived home, Calle rinsed the dust and sweat from her face and Beely snuggled onto the couch for a nap. He rolled over playfully hoping for a belly rub as Calle sat down next to him. Closing his eyes, he pawed the air like a kitten. When her fingertips touched the cobalt blue marking on his chest, he began to purr and as she began to massage his torso, he surrendered completely.

"You're spoiled, you know that?" Beely didn't care, he was in seventh heaven. "No wonder you're a ball of energy on our hikes, you sleep all the time," she teased. After a few minutes like that, he opened a groggy eye of disappointment when she picked him up and placed him on her chest as she joined him for a nap. He maneuvered himself into a ball of warmth on her tummy and she placed a loving hand on his hip. As she fell asleep, he closed his eyes but not his ears.

A swath of peace embraced her as she slid past any semblance of a dream. Her body and soul needed uninterrupted slumber. Any recollection of what happens when a soul reinvigorates its connection with its body is always kept secret, one only God knows, but never shares. It is essential any living person's health, but for an active dream trekker, it is even more vital.

Calle relished these times, but only when she awoke. It was then when she could realize what had happened and enjoy the gift of clarity that accompanied the experience. Often times, when she slept deeply, upon waking, she would have a brief lucid moment that would go out of body. It was usually intense, but fleeting. It appeared like the universe playing peek-a-boo with her, a snapshot pulsing once very quickly.

The flash of insight hit her astral being like déjà vu. Unexpected and tempting, almost mocking her, making her question herself. The image of Mona's house then a passing glimpse of the Lewis home signaled significance. It was important, but as usual, vague and ambiguous.

Calle awoke with a start, but lay still beneath her cat. Beely, stirred on her abdomen, stood then arched his back and yawned, exposing his razor-sharp teeth.

He made eye contact, then slipped to the floor, off duty while Calle grappled with the meaning of her vision.

She got up and on the way to the bathroom, mulled ideas over in her head. She wasn't completely sure what to do. It wasn't like her normal déjà vu on the physical plane, where she would simply watch and wait for the vision to come true. This was different, it was astral and it required action.

Calle paced back and forth on her patio with her phone stuck to her ear. Suddenly she stopped and began to talk, Lucy had finally answered her call.

"Hey, what are you doing the next couple days? Want to go to Portales with me?"

"What? Go where?"

"Portales."

"Texas?" Lucy asked into the phone. "No, thank you," she said away from the phone to someone nearby.

"New Mexico, I need to…" Calle started excitedly, but Lucy cut her off.

"Just a minute," Lucy said.

Calle waited impatiently as Lucy talked to the other person. After another 'Thank you', Lucy returned. "Sorry, I'm at Baja Taco, what were you saying?"

"I need to go to Portales, want to go?"

Calle explained her idea and Lucy thought if nothing else, the trip would be an interesting diversion. Always up for adventure, she agreed and since she worked for her uncle and had him wrapped around her little finger, she could usually come and go as she pleased. So, the next morning the intrepid travelers set out to the eastern plains of New Mexico.

Neither woman had been to this neck of the woods before and were surprised when the mountains gave way to the Llano Estacado, or the Staked Plains as it was referred to in English. The grasslands stretched on for as far as the eye could see. In the distance, rolling hills met the clear blue horizon and in the basins, large arroyos lay cleft into the face of the earth revealing hidden glens of pine and elm. Barbed wire, dirt roads, and train tracks braided the immensity as freight trains, each easily a mile long, muscled their cargo along the rails.

Aside from an occasional truck or car on the highway or a ranch house in the distance, there was little indication of any human habitation at all. Instead, the land belonged to the wind and frequent herds of cattle and sheep. Occasionally there would be a small group of antelope or a lone red-tailed hawk, but otherwise the landscape was open, desolate, and mesmerizing.

They shared a laugh when the last jarbled radio signal faded and the scan feature could no longer pick any signal at all. But when their cell phones lost service, they felt like they had fallen off the face of the earth. Having spent their entire lives connected to the media, the naked silence mocked like a broken radio on the dark side of the moon.

At first, they found it amazing there was even such a place that still remained in America. But devoid of any electronic intrusion and with nothing left to distract them, a mild uneasiness settled over the pair of adventurers. Lucy euthanized the scan feature when she clicked off the radio and the drone of the pickup's engine added to the feeling of isolation. But it soon passed and the natural silence stirred something fundamental about human beings. They began to talk.

"So, we're going to visit someone you met in a dream?"

"Yeah, there's this kid that reached out to me and I got involved."

"Involved?"

"He's being abused by his uncle, but I think his grandmother can help."

"Abused? Like physically?"

"Yep. I can't turn away; I've got to help."

"What are you going to do?"

"I really don't know yet. I'm going to talk to his grandmother and see if I can find some leverage to use against his uncle, he's a real bastard. I guess I'm just winging it."

"Alright, hmm, how can I help?"

"Just be there for moral support. I didn't want to go alone, so, you're already helping."

The conversation paused as they entered an almost abandoned town. Calle slowed the pickup as they surveyed their surroundings, marveling at the spectacle. Sometime in the past, the town must have been thriving, but now, it looked like all the inhabitants just got up and left, leaving the town to die a slow ugly death.

"How would you like to live there?" Lucy smiled in disbelief as they drove over a train track overpass bordered by a large cemetery.

"I wouldn't, but someone does. Did you see that guy in pajamas walking his chihuahua near that dilapidated motel?" Calle chuckled.

"No, I must have been looking out the other way." Lucy checked her phone, still no service. "I don't know how anyone could live here. I hope all the towns don't look like this." But they did.

At a road side rest stop just this side of nowhere, Calle idled her truck to a stop along a single cabled fence that enclosed two garbage barrels and a couple picnic tables with the unending landscape looming in the background.

"Sorry, but I have to pee."

"No problem, I'll just stretch my legs a bit," Lucy said.

After the initial hesitance about doing her business beside a state highway, Calle realized that the wind was a messier concern. As desolate as the road had become, she could have peed in the middle of the highway and nobody would have noticed.

Lucy had already returned to her seat as Calle paused at the tailgate to take in the wild expanse. In their own way, the eastern New Mexico plains were magnificent. That sentiment vanished when she caught an abrupt movement on her periphery. She flicked her eyes that direction only to see the grass swaying in the wind. Gooseflesh began to tickle her shoulders as a familiar stench pillowed across her face. She looked again for any sign of a presence, but there was nothing but wide-open plains. In that moment, standing alone behind her truck with the wind, she recognized the subtle warning.

Calle shared with Lucy what had happened. For the next forty-five minutes, she tried her best to convey the seriousness of her astral situation, but her words paled in comparison to the reality. She answered questions, but as she did, she began to hear her answers and decided she was beginning to sound schizophrenic. It was a case of you would have had to be there to understand, so she quit trying to explain any further. At least Lucy listened and tried to relate. Calle secretly thanked the heavens for such a true friend, but knew Lucy fathomed only an inkling of the truth.

As the adventurers trucked toward a massive railroad underpass, civilization appeared below the horizon in the lower Pecos Valley. It manifest itself in the form of cell service and modern convenience.

A small farming and ranching community straddling the slow meandering Pecos River, Fort Sumner was a quaint little hamlet with a storied history. Billy the Kid is buried there, but Mescalero Apache and Navajo natives detest the place due to the Bosque Redondo Reservation they were forced to inhabit starting in 1863. Unaware of the history on which they trod, to the two road weary urbanites, the rustic town was a godsend.

It's amazing what a fresh cup of coffee and a few friendly faces can do for one's attitude. That, and the final leg of the journey was a lot more eventful than it had been up to that point. With military fighter jets from Cannon AFB making low flybys on their way to strafe the Melrose bombing range and a small herd of mule deer bent on hogging the highway, the remaining miles flew by like a carnival ride.

Portales, New Mexico is a college town surrounded by a land of agriculture. Hemmed in by dairies and fields of peanuts or cotton, it is a living time capsule. Eastern New Mexico University is the center piece of the community, its brown stone architecture complementing its beautifully manicured grounds, giving the place a back east academic feel. The campus was sparsely populated however, partially because of the summer break and partially, like all schools nowadays, due to remote learning.

Calle and Lucy got a good look at the university because Spencer's grandmother's house was literally just down the street. The house was exactly like Calle remembered it from her dream. Her heart rate sped up as she parked the truck curbside in front of Mona's cottage. When her foot hit the pavement, her anxiety flared, pushing her to the edge of a panic attack.

*What was she doing here, coming unannounced? What was she going to say? Hi, I saw you in a dream?* What once sounded like a good idea now felt like a handful of salt in her throat. She halted, holding the pickup door open trying to catch her breath.

"Are you okay?" Lucy said rounding the front of the pickup to Calle's side. Calle closed her eyes and slowly let out a breath as Lucy put a hand on her shoulder. "You can do this, it will be alright," she reassured.

They were standing by the truck for a moment when the screen door to the house opened and a maternal, concerned voice called out from the porch. "Is everything alright?"

Hearing that voice, combined with Lucy's solace, shook Calle from her personal dilemma. Damn PTSD! She opened her eyes and when they met those of the kindly old woman wringing her hands on the porch, recognition sparked between them. Mona took a step back as Calle and Lucy introduced themselves.

Mona, despite her concern over Calle's presence, adhered to the rule of true Southern hospitality and invited the pair in, though it was clear, Mona was rattled a bit. She had never dreamt of someone then a few days later met them face to face. Fortunately, her curiosity was stronger than her superstition and soon the ladies settled into comfortable conversation.

Calle explained why she was there, never letting on that she knew about the dream. That would be way too much for the sweet old grandmother to comprehend. Calle wanted to help, not confuse and alienate the woman. So, the dream hovered in the background as Mona confided that she was embroiled in a custody battle with Spencer's uncle. If Howard would only give up his claim for custody, Spencer could come live with his grandmother permanently.

"Why does he want custody of a child he doesn't love?" Lucy's question came awash with innocent logic, but Mona's answer outlined the root of the problem.

"He thinks, Spencer will be a cash cow. That Social Services will shower him with drinking money." Her eyes swelled up with tears. "But he's wrong and my grandson is paying the price." She began to cry in earnest and shivered at the thought. Mona had had enough; she couldn't talk about it anymore. Her poor nerves were so frazzled, she said she had to go lay down.

As they were leaving, Calle thanked the woman and told her she would go talk to Howard. She mentioned she and Howard had met, but didn't go into detail about how or where. They left Mona's house knowing the trip was well worth the effort. Now to deal with the abuser.

Howard Lewis lived nineteen miles away from Mona in the city of Clovis. As the women motored north, Lucy questioned Calle's bravado.

"How do you know he won't attack you? He's a bully."

"I don't really know, but if he recognizes me from his dream, I think it will freak him out. Plus, you're going to be standing right beside me."

"Aha, I knew there was a catch."

Finding Howard's run-down shanty was not a problem, Calle had been there before. The women girded themselves for the inevitable confrontation and mounted the porch steps as gangster rap music rumbled the windows. They shared a look when the singer grunted a hate filled lyric about killing the bitch and slapping the ho.

Shaking her head, Calle rang the doorbell. She was shocked when it worked and doubly so when someone was actually able to hear it. The music was abruptly shut off and they heard shouting coming from deep within the structure, then boots clomping towards the door.

Howard Lewis was in fine form when he yanked the door open. His greasy hair was glued stiff to the side of his head and his pupils constricted as the daylight shone on his pickled features. When his vision finally came into focus, it was predictably all over Lucy. He cracked a self-gratifying grin featuring a few yellowed teeth and one rotten incisor set in blackened gums. Scraping a filthy fingernail under his bottom lip, he scooped out a finger full of Skoal and flicked the spitty residue into the dirt and leaned against the door frame like he was God's gift to women.

"Well, well, well, what can I help you ladies with?" His gaze turned to fantasy as his eyes fondled every inch of Lucy's form, stupidly missing the scowl on her face.

"Howard Lewis," Calle's voice attacked like a drill sergeant.

Obviously annoyed, Howard turned his attention to the other woman on his porch. His intention was to issue a rude reply, he didn't like strong women. But when his eyes met those of the nemesis of his dreams, he let out a scream like a scalded pig and nearly jumped out of his skin. Calle thought the man might pee his pants on the spot. Lucy would have preferred to break his nose.

"Oh my God, you're real!" His scrutiny bounced like a ping pong ball between Calle and Lucy. He was confused and scared, his inclination was to run. He stepped back, screamed, "Leave me alone, you bitch," and slammed the door with so much force a stick of molding fell from the jamb, clattering to the porch floor between the women.

They could hear yelling and the crashing of cabinets, then a gallop of footsteps back toward the door and the dead bolt banging into place. They were sure he was looking out the peep hole when Lucy turned to Calle with a grin, "I never would have guessed you were a bitch, but you wear it well."

Calle didn't hear the jibe, something inside her had clicked. Lucy changed her tactic and tried again, "You scared the crap out of that guy." But the words bounced off, never to be heard.

Calle's grim continence turned black as she stared down the peep hole, then yelled loud enough to carry through the closed door and half way around the block, "I'm not done with you, you abusive sack of shit. I'll be back."

*The Terminator* might have said it first, but the acidic venom seeping through the door burned like a prophecy. Any fool knew that a creepy android from the future was no match for a pissed, resolute woman protecting a child. Lucy gawked at her possessed friend then to the door, she was sure Howard knew it too.  He better.

# ☽ 17 ☾

"I don't know what came over me. I just snapped," Calle admitted as they drove back through Portales.

"Snapped? More like Atilla the Hun on steroids. You were magnificent!"

Calle side grinned to her friend. "I would rather be level-headed, but that guy really gets to me."

Lucy beamed, "I couldn't be more proud of you." She continued enthusiastically, "What are you going to do? Boil his balls in hot oil back in dreamland?"

"What?" Calle laughed. "You're one sick pup, aren't you?"

"Yeah, but you love me. So, what are you going to do?"

"I'm not sure." Calle slowed the truck as they approached a ranch style home with horses grazing in a pasture out front. "Is this it?"

Lucy leaned forward and squinted through the bug splattered windscreen and into the setting sun at a sign that confirmed they had found their lodging for the night.

"Yep, this is the B&B. Turn right here," Lucy pointed with her phone.

The family home turned hostel had three cute little bungalows out back surrounded by pastures of grazing livestock. The pastoral setting was a steal compared to the boxed lodgings across town along the railroad tracks where those mile long trains rumbled regularly. Located south of town on the Dora highway and hosted by a pair of charming, eclectic professors from the university, the place was the perfect refuge for the two drained travelers.

That night as they relaxed in their beds, Lucy started up.

"This running around all over the state trying to save the world is sure a lot of work, I'm exhausted."

"Amen to that."

"Just curious," Lucy mused aloud as she shuffled pillows trying to get comfortable. When she settled, she let out a sigh then continued, "So, are you going looking for Howard tonight?"

Calle clicked off the muted TV, rolled to her side, and pulled her comforter up to her chin. Her bed squeaked when she leaned over to click off the lamp on the night stand between them. With the light of the full moon beaming from the skylight, she responded, "It's not that easy."

A cricket began to sing in the distance and a fairy tale stillness marinated in the semi darkness as the night began to lull them toward sleep.

"If you kill him in his dreams, will he die in real life too?" Lucy's question barely a whisper.

It was a simple question, but implied a mountain of uncertainty. Calle had no idea. She lay wondering if that was a possibility or not. Her quiet contemplation only amplified the silence. After a moment she said, "I don't know. Maybe."

"If you killed him in his dreams and he died out here too, no one would know you had anything to do with it.

You might have a license to kill."

The idea sank like a depth charge in Calle's stomach. She didn't want that kind of responsibility.

"I don't have any intention of killing anybody and I'm not James Bond. God, can you imagine?"

They shared a veiled laugh then Lucy said, "My grandmother used to tell me dreams were full of symbols. She would say, 'If a snake bites you in your dreams, kill it before you wake up or someone you love will die soon'."

"Hmm, psychologists say dreams are full of symbolism too, but I haven't found that to be true at all."

"Sounds about right. Child psychologists who don't have children and marriage counselors who have never been married, what could possibly go wrong?" Lucy joked.

"I know, right?" Calle joined in. "Dream analysts that have never been lucid or out of body," she added with a giggle.

"It's funny how people with a title or credentials automatically assume they know more about you than you do."

"I once had an algebra teacher that always lectured us about what it was like in the real world." Calle scrunched mock quotation marks in the air with her fingertips. "He had taught school for thirty years and was an expert on everything. A self-congratulating know-it-all if there ever was one. Then one day, it occurred to me, he had spent twelve years in public school, four years for as an undergraduate, another two in grad school, and the rest of his life working in the classroom. He had lived his entire life in school, one way or another. How on earth would he have a clue about the real world?"

"Isn't that the truth, geez," Lucy agreed. "But that happens in all walks of life. Just give someone a little authority and they think they have the right to tell you all about it," she laughed.

They merrily continued citing examples from armchair athletes to assistant managers to auto mechanics and to every kind of bullshitter they could think of until their last bit of energy was spent. The high-spirited cynicism was a pleasant closing to an eventful day, but it began to fade as exhaustion overtook them. Before long they were both fast asleep.

That's one thing about astral projection, you never get tired. Your mind may get weary or your heart grow heavy, but your footsteps will always light and airy. Not that your footsteps matter all that much when you can fly, but hey, it is what it is.

Maybe it was because they were in such close physical proximity or maybe it was just dumb luck, but Calle soared into Lucy's dream as easily as a joey into its mother's pouch. In its own way, it was just as comfortable. Nothing like the trouble she had entering Howard Lewis' dream. Calle didn't take the time to figure out why as Lucy shone like a beacon floating in the clear blue sky over the Taos Gorge bridge aboard the Spider Pig hot air balloon, she just went with it.

"Mighty fine view from up here, ain't so?" Calle smiled as her bare feet touched inside the gondola next to her closest friend.

"That's for sure," Lucy answered as if Calle had been there all along. "See the bighorn sheep down there?

They're halfway to the river, see?" she bristled, patting Calle's hand and pointing downward.

"It's amazing how they don't fall off those steep cliffs," Calle observed, then leaned back to survey Wheeler Peak and the northern most part of the Sangre de Cristo range all the way into southern Colorado.

Lucy certainly had picked a beautiful setting for her dream. Calle was disappointed when she realized they couldn't linger to enjoy Lucy's dream at its natural pace. It might have been fun, but she knew this might be her only chance to help Lucy with her romantic dilemma. So, she pulled Lucy's hand into hers and asked sweetly, "Luce, do you want to go to Fairview?"

Lucy's carefree demeanor swirled into understanding as she met Calle's gaze. A look of excited expectation flickered across her features; one Calle couldn't ever remember seeing on her friend's face before. Lucy replied enthusiastically, "I would love to, let's go."

It was Calle's idea, but she didn't have a plan. Should they fly the many miles or should she teleport them there instantly? Take the scenic route to show off a bit or wham, bam, get the job done? Not surprising, the situation was all new to Calle.

A feeling of pride swept through her as she pulled her dearest friend into flight alongside herself. Her choice was to fly, but not like an airplane or a bird, but in a Tinkerbell sort of fashion, hand in hand, like two enchanted fairies on the wind.

They glided inches over the waves of the Rio Grande and wheeled beside the rock face of the gorge, then soared like lazy swallows surfing the breeze. Along treetops and over mountain peaks they sped as swiftly as a herd of snails. The journey was of Calle's making and she relished at each gasp of astonishment Lucy exhaled.

There's something about the astral plane that intensifies the connection between kindred spirits and makes even the slowest, most deliberate of actions fast. Calle felt it with Ethan and now again with Lucy. Whatever it was, it was wholesome and natural. It fit.

With that thought fresh in her mind, Calle landed them at the back of the graveyard, trying to recreate what she remembered from Lucy's description of her dreams. She released Lucy's hand and her friend took two steps forward then turned back to Calle with a look of uncertainty in her expression. Calle tilted her head in reassurance, then said, "It will be alright. Let's go see what happens." With that, they entered Fairview cemetery.

The second Lucy's sole touched the sacred soil, an elegant classical guitar etude embraced her arrival. It resonated as Celtic with a Flamenco flare. An ancient melody conjured by a master musician. It was a love song crafted from pure adoration performed flawlessly for one so beloved, the finest gift a musician can give.

Calle followed Lucy inward. The tones softened as the two lovers' eyes met. The guitar player ended his tribute and stood to greet Lucy with a kiss. She returned his affection and as they broke their embrace, Calle noticed a wispy glow that lingered between them, like their spirits were somehow entwined. It was strangely reminiscent of her own experience with Ethan, but she didn't have time to think about it as the guitar player tore his gaze from Lucy to her own.

Feeling like an intruder on their wedding night,

Calle sheepishly smiled and ventured a meek, "Hello."
Her greeting was met by a stare of curiosity.

From the moment she laid eyes on the man, Calle
knew what she was dealing with. By the empty look on
his face, the ghost of the handsome guitar player wasn't
nearly as sure. She had suspected Lucy's paramour was
a ghost, but in the astral world, she had learned to take
nothing for granted. Don't believe anything you hear
and only half of what you see, her grandfather's sage
advice playing in her head.

With dead people, communication was always a
fiddly endeavor. From personal experience, she knew
the dead could be open and clear, like her husband or
translucent and quiet, speaking only in pictures, like
the victim of murder she had once met. The choice, it
seemed, was up to them.

Lucy moved to take Calle's hand, then pulled her
close and said to her man, "This is Calle, the one I told
you about."

Awe replaced misgiving as the guitar player uttered,
"¿Soñador lúcido?" His antique Spanish dialect lagged
like an echo as the words translated themselves into
modern American English in Calle's ears.

"Yes, I'm a lucid dreamer," Calle replied, supposing
her gift served as a natural translator. "You can speak,"
she continued.

"Sí, puedo, pero Lucy no puede oírme," he answered
Calle's question as she asked it.

"I see... But Lucy cannot hear you."

"Si. You are special, no?"

Taken aback, Calle eyed him suspiciously.

"Lucy is dreaming, but you are something more," he
declared as a matter of fact.

206

That, she could not deny, but what was she supposed to say? I can talk to the dead, but Lucy can't? Instead, she redirected the conversation.

"What's your name?" she asked, taking the lead.

He smiled, "I am Rey Alba."

The conversation tumbled, then began to twitter between the trio like excited otters playing in the snow. With Calle in the middle, Lucy and Rey expanded their already close connection. It was quite odd actually because she, an English speaker, was acting as translator for two people both fluent in Spanish.

Rey explained that when people die and they are strongly convinced they have unfinished business, their ghost can remain on earth indefinitely. There they will remain, in limbo, until their conundrum is satisfied. He was one of those few. When he died, he had never met his soul mate and his stubborn vow to cling to life until he did, kept him tethered to the cemetery.

As fate would have it, as a child, Lucy grew up only a block from the cemetery. Rey had watched her since she was baby, then as a student at the Catholic school nearby. Recognizing a kindred spirit, he played games with her in her dreams, sang lullabies to her when she couldn't sleep, and consoled her when she was sad. As she grew, he fell in love with her and now that she was an adult, he revealed himself to her, hoping she would feel the same way.

On a basic level, Lucy was already in love with him. His unconditional affection, regardless of her physical search for love, never wavered. And when he came to her as a man in love, she saw him clearly for who he was, a perfect match, the man of her dreams. So, there they were, stuck in two different worlds trying to make it work.

Calle watched as he assured Lucy that he would wait and she readily accepted his promise. True love isn't concerned with time and age means nothing. A heart knows when its met its match and once it does, it will do anything for the one it cherishes.

Bliss is indeed a marvelous thing, but even on the astral plane, it is a passing sentiment that flourishes under the surface. Its fleeting bloom is sweet and its effect can be felt for a lifetime, but human existence is not tied to a single moment. It is dynamic and constantly changing. A roller coaster of ups and downs, a kaleidoscope of experience, many good and many not so much.

"How convenient, the fly has returned to the web."

The sour guttural syllables shattered the crystal chandelier around Calle and her friends.

In the split second it took for them to face the voice, its owner was already lunging for Calle. A three fingered talon with long, splintered fingernails, burnt umber in color and intent on destruction, slashed at her face, missing only by inches. The surprise attack scattered the three friends as they scrambled for safety. When the creature halted in their midst to survey the situation, they got a good look at their cunning adversary.

A long, cavernous face like that of a starved mule, sat at a smug angle a top a masculine body dappled by shaggy and matted fur. Despite, being outnumbered and surrounded, he bristled confidence. Fiery, intelligent orbs recessed into his skull jittered crimson fury as he plotted their demise. His leathery chest was bare and heaved a breath through his nostrils that came out like sulphuric steam from an angry locomotive. It hung in the air as the creature pivoted on cloven hooves, moving his attention from face to face, looking for weakness. Almost human in form, the demon stood cockeyed like the prehistoric love child of a bow-legged neandertal and a molting muskox.

Having sized up the competition, the demon leapt again for Calle. His single-minded obsession was fast, but she was ready this time. Though still a novice, she was still a quick-witted dream trekker, catching her on this plane would not be easy.

The demon tried to materialize next to her, but she had already teleported behind him. Spinning on his heel, he turned to face her. Slow and deliberately, he began to stalk like a tiger in the bush. The new tactic seemed foolish since she could see him clearly, but she had made the mistake of locking eyes with him. A hypnotic stupor began to fill her mind as she tried to break away from his spell. Now his words made sense, she was indeed trapped like a fly in a web.

With his conquest seconds from reaching climax, his focus faltered. Something distracted him. He was stopped mid-step as a cylindrical light emerged and coalesced into a young maiden between the spider and the fly. A child's voice rang out steady and true, hammering a declaration into the demon like a stake in his chest.

"Cuün, you will go no further," she said as she raised the lantern in her hand to eye level, a cloud of sky-blue light glowing from its center, engulfing the demon.

The demon's fur stood on end in razored edges as he shouted to the girl, "Isla, you pitiful orphan. You've been abandoned again; you're not even a real angel."

Cuün leveled his glare at the child and continued, "But I will have mercy on you. Give up and I will strangle the light from your soul."

Isla did not respond with words, instead determination swept her features as she intensified her attack. The blue light darkened into cobalt chain lightning that encompassed Cuün like a prison cell.

With surprising dexterity, Cuün blocked the maneuver with a miniature cyclone, effectively shielding himself from contact with her high voltage attempt to ensnare him. The two circled each other, slashing and dodging like two evenly matched swordsmen. After a few minutes, it became obvious, with Isla on guard, Cuün could not reach Calle.

Patience is a virtue for which demons are not known to possess. He knew he could not best Calle's guardian under these conditions and the little patience he did have had long since evaporated. He needed a new tactic and it came to him as his frustration exploded. His abrupt disengagement of Isla caught everyone off guard as he shot from the fray to snatch Lucy off her feet by the neck and throat.

Lucy tried to defend herself, but she was way out of her element. Cuün had her in his grasp before she knew what was happening. Calle was caught flat-footed as well and her attempt to help her friend came too late. Cuün held Lucy aloft and dangled her like a rag doll, taunting his quarry with the torture of her best friend.

Though the demon was an expert astral entity and was in control, Lucy fought valiantly. She gouged her slender fingertips of her left hand into his orbital socket, ripping his lower eye lid from his face. Open hatred glared from his bare eyeball as she sunk her nails deeper into the flesh under his eye. Using the grasp of his cheek as leverage, she kicked into his exposed manhood as hard as she could while latching her right hand onto the single downturned horn sticking from his head, trying to wrench herself free. The furious counterattack would have incapacitated any mortal man, but her struggling only emboldened Cuün. Though he was enduring serious physical abuse, he seemed delighted by it.

Calle screamed to Isla, "Do something!" but Isla frowned and replied, "I cannot. I am sworn to protect only you."

Calle's mind was whirling at eighty miles a second. She couldn't think of anything astral to use as a weapon. She had never thought like that before. Should she attack the demon with her bare hands or would Isla prevent it? Instinctively, she sprang closer to help her friend, but Isla moved between them.

An eternal second ticked by as Calle watched Lucy wrestle for her life. Cuün was powerful and unrelenting, burning his finger into Lucy's arm as she struggled in vain. Calle knew Lucy couldn't survive much longer, but she also knew Cuün would drag her death out as long as he could. A startling thought crossed her mind. If Cuün kills Lucy here, will she die physically too?

In desperation, Calle shrieked as she sidestepped Isla. "Take me! Leave her alone, you want me... Take me. I give you, my soul."

Everything was a blur up to that point, but when Calle made her plea, time came to a screeching standstill. Lucy was spent. She had no idea how to control her dream and Calle was at her wits end.

Cuün, sensing victory at last gloated out a reply. "You are already mine dreamer and your friend means nothing. You will watch me devour her soul bit by bit, then you are next." He flung a slight condescending nod to Isla and continued, "And her, she is weak. She cannot protect you; she doesn't even have wings."

Immensely satisfied with himself, he licked his lips, grabbed Lucy's left index finger, and started to pull it off.

In an instant, time jolted back into gear. Calle screamed, "No!" and rushed Cuün while Isla bristled blue lightning around her. Cuün could not contain his mirth and began to laugh hysterically, but no one noticed the dead guitar player hoisting a copper clad holy relic from his grave. Not a soul heard the ghost as he sailed with the pointed, wooden cross poised in his grasp across the graveyard behind the wicked devil. But everyone knew it when Rey plunged the crucifix to the hilt deep into demon's back.

Cuün roared in agony as he flung Lucy to the ground. His skin began to blister as the relic's power nobbled into his body like the venom of a black mamba. He flailed frantically to reach the impaled artifact, but his futile efforts only infuriated him past the edge of sanity. Calle immediately sprang to Lucy's side, engulfed her in a protective embrace, and teleported her to safety away from the crazed demon.

Reduced to his essence of pure evil, Cuün lashed out in fury to the nearest and most despised person within arm's reach. He clutched Rey by the chest and began to rend his essence to shreds. Calle and Lucy watched on in horror as Cuün crammed pieces of Rey's spirit into his maw and swallowed them whole. They did not know that a ghost could be unmade, but as Lucy met Rey's heart-rending grimace, she knew his fate was sealed. He was giving his afterlife to protect her.

He extended his remaining hand toward her in one final attempt to touch his beloved. As she stretched out her bloodied fingertips in response, his ring tumbled from his dissipating finger and rolled to her feet. She picked it up just in time to see the fading glimmer of Rey's soul settle on the astral wind like twinkling ions of Verga, evaporating midair before they can turn into a single raindrop.

Sensing Calle's emotional vulnerability and seeing Lucy's shuddered face, Cuün ambled unevenly toward them. Still agonizing with the cross stuck in his back, but reeling from the ecstasy of Rey's murder, he locked Calle in his hypnotic stare.

With his focus solely on his prey, the demon hardly noticed as the thinly braided, golden chain slid over his head. He almost didn't recognize the seriousness of it as he moved within a sniffle of Calle's face. But when Isla cinched it tightly around his throat, his putrid breath caught, and reality dawned on him like the second coming of Christ. Cuün, the Swindler of Souls, was captured.

Isla yanked him off his feet and dragged him toward the mausoleum. No matter how hard he resisted, how angry he became, or how much power he tried channel, he could not break free. Rey's sacrifice was not in vain. The dreamers looked on as Calle's guardian secured the howling demon to the defiled grave marker like a dog to a dog house.

Calle awoke with a start, her eyes wide and alert. Lucy was already awake and sitting staring out the window at the waxing moon listing in the clear night sky. With her hands wrapped tightly around her coffee cup and her knees pulled up to her chin, she looked like a lost child.

There wasn't any sense in trying to go back to sleep. The unbelievable events of their shared dream clung to them, much too raw and poignant to ignore. Instead, they sat in the dark reliving the episode.

It started with a whisper from Lucy about Rey. He had only lived in her dreams and she hadn't been sure he was even real, but now, she could hardly believe he was gone. It was all so new and fantastic, she didn't know what to think, but she swore she could feel his ring on her naked finger. Calle let Lucy vent. Heartbroken and shocked, she yammered on about the demon, Calle's guardian angel, and how she could hardly believe the astral world could be so real or so cruel.

When Calle confirmed everything about the dream from the hot air balloon to the golden chain, Lucy slowly began to comprehend the gift her friend possessed. Calle apologized about being ambushed and almost getting her killed, but Lucy knew it wasn't her fault.

In the way troubles and tribulations often do, the ill-fated dream brought them closer. Lucy had paid a high price, but now knew the extent of Calle's loyalty. They had shared something severe and uniquely their own. By surviving the nightmare, their spirits would always share a common thread. The truth was bittersweet and could never be undone.

Wide awake and antsy, there was no reason to hang around in Portales any longer. So, at 3:13 am, they loaded up into Calle's pickup and headed north. As the lights of town flickered in the rearview mirror, Lucy showed Calle the scar on her arm where Cuün had burned her and the black stains on her fingertips. Calle nodded in acknowledgment. Another a physical reminder of just how real dreams can be.

The sun peeked the amber rays of a new day over the tree line of the Sangre de Cristo mountains as the women motored quietly along wrapped up in their own thoughts. As they coasted to a stop at a traffic light in El Dorado, a homemade RV converted from an old school bus idled at the cross street. It labored into motion as the light changed and as it passed, hippie flowers and the words *El Rey Music* were crudely hand painted on its side.

Knowing exactly where Lucy's mind went, Calle side-eyed her companion. Lucy's stoic expression revealed nothing, but Calle knew her thoughts were reeling. She supposed they always would from that day forward, how could they not? As the bus disappeared down the road and the light changed again, she pondered Lucy's loss and the loss of her own husband. Love truly is an amazing and powerful thing, but does it always have to be accompanied by such extreme heartache?

# ☉ 18 ☾

The crisp, clean morning was in its infancy, but after Calle dropped Lucy off, all she wanted to do was go home and rest. It had been quite the adventure. When her mailbox came into view, she blew a sigh of relief. Soon she would be safe and cozy in her casita and she couldn't wait to put the world behind her for the next few days. But as she slowed to enter her driveway, her plans were jilted by the ruddy cargo van parked in her driveway.

Frustration compounded by exhaustion welled up inside her as she crammed her truck into park and got out to investigate. The van was parked close to her shed with its rear overhead sliding door hanging partially way open. Walking past, she glimpsed through the opening to see a horde of carpentry tools, saddles, and a riding lawn mower. When she rounded the front of the van, she spied Beely crouched on a saw horse near her trash trailer watching over the scene.

As she approached, her cat jumped down to do his death-defying figure eight routine between her ankles. It was as if he had been waiting for her and wasted no time welcoming her home. Purring loudly and bumping her shins vigorously with his head, she picked him up and cuddled him close to her face.

"Did you miss me kitty?" she whispered and kissed

him on the nose. As usual, he immediately wanted down, so, she complied. When his paws hit the dirt, he began to circle and pompously flick his tail. He was awfully proud of himself for some reason. "What's the matter Beeler, cat got your tongue?" she laughed at the worn-out joke.

At the sound of her voice came a stifled voice from her shed. "Hello? Is anybody there?"

Surprised, Calle went to the door of the shed. The lock and hasp lay broken on the ground nearby. Cautiously, Calle tried the door. It was bolted from the inside.

"Hello?" she ventured as she picked up the shovel leaning against the wall. "Who's in there?"

Amid a flurry of heated whispers, something clattered to the floor inside then a single voice responded. "Is it still out there?"

"What?"

"The cat, is it still out there?"

Calle looked at Beely, who was back on the saw horse like a king on his throne.

"Yes, he's right here."

"Then we're not coming out."

"Okay," Calle muttered then dialed 911. She considered quizzing them through the door, but the whole situation was too bizarre and she was too tired to fool with the likes of these guys. Hoping they would stay true to their word and remain in the shed; she hiked her butt up next to Beely on the saw horse to wait.

The calvary must have been in the area, because within a few minutes, a sheriff's SUV pulled in behind her truck. Before the deputy could get the men to exit the shed, another officer and a K-9 unit had arrived.

With her tonsils beginning to float, Calle made a bee line for the bathroom as the officers did their duty. She was back out in time to watch as three scruffy twenty-something men were handcuffed and loaded into the police units. With the men secured, the sheriff approached her.

"Looks like you caught the guys who've been terrorizing the neighborhood. Good job. What happened?" He slid a weathered notebook into his lapel pocket and removed his sunglasses.

She met the cedared hue of his eyes and replied, "Nothing really, I've been out of town. I just got home and they were locked in the shed. It was weird."

"Really? That is strange. They claim they were trapped in there by a large black cat. A mountain lion or panther. Can you believe that?"

"Well, my cat was watching the door, but as you can see, he's just a housecat." As if he knew they were talking about him, Belly strutted by like the national champion at the cat show. The officer eyed the sleek feline.

"He's a beautiful animal, are his eyes blue?"

"Yes, he's very unusual." She didn't elaborate.

"Maybe that's why they freaked out. I'm pretty sure they're high on something. Maybe those blue eyes flipped them out."

"That makes sense," she agreed. "Whatever the case, I'm glad they are off the street. Thank-you."

As a tow truck arrived, he asked her to move her pickup and if she was missing anything. When she confirmed none of the stuff in the back of the van was hers, he shut the sliding door and went to take some more pictures.

With his card in her hand, she stood and watched as they hitched up the van and drove off. With the last groan of the tow truck's engine echoing down the bosque, Calle glanced at Beely. He was magnificent with his sapphire eyes and camouflaged indigo sunburst marking on his chest, but could he have captured three grown men by himself? She was convinced the officer was right, the thieves must have been high.

Exhausted, she crunched her way back toward the front door of her casita. With her mind whirling everywhere but down, she never noticed her footprints as they etched themselves over the fresh prints of a very large feline predator.

The morning was already heating up, so, Calle flung her flannel shirt on the couch and kicked off her shoes. Barefoot and in a t-shirt, she padded into the kitchen for a fresh cup of coffee. As she waited for the Keurig machine to bubble out a mug of steamy goodness, she dialed up Lucy to fill her in on the unexpected welcome she had received.

"When it rains, it pours," came Lucy's level response. She was still numb, but getting used to the high drama that seemed to follow Calle everywhere she went.

Calle had to agree. Enough already, for goodness' sake.

After unpacking her overnight bag, she sliced an avocado for breakfast, grabbed her smoking tin, and headed into her warm, sun dappled backyard. Immersing herself in her favorite therapy, she closed her eyes and let the sounds and aromas of nature massage the fatigue from her body and spirit.

She easily slipped into a light trance. Sometimes

it came to her so comfortably she didn't even realize she was meditating. Drifting along just this side of slumber, her mind was able to sort the necessary from the trivial, defragmenting all the ill-fitting thoughts and feelings that accumulate over time. Its healing effect was similar to a spring clean or the relief that comes when you finally eight-six all the crap you've been hording, but haven't used in years. Like an internal reset button, it cleared her mind and left her rejuvenated.

After a much appreciated, lazy afternoon of yoga and reading, Calle spent the rest of her day in the kitchen. Not necessarily the finest chef in town, she did have a few recipes that she had mastered. As her last batch of banana nut muffins with cranberries went in the oven, her phone jingled to life.

"Hey Babe," Matthew bade over the tinkling of glassware in the background. He went on to tell her about his trip so far and how he missed her. For some reason, she felt detached. Though she had tons to share, she mainly just listened.

"I had a dream about you." His words snapping her to attention. "Well, actually, it was this guy telling me about you. Like he knew you better than I did. It was strange. He said you were a dream come true, but I already knew that."

"Hmm."

"Pretty weird, huh?" he laughed.

For the forty-eleventh time she wanted to tell him about the other side of her life, but again, she didn't. He was pragmatic and practical, close minded about anything that was not physically tangible. He regarded dreams as fantasy, something to laugh about, certainly not real in any sense.

As he talked, she remembered visiting one of his dreams. In it, he had said he loved her, but after he awoke, all he remembered was the ring on her thumb, nothing about what he had said. So, she let it go. She wondered if she should visit him again and reveal her ability, maybe force him to take her seriously, but that didn't feel right. Love should come naturally; it shouldn't have to be coerced.

She was convinced, 'the man in his dream' was Ethan and if Ethan couldn't persuade him to take the astral world seriously, what chance did she have in doing so?

With each passing word, she felt further and further away. Matthew was a good man and meant well. She was sure he loved her in his own way, but there was more to her than he could ever comprehend. She wanted desperately to tell him about Spencer and her visit to Portales, but the gap between them had grown into a canyon.

Growing up ridiculed because of her déjà vu and lucid dreams had made her wary of others' opinions and she didn't want to risk it with him. The fear of conflict over her double life made her so distraught, she didn't even tell him about the thieves that were caught in her shed that very morning. The ding of the kitchen timer gave her the excuse she needed to exit the conversation. She rang-off feeling dishonest and disillusioned, wondering how she had let it get this far.

Starting a new book is an act of anticipation. Even if the book isn't brand new, cracking open the cover is like finding a buried locket in the forest and opening it for the first time. There is no telling what secrets could be hidden within. But the contents of a book, unlike lost jewelry, reveals itself slowly, page by page, until you are in so deep that only the author can save you.

Calle knew the power of books. She had loved reading since before she could decipher letters. She was a willing pushover for any writer who had moved her before and the unread story by her latest favorite author in her hands beckoned like manna from heaven.

Slowly and deliberately, she followed the tale, taking extra time to immerse herself in the details. With a book so promising, she was tempted to plow through it and devour it like a ravenous vulture, but experience had taught her to chew her stories thoroughly and savor each bite. So, she limited her reading to only two chapters, tops, though sometimes in the heat of the moment she might splurge to three or four.

She reluctantly laid the book on her dresser and clicked off the light. Lying in the darkness, she contemplated the quirky heroine. The woman was different, unusual in her world, and her uncommon circumstances thrust her into genuine human conflict, one of virtue and survival. A strong feminine character with which any woman could identify, but it was the different and unusual part that resonated deeply with Calle. To tell the truth, there were many times she felt like fiction herself. With an assuasive sense of belonging, Calle slipped off into slumber.

Like a gymnast finally getting into shape, Calle went lucid and out of body without any problem. Even finding Ethan was as simple as knocking on a door. The gleam in his green eyes melted her heart and the distance they had endured only made their reunion all that much sweeter.

"What's up?" she feigned nonchalance with a smirk.

They both knew it was loaded question. But her cute remark cracked the ice between them in a single blow. He was overjoyed to be close to her again and she wasn't nearly as angry as she imagined. He couldn't contain his mirth and drew her into a sweltering kiss. She readily returned his passion until they both fell laughing on the grass.

Lovers whose love is true, never pass up a moment to satisfy one another and when they have been separated by misunderstanding, they eagerly submit to their desire. Sex is a mental connection that coalesces into carnal pleasure, but it doesn't necessarily have to be physical. In fact, spiritual intercourse is not only climatic, it is enduring. A relation on this level is mutual in every sense of the word. In respect, in adoration, in yearning, in fulfillment, and as Ethan's essence entered her, Calle released a frenzied orgasm, teasing him deeper and deeper into wave after wave of tsunamic bliss.

Astral travelers don't get physically tired, but after a while, they can be satiated. As close as two spirits can become, they are still separate entities. Granted, they are irreversibly connected, but independent nonetheless. It is that difference, that distinct separation, that draws them back together time again and time again.

Calle brushed a strand of hair from her eyes as Ethan took her hand is his.

"Come, walk with me, Sweet Leaf," he beckoned.

Hand in hand, they began to walk and talk in a secluded mountain glen along a bubbling creek somewhere in the wilds of Europe. It was one of Ethan's favorite getaways and as Calle took in the magnificent scenery, she began to ask the questions she had been brooding over for the last few days.

"So, why were you restricting my trekking?"

He pulled her close and their shoulders bumped. "It was only temporary. I was trying to protect you from the demon, but you were too clever for me."

Calle smiled inwardly knowing she had outwitted her teacher. Reading her body language, he returned a smile of his own.

"You and your friend were in grave danger," he continued, his continence turning somber.

"I know, but it all worked out, right?"

"Yes, it did, but at what cost?"

Calle shivered as she remembered the last look on Rey's face just before he was unmade.

Ethan continued, "It would have been very different if your angel had not intervened, she saved your souls."

"But why was Cuün chasing me anyway? What did I ever do to him?"

"Not him, but the witch that summoned him."

Calle's thoughts went straight to the dead rats and the curse she was under. "The hex is a demon summoned to kill me?"

"Yes, the witch sold her soul for his assistance. Cuün will pursue you until the curse is fulfilled, so you are still a marked woman. Thankfully, he is captured and under constant surveillance, but don't ever forget about him."

"Oh marvelous, so I have to watch over my shoulder forever until the curse is lifted? How does that work? I mean, what can I do?"

"The curse will only end when Cuün is satisfied. Since the witch sold her soul for you, he will pursue you until he catches you or the witch dies. Whichever comes first, either way, he gets a soul."

"Isn't that just peachy."

"Buck up, Sweet Leaf, he is imprisoned and probably will be for a long time."

Calle tilted a glance his way, "That's not very comforting."

Ethan laughed, "But it's the truth."

"Mmm hmm," Calle sighed and fell into inner contemplation. They paused for a moment as a grand expanse of smoky orange flowers with hundreds of tiny yellow butterflies laboring over them came into view. Calle released Ethan's hand and stretched her arms over her head then resumed walking beside him. She changed the topic.

"So, I hear you've visited my boyfriend's dream," she stated as if it was the sort of thing that lovers talk about all the time.

"Matthew? Yeah, I tried to help him understand this side of reality," he answered, no hint of jealousy in his voice.

Calle stopped walking again and turned to face Ethan. "Why?"

He met the seriousness in her gaze. "I thought I could help you, but I was wrong. He was unconvinced."

"Thanks, but why?"

"Why what?"

"Why would you try to help a rival?"

"I don't see it that way. I don't own you; I trust your judgement. I want you to be happy."

That was a sentiment Calle couldn't quite fathom.

Ethan was like no other human being she had ever met. He was always surprising her, maybe that was why she loved him so much.

"Okay," she moved on.

Midstride, she twiddled her fingers behind her back and took a moment to organize her thoughts.

"If a person dies in their dreams, do they die physically too?" she asked.

Never missing a beat, her mentor replied, "Yes, they do, but lucid dreamers are not easy to catch and weak-minded dreamers are of no interest to dream trekkers, usually."

Her mind conjured up a vision of Ab Pistola and Lily Lassiter.

"Hmm." Having fun running the quiz show, she fired another question. "What were you reading to me when you had me trapped on the monolith?"

He chuckled at her description of his effort to protect her. "Trapped? You? I don't think anyone could trap you for very long. Besides, I like you just as you are. Free willed and free minded." They started to amble along again in silence. He was formulating more to his response and she didn't press him.

Finally, he said, "They were subliminal lessons. Things I've learned that maybe you can use when I'm not around." She studied his handsome profile a second, then began to speak.

"When you're not around? Are you going somewhere? When are you not going to be around?" She slowed her steps. Reasonable questions she knew she had a right to know, but she also knew he wasn't always the easiest person to locate.

"Like in the cemetery. Not that I'm a match for an

angry demon, but times like those," he deflected, but she was already one step ahead of him.

"Are you still sick?"

He shook his head no, but said, "Yes, but don't worry about it. I'm okay, everyone gets sick. It's no big deal."

She played her only ace. "When can I meet you face to face?"

He started to say, 'Here I am,' but she interrupted. "I mean when we're awake, on the physical plane, face to face."

She had him cornered.

He hadn't wanted it to come to this so soon, but he couldn't deny the woman he loved. "Soon, Sweet Leaf. I'll contact you when the time is right. I promise."

She could feel the dream trek losing its intensity, the periphery began to blur. They had been together for longer than usual, so she couldn't tell if he was ending the dream or if it had just run its natural course. Either way, she settled back into her body elated to have had him with her for so long, but sad it was over. And his parting tone left her suspicious and confused.

Why does love never seem to go as planned? As she crawled out of bed, she remembered something she had once read. It went something like this: Best laid plans never survive contact with the enemy. She could never consider Ethan an enemy, but the analogy of plans gone awry described her love life exactly.

# ☉ 19 ☾

Sometimes the best company you can keep is yourself. Life has a way of dragging you into everybody's business like it's your responsibility to solve every little problem that comes up. Most certainly, it is important to help others, especially those who can't fend for themselves or a friend in need, but if you don't take care of yourself, you are useless to others and risk becoming an emotional wreck.

That's where Calle had worked herself, painted into a corner of her own making. So, she used her remaining time off work to regroup. She pictured herself walled away from the world in her casita like a minor prophet whose only contact with the general population was through her blue-eyed cat and the green-eyed blue jay that came daily to beg for peanuts.

No thieves, demons, lovers, or people in comas allowed. That is not to say that those people were not alive and well in her mind, they were, but by detaching herself from their immediate company, she was able to gain a better perspective. One she desperately deserved and one she cherished like a pearl diver coming up for air. Her personal hiatus ran its course and after a couple days, came to a satisfying end when her phone jingled to life that particular morning. It was time to jump back in the ocean, a magnificent treasure was waiting to be discovered.

"I'm near Camel Tracks, I'll be there in a few." Samantha's voice issuing notice as she motored past the time worn entrance to the Caja Del Rio.

Minutes later, she was sitting on Calle's back porch sipping iced tea and chatting excitedly. She then produced from her pocket a small leather pouch filled with mysterious items and cinched tightly with a hemp cord. As she presented the talisman, she grasped her hands around Calle's. With the pouch in the center of their grasp, she uttered an incantation under her breath. As she released her grip she added, "It's got some valuable things in there, but don't open it. Keep it with you and I promise it will help."

With the main purpose of the visit fulfilled, Samantha relaxed a little and they continued their conversation. Calle explained the incident in Lucy's dream and the fact she knew the demon had been summoned by a witch. Samantha was one of only a few people who would take Calle's revelation seriously. In fact, she suspected the witch in question, was an old friend turned foe, Clarita Salazar. After Calle described her encounter with Jamaica and the purple haired crone in the Pérez cemetery, Samantha was certain of the witch's identity.

"Why me?" Calle questioned.

"Remember, when Elise died in your arms a few months ago?" Samantha reminded.

How could she possibly forget? Elise tried to kill her, but died in the attempt. It was a hairy episode Calle would always remember.

"Clarita is Elise's aunt. She's out for revenge."

"I didn't kill her niece."

"I know, but Clarita doesn't care about that. She is spiteful and blames you for her death. Remember I warned you she was clannish and couldn't be trusted?"

Calle did remember the warning, but at the time, couldn't conceive of anyone being so vindictive.

"So, she's out to kill me?" Calle shook her head in disbelief. "Is she powerful enough to summon a demon?"

"It appears so," Samantha stated with obvious concern. "But you said the demon has been captured?"

"Yes, chained to the mausoleum."

"Well, keep the medicine bag with you anyway. There's no telling what that woman will try."

As Samantha departed and Calle readied herself for work. *Out of the frying pan and into the fire.*


Verna Lloyd had it bad for the handsome Michael Pérez and she shamelessly greeted him as he walked under the pavilion with Ezra. She met his gaze with a flirty, "How about a drink?" and Ezra ambled along beside wondering if he was invisible. The trio settled into a shady spot for a break and Calle disappeared into the kitchen to check on something in the oven.

The Sister Cities' grand finale week was underway at the Pérez mansion. It would be a couple evenings of dining and presentations by the guests, then the all-day event on Friday, an elegant gala with the artwork of a renown Asian artist on display as the centerpiece. The artist, who would also be in attendance, would be available for autographs and insights about her work. It was all very sensational and the old hacienda was abuzz with anticipation.

"I don't know why the old man was always so uptight, his job is easy," Michael bragged to Verna as Calle and Jill lugged buckets of ice to the salad bar. "Ezra and I haven't even broken a sweat all week. If Otis doesn't come back, I won't miss him," he continued.

Jill hung her head and disappeared behind the fountain.

Calle set her bucket down and approached the table. Ezra winked to Verna, then chirped, "It's a whole lot more fun than waiting tables."

Verna shot him an angry glare and he returned a mischievous grin just as Calle was about to end their break and send Michael packing. But before she could assert her authority, Jill came screaming from behind the fountain waving her arms frantically with a lone honeybee in hot pursuit.

With her prayer cap askew and her long blonde hair flying like she was on the back of a speeding Harley Davidson, she zigged and zagged around the dining area dodging the angry bee as if her life depended on it. For such a tiny insect, he was quite tenacious. Her exasperated antics spurred laughter from her coworkers, but it was Michael who valiantly sprang to her rescue.

With a wide smile on his face, he jumped up and pulled Jill into a protective hug and with a swat of his cap, knocked the bee to the ground. Before he could squash the assailant into the grass, the bee bumbled a hasty retreat. With a terrified Jill in his arms, Michael beamed like a hero while Verna simmered a nasty scowl.

As the scene settled and as Calle righted a fallen chair, she commanded, "Alright, alright, that's enough. Show's over, let's get back to work." Turning to Jill, she asked, "Are you alright?"

The girl, distraught and embarrassed, peeled herself from Michael and under Calle's embrace, they exited the dining area. In the quiet of the women's restroom, Lisa Jill confessed, "I'm allergic to bee stings."

Calle reassured her that everything was alright and they returned to the pavilion. *The apple sure didn't fall too far from the tree.*

When they arrived, Calle sent Jill to work in the kitchen and went to deal with an unexpected problem.

Gloria and her oversized boyfriend were lounging just inside the shade at the far end of the dining area. She was ordering drinks and expecting service as if she were in a restaurant. Didn't she realize this was a catered event and not open to the public? Calle didn't need this kind of nonsense, but she joined Verna as she was delivering cocktails to the mansion's demanding matriarch.

With as much tact as she could muster, she approached the woman.

"Good afternoon. I'm sorry, but we're not ready to serve guests yet, perhaps you could go to the restaurant for lunch," she gestured toward the main building.

Her suggestion was met with self-righteous entitlement and condescension.

"Listen here missy, let's get one thing straight, I own this place and you will do whatever I want you to. Get it?"

Verna took a step back as Calle squared herself to face the geriatric tyrant.

"That may be true, but we don't work for you. We have an event to prepare for, so if you please, go somewhere else to eat your lunch."

Gloria fumed. Unaccustomed to backtalk, she spat, "I've already called my daughter and when she gets here, you will be gone!"

Fen pushed his chair back, began to stand, and for a second, Calle thought he might attack her, but before the situation could escalate any farther, a shout from Teresa broke through the tension.

"Mother!"

Fen, now on his feet, leered at Calle, but as Teresa got closer, he turned and went to fetch their golf cart.

"Mother what are you doing?" Teresa implored like she was chastising a toddler.

Calle stepped back as Gloria threw a raging fit. She exchanged a sympathetic glance with Teresa as the frazzled woman dealt with her unstable mother.

Calle touched Verna on the elbow gesturing for a hasty retreat. Calle had to redirect her crew back to work as Teresa and Fen assisted Gloria into the cart. Before Fen joined his girlfriend in the vehicle, Teresa whispered something in his ear. Then as they tore away, Teresa turned back to the stunned catering crew and with an apologetic look on her face, approached Calle.

Never having had children, Calle really didn't know what it felt like to have to deal with a meltdown like that in public, but it didn't take an expert to recognize the humiliation on Teresa's face. Not surprisingly, Teresa motioned for Calle to join her in a walk so they could talk in private. As they strolled under the willows, Calle listened to Teresa vent.

"That woman is going to be the death of me," she began. "I'm so sorry."

"Don't worry, it happens," Calle said, but thought, *that woman should be sedated and incarcerated in a long-*

*term care facility.*

"But there's a bigger problem," Teresa's words jarring Calle back to attention.

"Bigger problem?"

"Yeah, we lost our headliner for the weekend. The truck with all the artwork got into an accident, I guess some of it was damaged. They won't be able to do the event. We're officially screwed," Teresa lamented shaking her head.

"What are you going to do?"

"I guess hire a band or something, but on such short notice, I don't know," Teresa said dejectedly. "Probably get sued," she finished.

"Hmm, not good."

The two strolled along in silence a few more steps, then Calle's voice pierced the air.

"Maybe, I can help."

Teresa looked at her like she had antlers sticking out of her head.

"Oh, yeah?"

Calle had to smile at the look she received. "I know this local artist. Pretty famous actually, Samantha Cloaker. Have you heard of her?"

Teresa cocked her head in disbelief.

"You've got to be kidding, you know the Samantha Cloaker?"

Calle didn't know there was a 'the' Samantha Cloaker, but she replied, "Yes, she was at my house this morning."

A feeling of pride and importance swept her continence as she suggested Samantha as a solution for Teresa's predicament. She absentmindedly touched the medicine bag hanging around her neck beneath her blouse and continued.

"I'll call her right now."

Samantha answered concerned about Clarita, but Calle covertly assured her things were alright on that front, then described the situation at Pérez mansion. Relieved about Calle's safety, Samantha was also agreeable about the showing. Calle handed her phone to Teresa and after a short conversation about agents and the scope of the event, the women had reached a tentative agreement.

Beaming like she had just been plucked from a pit of quicksand, Teresa thanked Calle profusely. And as Calle returned to her crew and Teresa departed, both women were pleased as punch and their minds spun with new ideas and plans for the grand finale.

The rest of the evening went smoothly and after everyone had left, Calle thought about the day as she closed up shop for the night. The guests were satisfied and the wait staff had earned generous tips, so, despite Gloria's asinine behavior, Jill's bee incident, and the diverted disaster of the headliner canceling, Calle was happy with the way it concluded. She went to the break room to turn out the lights and as she entered, her feeling of accomplishment was squashed by the heartbreak that was littered before her.

On the table, next to a toppled Dixie cup and soaked in spilled soda pop, lay the rigor mortised body of El Gordo. She was shocked, then saddened by the death of the creature she had come to love, but then a sense of menace crept into her thinking. Lifting the cup to her nose, she suspected it was tainted with something toxic. Her mind ran riot over her suspicion. She was sure the cute little mascot had been poisoned, but not intentionally, it was meant for someone else. A scribbled 'LJ' in black Sharpie on the red plastic cup fueled her misgiving and told her all she needed to know.

# ☽ 20 ☾

She couldn't stand the sight of the bloated little chipmunk any longer. Her first inclination was to bury him, but she knew hungry animals often dug up buried pets and ate them. She didn't want to accidentally poison another wild animal so, she wrapped his sticky body in parchment paper and put him in a cardboard box, then took him to the dumpster. It was a sad ending to such a beautiful creature that had brought so much joy to so many.

As she cleaned and sanitized the breakroom, her mind spun circles around the incident. Her thoughts raced backward through the events of the afternoon and evening. Any number of people had access to the breakroom and with the crew so busy with the clientele, no one would have noticed any activity back there. The poisoning would have had to have happened later in the day, closer to closing, but still that left a number of suspects. Verna's angry face kept popping up. It was hard to imagine, but could Verna have been so jealous that she would've resorted to something so sinister?

After only two rings, Detective Ramirez answered. Calle honestly thought she would have to leave a message or talk to a screener, but he had given her his personal cell number. She described what had happened in the breakroom and that Lisa Jill claimed to be Otis' long-lost daughter, but Shawn dismissed the incident as coincidental. No one was hurt and there was no proof of poison. The police would not investigate the death of a rogue chipmunk, no matter how cute. Furthermore, there was no proof that Lisa Jill was actually related to Otis.

After talking with him, she felt foolish and began to doubt what she had seen. Maybe paranoia was getting the better of her. Then Lucy's joke about romancing the lead detective replayed in her mind. Was Shawn only pretending to find interest in this case or was he just trying to get a date? Calle was starting to think Lucy might be right.

As she saw it, his flirty overtures were in sharp contrast to the seriousness of the evidence. He asked her to report suspicious incidents and she did, but he downplayed all she reported. She didn't like being patronized. Feeling played, she lost all faith in the police and decided she couldn't count on Detective Ramirez.

Regardless of what the police thought, she was sure El Gordo was poisoned. She might be a little paranoid, but she was going to keep a close watch on Jill anyway. It was better to err on the side of caution.

It was getting late, she was tired, and she should've gone straight home, but instead her truck angled into a well-lit parking space on the lower level at St. Vincent's Hospital. She was just locking her vehicle, surveying the parking lot up the slope looking for the easiest way to the upper-level entrance, when a familiar silhouette graced the doorway. Illuminated clearly by the bright portico and entrance lights, out strode Teresa Pérez.

Calle paused to watch unnoticed as the graceful woman approached her SUV. Teresa was alone, walking with her head down, lost in introspection. Oblivious to her surroundings, and caught up in her own thoughts, she hopped in her vehicle and motored away.

Inside and up on the third floor, Calle met a nurse leaving Otis' room.

"How is he?"

"He's doing well now, but please don't touch the equipment. Someone accidently unplugged his monitor," the nurse informed.

"Uh oh."

"Uh oh is right. Just be careful."

"No problem," Calle assured as she entered the room.

From the doorway, she surveyed the scene. Otis' swelling had eased and he looked closer to alive than last time she had seen him. Closing the door, she could see that he was attached to the monitors and IV's and everything seemed to be working properly. He was better, but he was still unconscious and remained in serious condition.

The room was stark and dim. The only bright spot was the beautiful bouquet of roses Teresa had left. Otis must not have many friends, Calle thought. The somber mood of the room washed over her as she sat in the chair by the window. Sitting quietly, she wondered what someone said to unconscious loved ones. Did visitors simply sit and hold their hands, maybe utter a prayer or two? And what about acquaintances like herself, what were they supposed to do?

Suddenly, she realized she didn't really know why she was there. What she hoped to accomplish, she didn't have a clue. But some internal compass had drawn her there and despite her second thoughts, she remained in the austere silence of the hospital room with a comatose man she barely knew.

Her visit may not have been all that beneficial for Otis, but it was proving to be a comfort to her. She felt detached, hidden from her life for at least a few minutes. It was similar to how she felt when she visited cemeteries by herself. There was something that attracted her to places like these. She relaxed and lingered, gazing at the night sky through the window as her thoughts began to unwind.

It is funny how one can be daydreaming and then dreaming without ever realizing they have fallen asleep. Even for Calle, the transition often happened smoothly without notice, but once in the dream, there was no doubt for her where she was.

Death is often referred to as 'The Big Sleep', but Calle knew it was something else entirely. A coma, however, was indeed a big sleep and every sleeping person dreams. Do big sleeps facilitate big dreams? She wasn't sure, but the dream Otis was enjoying seemed common enough to Calle, but was probably pretty big to him.

She strolled into his dream as if she'd bought a ticket. She sidled up behind the younger version of the man, full head of sandy blonde hair and all, then stood next to him as he watched a striking young woman slicing a watermelon. Calle watched as the woman, really more of a girl, turned to share a slice with Otis. Her lithe movement was surprisingly familiar and when she shared a smile with Otis, Calle's breath caught. Otis was dreaming of Lisa Jill.

Shocked, Calle instinctively put her hand on Otis' arm. Her touch tore Otis' adoring gaze from the young woman, inadvertently interrupting the flow of his dream. His expression screamed, 'What?', but he only stared at her.

Now on the spot, Calle said the only thing that came to mind. "Do you know her?"

She was struck at how handsome he was, but didn't get distracted by her comparison to the man she knew and the man talking to her now.

"Of course," he said as if she were daft.

Confused, Calle plodded along. "How can you know her?" she asked, wondering if somehow in the spirit world, parents knew their children before they were born.

"I've known her my whole life," he added to her confusion.

"What? How can you know Lisa Jill?"

"I don't," he responded like she was joking. "But that's my Jessica," he pointed with his chin. "Not Lisa Jill."

"Jessica?"

"My true love. She's waiting for me," he said. "And it won't be long now. I can feel her getting closer."

Calle didn't know what to say, but this Jessica had to be Lisa Jill's identical twin. Jessica's image dissolved as Calle tried a new tactic.

"You know this is a dream and you're in a coma, right," she ventured cautiously. She had never told anyone they were dreaming before, let alone that they were in a coma. She didn't know how they would react.

"I know, someone with painted fingernails pulled a sack of bees over my head," he said as if it was common knowledge. "I couldn't get to my pen in time. I'm dying," he said as he faced her squarely, a look of contentment in his eyes.

Then she realized, he was aware of his situation. He

knew he was in a coma.

"But this is just a dream, you're still alive."

"So what? It's real to me," he stated matter-of-factly. "And I don't want to go back. Jessica is alive in my dreams. I don't want to live without her anymore." His sincere statement struck a chord. True love was enduring, it was larger than life.

For a second, Calle felt guilty for saving his life, he would have preferred to have died, but she was sure she had done the right thing.

Then like a revelation, the bigger picture came into focus.

"You have a daughter," she blurted out trying to rekindle his zest for life. When excited, subtly was not her strong suit. "She has come to meet you."

By the look on his face, her shot in the dark must have struck a chord.

"A daughter?"

"Yes, she looks just like Jessica," Calle said as something bumped into her foot.

"Sorry Miss." Calle heard a woman's voice. *Oh crap!* Consciousness was tugging on her spirit. She was waking up.

"Lisa Jill is your daughter!" she shouted in desperation as his face began to dematerialize.

Finally grasping the truth in her words and sensing the end of their connection, Otis stretched out his hand as she faded and frantically screamed, "There's a box under my bed, give it to her!"

His message trailed off into the ether like a contrail vaporizing into the stratosphere. And as the last semblance of her visit dissipated, she exited his comatose dream.

When her eyes opened, Calle was sprawled in the chair with her head leaning against the window. The nurse standing next to her with one hand on a vitals trolley and the other holding a blood pressure cuff smiled and began to speak.

"Sorry, I didn't mean to wake you. I am here to check on Mr. Delve."

"No problem," Calle said as she rubbed the blur of sleep from her eyes. She sat up, gathered her purse and her wits, then continued, "I was just leaving."

# ☽ 21 ☾

Her secret revelation weighed heavily on her mind all morning and she was glad the breakfast rush had come and gone. Lucy and Fiona had agreed to help with the upcoming weekend finale and had just arrived. After a few minutes of orientation, Calle left them with Verna and Ezra for their final training. Phillip wasn't there yet, but he would soon join her ragtag entourage of waitrons, but it was Lisa Jill Calle she called over in private.

"I need you to help me," she said trying to tame her enthusiasm.

"Sure thing," Jill replied as they hopped on the ATV and rolled up the hill towards Otis' tree house.

Sensing something askew, Jill asked, "What's up?" She twirled a prayer cap string around her index finger, eyeing Calle with suspicion.

"I want to show you something."

"I'm not in trouble, am I?" Jill's misgiving solidified; she knew something was going on.

"No, no, just wait. You'll see," Calle assured with smile and a pat on the girl's knee.

As they idled to a stop just below the wrap around porch of the tree house, Jill placed a hand on the ATV's windshield spar and leaned out of the cockpit to get a better view.

"What's this?"

"This is your father's house. Come on up," Calle said as she eagerly took to the stairs.

Lisa Jill followed, but at slower pace, taking in all the oddity and beauty of the structure. She stopped at the top of the steps and spun a full circle to survey the scene.

"This is incredible," she marveled. "It's like a fantasy come to life."

"Pretty cool, huh?" Calle said as she watched the young woman. She was amazed by the awe and admiration on Jill's face. It was heartwarming to see someone so willing to celebrate the simple joys in life.

"Over here," she said as she stepped to a nearby wicker chair, inviting Jill to join her with a gesture to the empty seat beside a matching coffee table.

As Lisa Jill sat down, she spied a scuffed, simple pine jewelry box on the table, then lifted her eyes to meet Calle's.

Calle didn't know where to start, so she jumped right in.

"I found something of your dad's that you should see," she said, purposely leaving out the details about how she knew where to find it. Hopefully, that wouldn't come up.

She reached for the box, then handed it to Lisa Jill.

"This is your father's. I think he would want you to have it."

Lisa Jill held the box reverently in her hands like it was the Ark of the Covenant, afraid to draw it any closer and uneasy about its contents. She looked from the box to Calle then back.

"Open it," Calle nodded encouragement. "It's

important."

Lisa Jill set the aged chest on her lap and creaked open the lid. The box was filled with personal treasure, a motherlode of yellowed envelopes and photographs. As Jill thumbed through the contents, a silence so sacred fell over the porch that even the forest stopped to listen. Tears filled the orphaned woman's eyes as realization swept through her spirit.

"These are post marked Pennsylvania... From where I grew up," Jill said. "And this woman looks just like me," she continued as she held out a polaroid for Calle to see. "Here's one of her with a man. They look so happy."

"That man is Otis. I think that's your mother with him," Calle spoke what Jill was thinking.

Indigo irises implored chestnut rimmed pupils.

"Her name is Jessica and the letters are love letters to your father. I think your mother's name is Jessica."

Emotion overwhelmed the pair and Calle pulled Lisa Jill in close for a hug. As they broke the embrace, Calle continued speaking.

"Now that we know her name, maybe we can find her."

The statement opened the flood gates of supposition and speculation. They sat there chattering for a good hour hashing out what-ifs and maybe-so's until they couldn't come up with any more ideas. And as the novelty began to settle in as reality, Lisa Jill asked the question Calle was hoping to avoid.

"I can't thank you enough for what you've given me, but how did you come by the box?"

Sometimes fate offers a person the slimmest glimmer of opportunity and Calle seized hers as it buzzed by in the form of a lazy honeybee.

"Is that a bee?" Calle exclaimed in over-exaggeration.

"What? Where? Oh my..." Jill sputtered as she hastily piled the box's contents back inside and joined Calle for a swift exit from her father's porch.

There are places in the world that attract and hold the human spirit to tickle it with the exquisite seasoning of dimensions just outside the limit of full perception. Like the aroma of a delicious barbecue wafting through the countryside, they tease every nostril within their magical olfactory range. They color the physical world with vivid hues we cannot directly see and the lingering flavor is so poignant, it is unmistakable on our palette of every day experience.

Santa Fe, New Mexico is such a place. There's something about the town in the fact that everything that is real seems like it's not so much and things that aren't, seem all the more. It is a place where imagination and reality share the same space at the same time.

Some refer to the old city as, 'Fanta Se, forty square miles surrounded by reality'. While the reference is meant as a joke, it is more frequently nearer to the truth than one might initially anticipate. An ever-evolving collage of the fantastic and the mundane, the city of Holy Faith has deep spiritual roots. It is often tantalizing and sometimes comes in a bit blurry, but it is never hum-drum.

So, later that evening when a tall tree snag decorated with Mr. Potato Head facial features called out, "Hey, where are you going?", it was easy to believe it was a real, live Tree Ent acting as a sentinel. Similarly, it wasn't that much of a stretch to trust that when a born-again Wiccan beckoned you into her home with ringed fingers and a gleam in her eye, that you were entering into a witch's lair. And when that same witch boasted of a magical book maven that had the uncanny ability of matching the perfect book to any reader, it wasn't only plausible, it was taken as absolute fact.

"In Bernalillo, on the main drag, near I-25," Samantha said. "*Under Charlie's Covers* is the name of the bookstore. It's quite popular, but the it's the maven's skill that makes the difference." Waving an ancient, title-less, black, leather-bound volume in her hand, Samantha expounded, "She's able to find books for me when no one else can. Nothing verboten, I suppose, but I don't ask nor do I care." Calle raised an eyebrow and exchanged a dubious glance with Lucy.

"Yeah, we stopped in there on our way up from Tech," Fiona chimed in. "I found a great book about a mathematician who travels in time. Samantha got it for me and she gave me this too..." She added as she fished a silver figurine attached to a thin necklace from under her t-shirt collar. "For my birthday," she finished proudly, hanging it over her thumb and under her chin for all to see.

Lucy and Calle crowded in closer to get a better view.

"His name is Festus," Fiona crowed.

The small figurine was a finely cast silver dragon with scales, talons, and detailed bat-like wings. In fact, it was so realistic, Calle thought she could see his eyes follow her as she moved.

"He's cute," Lucy complemented as she fingered the

ornament. "It feels warm."

"Probably because he's been under my shirt all afternoon," Fiona said as she pulled away and quickly slipped the dragon back out of sight.

"Hey, you guys, grab a drink and let's go to the studio. I want to show you something," Samantha interrupted. "We can sing 'Happy Birthday' back there."

Since Samantha was throwing the party and was a world class painter that shared her extensive studio with other accomplished artists, the women eagerly complied. There was no telling what amazing artwork she had cooking up out in her studio. Samantha's dogs, a huge black Lab named Orlie and a feisty Maltese mix named Wilber, happily joined in the jaunt up the hill behind the house.

With Samantha in the lead, the intrepid clutch of curious women entered the large warehouse. Inside were several artsy stations divided by moveable plywood partitions, each containing various masterpieces in progress. It was like stepping into the southwestern branch of the Smithsonian, if there ever was such a thing.

In one cubicle, Native American pots, some finished, some unfired, were stacked around a kiln and a dusty pottery wheel. Adjacent to that cubby sat a half-finished clay sculpture of a covey of quail that filled a kitchen sized table. Next in line came a space dominated by a loom laced with what was in the process of becoming a beautiful orange, black, and ivory wool rug. Not every area contained artwork however, some looked to be storage places for tools like welders, shop vacuums, and air compressors while others held piles of art supplies and bottled water.

As the women walked and gawked along, a shuffling noise came from within the labyrinth of creativity. Samantha stopped and turned to her friends.

"That's Facundo, I need to talk to him for a minute," she smiled. "What I wanted to show you girls is around that partition." She pointed a bejeweled finger to an opening beside an exterior overhead door. "Go check it out, I'll be there in a minute." Then she disappeared through a tight crevice between a huge roll of canvas and cluster of slender latillas tall enough to build a teepee.

The space opened up along the expanse of the rear of the building. They could see the door to Samantha's private painting refuge past a maze of great, bulky items hidden beneath tarps and arranged haphazardly across the concrete floor. The scene was reminiscent of the abandoned rooms in an old haunted mansion where the furniture was covered in sheets, but the ghosts were replaced by a pair of happy duty dogs.

"I guess this is it," Lucy said as she fingered the tarp covering the nearest and biggest item. Then trying to match the flair of Houdini, she grabbed the cloth with both hands and pulled, but the tarp was bigger than she had expected and the grand unveiling came up short. So, Fiona hustled to assist in the disrobing of what was revealed to be a gigantic bronze sculpture.

"Oh my god," Calle gasped in awe.

"Holy Mother of John," Lucy added.

Fiona just stood stunned, holding the corner of the tarp and stared.

"That..." she ventured a wide-eyed stutter, "is the biggest penis I've ever seen!"

Before them, in finely detailed glory, sat the bronzed

ass end of a stallion. His tail flared majestically along his right hip and his flanks rippled with exertion. The musculature and physiology of the animal was incredible and anatomically precise. Its proportions were perfect and the veins looked real enough to pump blood, but it was the unbelievably accurate depiction of his testicles and phallus that grabbed the women's attention. Like the rest of the sculpture, it was astonishing and it was huge.

The initial collective reaction was as priceless as the piece of art they stood admiring, but it only lasted a second before laughter erupted and the jokes flew. As they circled the sculpture, actually only a section of a much larger piece, their light-hearted sense of perversion turned to genuine art appreciation.

"It is amazing how detailed something so enormous can be," Calle marveled.

"Said the quivering, curious virgin," Lucy quipped, not quite over the humor yet.

"Shut up, you," Calle laughed.

"I know, then think of how detailed Festus is... And he's tiny," Fiona added ignoring Lucy's joke.

"I guess all these pieces get welded together to make a gigantic statue," Lucy observed in a more serious tone, as she stood with another tarp in hand next to a bronze boot big enough to stand up in. "What's under that one?" She pointed to a covered piece near Fiona.

Fiona pulled the tarp off to reveal a conquistador's helmeted head. It was cast in as perfect detail as all the other pieces.

"Astonishing."

"It certainly is, isn't it?" Samantha confirmed over the clicking of her heels as she joined the party from

JACOB JANEY

the opposite end of the storage area. "It's going to be a conquistador on a mighty rearing stallion. It's destined to an airport somewhere south; I can't remember where exactly, but it was cast at Shidoni."

"I've been there," Fiona said. "It's totally cool. They let you watch as they pour at the foundry. It's in Tesuque, right?"

"Yes, just up the road, next to the glass blower. You can watch them work too. Then you can walk through acres of sculpture in the outdoor gallery or sit by the river and have lunch. It's a great place," Lucy added like she had been there many times, which she had.

"Okay, I thought you might like to see this before they ship it off," Samantha said. "But how about dinner? Anybody hungry?"

That evening, Fiona's birthday bash moved outdoors to a special gathering area behind Samantha's house. It was a low-key celebration, but filled with cheer and interesting conversation. The women, who had forged a unique bond a few months prior under the intoxicating influence of the Spring Equinox, enjoyed each other's company and had a lot to catch up on.

Calle idled around the blazing fire pit prodding the embers with a long juniper branch and sipping a goblet of homemade wine. She listened to her friends as her shadow danced disfigured geometric shapes against the five huge monoliths brooding around the space and as tendrils of smoke rose to impregnate the sky. With a quick glance to the heavens, she located her star, whose clear illumination assured her that Isla was still on duty and she was safe from Cuün. As her mind spun back to that fateful encounter, Lucy began to share what Calle was thinking.

"It's hard to explain," She paused to gather courage enough to relive the dream she had shared with Calle. "It was a dream, but it was so very real," she intoned, then revealed the scar she bore on her arm.

Emotion swelled inside her as she girded herself to spit out the name of the demon. Lucy's remarkable fortitude was on full display as she continued.

"Cuün, was after Calle, but he got to me first. He was too strong for me and Calle saved my life."

A collective pall fell over the women. Only the crackling of the fire had the nerve to make a sound, until Calle used her now flaming stick to emphasize a point. Jabbing it in the air like a military general describing a plan of attack, she added to Lucy's tale.

"Actually, it was Rey and Isla who saved us, I was just as scared as you were," she confessed.

The exchange opened up the conversation full bore. Calle explained who Isla was then Lucy told of Rey and his sacrifice. Samantha and Fiona could hardly contain their empathy for their friends as Fiona thumbed through Samantha's new book.

"So, Cuün was summoned by Clarita Salazar, I'm certain of it," Samantha stated. "This has the all the markings of Dark Magic. Clarita must have lost her mind to join in league with such a creature."

"Here he is," Fiona spouted, pointing to a picture in the book. "He's called the *Swindler of Souls*," she revealed as a matter of fact, a fact of which, of course, Calle and Lucy were already well aware. "He's an astral assassin. He makes deals with mortals to kill in exchange for souls."

"Well, he's being detained right now by Calle's guardian angel," Lucy said flatly.

"Here's an artist's rendition of him, does he look like this?" Fiona thrust the book in front of her friends.

"Not anymore. She..." Calle thumbed in Lucy's direction, "Ripped off his eyelid and now he has a cross sticking out of his back." Samantha and Fiona glanced at Lucy, whose continence had turned grim at the sight of the demon in the picture.

"Drippy." Fiona said as she leaned back with a grin, closed the book, and crossed her legs under herself. "That's why I want to study the occult."

Her statement caught her friends off guard. No one expected the conversation to turn in this direction, but they were starting to get used to Fiona's mammoth intellect leading them into uncharted territory. They knew the young woman was about to share something profound.

Fiona laced her fingers together and placed her elbows on her knees cradling the book in her lap. With thumbs on her chin and her fingertips tented on her lips, she paused to organize her thoughts. The pads of her index fingers began to clap like little hands under her nose as she raised her attention to meet the curious stares of her friends who waited patiently for clarification.

"I think the connection between the spiritual, or astral, if you will, and the physical planes can be defined by science. It is clear, science has not addressed some things that are obviously facts. Such as the fact that every person is a spirit. That cannot be denied, but currently defies scientific description. Furthermore, contemporary mathematics is constrained by the exclusion of the act of dividing by zero. Which implies dividing things into zero equal parts, or many unequal parts, but that phenomenon occurs in nature billions of times every day."

Her friends sat listening in support, searching for the gist, but looked to one another in confusion. Not surprisingly, Fiona's point hadn't been received with the complete understanding for which she had hoped. She tried again.

"I believe that I am in a perfect position to solve who humans are and how they fit into the universe. I mean, with you guys so active in the paranormal world, I am privy to factual information no other scientist in the world has ever had access. With your help, I think it's possible."

"So, you think you can quantify the spiritual world?" Lucy asked. "Like, find the proverbial 'Stairway to Heaven'?"

Calle stared at Lucy, impressed by how insightful she was in spite of her distain for formal education.

"Or the 'Highway to Hell'," Samantha cut in sarcastically.

"Not exactly, but yes, I think, as a group we are very powerful," Fiona defended.

"Well spoken," Samantha agreed, clearly proud of her young friend.

"I don't think it's coincidence that on the first day of creation, God said, 'Let there be light.' And now we're learning that the speed of light is a monumental threshold to all our scientific understanding."

"Hmm." Lucy was warming to the idea.

"If geological time is aligned with the biblical creation timeline, then the era we are living in is still the Seventh Day. What happens on the biblical tomorrow, the Eighth Day, the Monday morning after creation?"

Fiona elucidated enthusiastically.

Her friends looked to one another as Fiona's logic began to kick into high gear. She saw their expressions and slowed her thinking back to her original conjecture.

"But I am diverging, sorry," she calmed herself a bit, then continued. "The point is simply this: Together..." she glanced from face to face, "We are a special group. A coven, in a way."

"But we're not witches," Lucy interrupted as Samantha shot her a 'speak for yourself' glare. "Well, not all of us," Lucy corrected with a grin that started them all laughing.

"A coterie then?" Samantha suggested. Lucy shrugged her shoulders with indifference.

"I guess the name doesn't really matter," Calle said, accepting the idea. "Does it?"

Like the wily teenager she was, Fiona seized the moment. "Then you'll help me like you helped Lucy?"

*Oh crap!* Calle knew she was cornered, but went with her heart. "I suppose, but it can be dangerous."

Samantha and Fiona shared a knowing look with Lucy then they all turned back to Calle.

"I trust you," Fiona said.

There are no more powerful words when spoken in honesty and were like honey to Calle's ears, but did she trust herself? She didn't really know, but it was too late to turn back now.

Though Fiona uttered the unsaid mantra aloud to Calle, it was a sentiment already shared by them all. It didn't matter who said it to whom, it applied to each equally and now that it had been verbalized, it bonded the already close group into a united entity.

A coven? Maybe not in the conventional sense, but it

was very much like *The Three Musketeers*. All for one and one for all.

# ☽ 22 ☾

The grand finale extravaganza of the Santa Fe Sister Cities convention at Pérez Manor was off to a good start. That is of course, if one takes in account the numerous minor adjustments that had to be made on the fly. Large scale, expensive galas involving elite clientele often go awry and program directors almost always have to scramble to make them appear smooth and polished. The illusion of easy is always hard and it's never a cinch to deliver a show as posh and as sophisticated as advertised.

Monkey wrench in the last-minute cancelation of the headlining artist and the event most likely will turn into a full-blown dung fest. Not so for the lucky Teresa Pérez however. Her chance introduction to the highly renown New Mexico painter Samantha Cloaker, was proving to be not just fortuitous, but advantageous.

Somehow the news of the replacement entertainment had reached the newspaper and reports were being shown on all the Albuquerque news channels. Although it was a closed event, there was a fresh sense of noble authenticity circulating amongst the guests and the members of Sister Cities International were thrilled by the change to a famous local artist. The gala was generating quite a buzz and everybody was riding a euphoric high as the day began, that is, except of course, the acting head honcho of Kokopelli catering, who was beside herself trying to slap together an extravaganza of her own.

Fortified by a distant, glib one-line text from Alby, wishing her the best, Calle faced the challenge like an Athenian General facing the Persian onslaught at Marathon. Thankfully, the nucleus of her crew was experienced and efficient, she would need their leadership as her friends filled in the gaps. It would be a long day and go late into the night as the dignitaries from the Sister Cities consortium conducted their final speeches and awards ceremony, after which, the art showing and ensuing party would commence in full until all were exhausted or they ran out of booze, whichever came first. The battle lines were clearly drawn and the game was already afoot.

Right out of the gate, it was clear, the alcohol service would need reinforcement. Phillip had drawn a crowd and was entertaining them by juggling glasses and bottles like the professional magician he was. The morning swillers were already well oiled and flocked around the bar in a festive mood. Between impromptu acts, he engaged them bravely like the only warm-blooded mammal inside a tent full of hungry mosquitoes. His performance was stellar and he was slinging drinks as fast as was humanly possible, but they were many and he was the lone barkeep.

But not for long, Calle saw his predicament and enlisted Lucy to barback for the overwhelmed bartender. It was a clever ploy because Lucy had experience mixing and serving while Phillip had a major crush on Lucy. With her expertise and his testosterone driven need to show off for her, they could handle anything this genteel mob could throw at them, at least until after lunch.

The over thirsty crowd wasn't the only unexpected crack in Calle's plan. Gloria and her big hunk of burnin' love had garnered a table near the waitron station and were behaving predictably like a turd in the punchbowl. Calle didn't have time to confront the old bat and decided to work around the pair, telling her crew to treat them as guests. Ezra's voice had begun to crack like a crystal wine glass during a soprano's aria and he was becoming too embarrassed to speak. A mute waiter would not go over well, so she decided to fight fire with fire and assigned him to Gloria's section. If she were lucky, the persnickety octogenarian would get aggravated and abandon ship, by then, maybe Ezra's voice would settle down.

Like a rowboat in a summer gale, the Kokopelli crew weathered the storm of spilled drinks, incomprehensible accents, and tipsy revelers. What had come over these people? Was there something in the water or had the convention been so tedious they were overjoyed for its end like college students clamoring for spring break? Whatever the reason, Calle was proud of her crew, especially Ezra, who screeched his way gallantly through the whole mess and somehow managed to placate the resident pain in the butt. They had survived the most raucous brunch rush she had ever seen and she was glad for the lull before the late afternoon move to the art gallery pavilion.

As the crew moved its focus to the outdoor gallery pavilion and began to set up shop there, Calle had a chance to chat with Samantha and her agent, Isabella Weft.

"What a magnificent surprise this turned out to be," Isabella gushed. "We've had the chance to meet several influential persons from around the world that are interested in showing Samantha's work. This could be the start of something really big."

Samantha side eyed Calle at Isabella's 'vision' and Calle understood completely. Samantha didn't really like to be on display along with her art and was doing the showing mainly as a favor for her. On the other hand, Isabella was onto the scent of money to be made and went after it like a barracuda loose in a school of cornered sardines.

Calle smiled a meek 'thank you' to her friend as Isabella enthusiastically reported excellent sales from earlier in the indoor gallery and her expectation for an 'Enchanting Evening Under the Stars', when the event kicked into full swing later on. Calle knew Samantha was more likely looking for a chance to escape and suspected the only enchantment that would occur that night would probably be an alcohol fueled 'Karaoke Under the Stars'. Her intuition proved to be spot on, except for where it wasn't.

As the sun began to slide beneath the horizon and the night owls were just beginning to hoot, Calle wandered the gallery pavilion admiring Samantha's work. Samantha truly was a gifted artist and the large tent was arranged in a mazy fashion in order to create a certain intimacy around each collection. Isabella must have hired a wizard because the presentation was nothing short of fantastic and Samantha's prolific past provided a wealth of pieces to view.

Scattered among the paintings were pieces from

some of Samantha's artsy friends.  A basket here, a multimedia piece there, some pottery arranged poetically on a hand-woven rug.  Calle had to chuckle when a miniature of the completed conquistador sculpture they had seen in huge graphic sections at Samantha's studio came into view.  The showing was rather extensive and it all added up to a brilliant display.

The adjacent dining pavilion had been transformed into a dance floor with a grand piano surrounded by a smooth jazz combo featuring a sultry female vocalist and a sensual saxophone lead.  It was the most sophisticated set up Calle had ever been a part of and it was hard to believe that it could come together so quickly and so professionally.  But it did and it all began with her small idea.  Chalk one up for the good guys.

Though the event was coming together nicely, Calle wasn't complacent.  She knew from experience that things could go from superb to abysmal in a heartbeat.  Any gathering could implode, instant disaster, just add alcohol.  She reminded her crew not to over serve, but she couldn't control what the guests did in private and if the morning rush was any indication, they were in for a wild night.

"It's amateur hour," her heavy drinking uncle would have declared.  "When people who don't usually imbibe try to drink like the professionals, that's when trouble starts."

But it wasn't only the guests that had Calle worried. She was still concerned about Lisa Jill's safety.  Even though she didn't have concrete evidence to support her suspicion, she covertly kept an eye on the young woman.  She could sense a coldness from Verna toward Jill, but nothing malevolent.  In spite of her jealousy, they appeared to be working together just fine.

It was the presence of Ned Luper and Rob Aragon that caught Calle's attention. The two men had driven past the event several times earlier in Rob's delivery van. During brunch, she caught sight of them leaving the kitchen when the crew was busy on the floor. After checking, she found nothing out of place except missing sandwiches and pieces of fruit. Maybe they had stolen lunch, but they had no business in the building in the first place.

And now, they were idling past again, eyeing the growing crowd with an odd interest. What were they playing at? She had meant to report their behavior earlier, but got sidetracked and forgot. As they disappeared up the service road, she went in search of her two-way radio, but in all the turmoil, she couldn't remember where she had left it. Her report would have to wait.

As the party picked up steam, the mischievous Santa Fe charm began to sieve into the veins of all in attendance. Like it had done for centuries, the magic of the place filled everyone with an intangible sense of enchantment. The mystic vibe carried its own intoxicating aura that stirred even the staidest of persons and fertilized the mood of the gathering, making it ripe for love and misadventure.

Calle stood in awe of Phillip's performance. What he was doing bartending in Santa Fe was beyond her comprehension. He could be working in Las Vegas for big money, but here he was thrilling her crowd with unbelievable tricks.

As he scanned the crowd, he caught her eye. He smiled to her and produced a gold coin from his pocket.

He expertly rolled the coin along his knuckles and made it disappear, then reappear. He was doing the trick he had taught her and as he finished, he pointed his finger at her and grinned, as if to say, "This one's for you" and then returned to his bartending duties.

His overture made her smile. Her friends had stepped up big time for her and she was awash with gratitude. She floated back to her duties and went to the kitchen to replenish some hors d'oeuvres trays. As she passed the breakroom, she stuck her hand in her pocket and felt for the poker chip Phillip had given her. Stepping inside for privacy, she took a moment to give her trick a quick try. He had made it look so easy; she would only be a minute.

As usual, she was able to pull it off with her left hand, but when she tried with her right, she fumbled the token and it rolled underneath the table. Wouldn't you know, it rolled all the way to the corner, back near the hole in the wall El Gordo used to use. Crawling on her hands and knees, finagling herself under the tablecloth, she mumbled to herself about her stupidity and the waste of time.

When she was completely under the table and within reach of the chip, she heard someone enter the room. She froze as a man's voice began to speak.

"If I could get her alone for just a minute, I could do it," he said. Then a faint, but audible woman's voice sprang from his phone.

"Now's the perfect time. With so many people around, they will never figure out who did it."

The man leaned his butt on the table only inches from Calle and clasped his fingers around the edge. She held her breath as the table sagged, his meaty fingertips twiddling on the underside of the table as he spoke. His colorfully painted fingernails danced a menacing jig as she recognized the owner of the digits and his call-in confidant.

"Grab the little bitch tonight before Teresa sees her. We'll get rid of her later," Gloria's heartless voice commanded over the phone.

"What about that catering woman? She's always watching the girl," Fen asked with a hushed grunt.

"She wouldn't be if you hadn't botched the poisoning," Gloria's tiny voice spat. "Kill her too if you have to, I don't care."

At the mention of him killing her, Calle bumped her head on the bottom of the table. The hope that he wouldn't notice died as quickly as the conversation on the phone. As he stood up from the table, turned around, and stooped to push back the tablecloth, she knew the jig was up. There was no sense waiting for the inevitable, so she launched herself from under the table like a sprinter from the blocks. If she could get to the door, she knew she could probably escape, but as she sprung from under the table, his burly hand latched around her forearm.

He jerked her to her feet and stood triumphantly holding her arm in one hand and his phone in the other. He snickered a contemptuous smirk in her face, shook her violently like a jackhammer to the spine, then tossed his phone on the tabletop. Through frazzled wits, she could hear Gloria's grouchy voice screeching in the background as he twisted to deliver the Coup de Grace.

But he had underestimated the tenacity of his intended victim. This was not the first time Calle had to fight for her life and despite his size, she went on the attack.

Without hesitation, she sunk her teeth into his knuckles like a rabid honey badger. Her ferocity caught him off guard, but he grabbed at her throat with his other hand, ripping the medicine bag from around her neck as she clawed at his face. She spun downward with all her strength and with a guttural curse from his lips and a smear of blood on her chin, she spit out a hunk of flesh, wrenched herself free of his grasp, and flung herself from the room and out the side door of the building.

For a very pissed off large man, Fen was surprisingly nimble. As Calle tore from the kitchen into the darkness, he was right on her heels. Her first instinct toward the parking lot proved to be a misstep. It gave him the advantage, leaving him between her and any assistance she might have found from the crowd.

Panic drove her further from the party and deeper into peril. She could feel her anxiety boiling under her skin and knew if she were to survive, she had to gain control of it. Fen sensing her inner turmoil, slowed his pursuit. Like the sadistic murderer he was, he was going to enjoy her suffering like a food critic savors a fine meal.

Fleeing frantically under the full moon, she mentally fumbled with her relaxation techniques as she tried to formulate a plan. As she skidded around the corner near the employee parking lot, she had an epiphany. Relaxation was the stupidest thing she should be considering at the moment, panic and anxiety were exactly the correct emotions for the situation. Now was the time for action not introspection. Dismissing her foolishness, she reacted.

Embracing the adrenalin rush cleared her cloud of indecision and with the agility of a rodeo clown and the clarity of a fighter pilot, she leapt into the seat of a nearby ATV and ripped up the service road like a NASCAR driver on meth.

Without headlights, the night flew by in a blur of desperate shadows. The trees and shrubs that in the daylight and at a reasonable pace were quite lovely, but now presented deadly obstacles just one mistake away from disaster. All she needed was to impale herself on a spindly juniper branch or crash face first into a cholla cactus.

Chancing a furtive glance over her shoulder confirmed what she feared most. Fen was barreling after her on another ATV. He must have grabbed a formula one version because despite his weight and size, he was gaining on her. Her only defense was the rip-roaring cloud of dust and gravel flying up behind her. If she were lucky, he would catch a stone in his teeth or a rock would take out an eye.

With the stables only seconds away, she hatched a plan to zip past them, then zing down the main pathway back to the party. It was a good strategy, if only she could keep Fen a bay, but his machine was pulling up beside her. As his front left wheel came alongside her right rear tire, he violent turned his ATV into hers. The collision knocked the rear of her ATV off track and sent her careening out of control.

Like a trucker sliding on ice, she braked and turned into the slide to regain control, but by doing so, she was pushed off the main path and was now aimed up the path toward the cemetery. Fen, having overrun her by a few yards, slammed his brakes then gunned his machine in an arc, spitting gravel and branches behind him as he beared down her again. She opened up her throttle and shot up the mountain trail like a jackrabbit juking a mountain lion.

She knew this was a dead end. Maybe she could make a stand at the grotto or hide in the forest. She looked over her shoulder once again to gauge her position. How she had gained such a considerable separation from him, she didn't know, but she hoped the distance would give her enough time to escape when they reached the cemetery parking area.

Calle leaped from her machine before it stopped rolling. She was already three steps behind the giant lilac stand when her ATV finally came to a rest, idling nose first in the bush. She thanked her lucky stars that there were no bees on patrol at night as she hustled up the rocky trail.

Her mind was whirling in circles with each step. Why was this guy so relentless? She tried to connect the dots between Fen, Gloria, and Lisa Jill, but her pressing need to escape kept interrupting her train of thought. As she passed the grotto, she stopped to take stock of her situation. The tiny trickle of water flowing from the spring under the full moon radiated beauty, maybe even romance, but with the fact that a mad man bent on murder was only steps behind her, the dribbling creek sounded more like ravening imps gathering for a bloodbath.

She could hear him laboring up the rocky trail several yards behind. She sprung back into flight hoping she could outlast him on the uphill hike. Moments later she was standing under the wrought iron gate of the cemetery.  Moonshine washed over the tiny necropolis illuminating a few stark headstones that rose from the shadows like zombic stalagmites thrusting themselves upward from the confines of Hades.

As Fen's lumbering silhouette rounded the path from the darkness, Calle dove to the ground.  Hiding in the shade of the rock wall, she hurried along on her hands and knees further into the darkened corner until she was completely swallowed by the night.  She shallowed her breathing and became as perfectly still as all the other permanent residents of the cemetery.

It felt familiar, lying there hiding in the shadows, like a child playing hide and seek.  She had been an expert then, never having been found.  Hoping her childhood skill would save her life, she lay motionless, an unexpected calm washing over her as she scanned her immediate surroundings.

She could hear Fen at the cemetery gate. He paused to catch his breath and then stepped into the graveyard.  She knew she had temporarily juked him.  A flash of hope crossed her thinking as she watched in silence as he began to search.

As he turned away from her to look in the opposite direction, she was tempted to jump up and flee. But as a skilled hide-and-seeker, she knew to be patient.

The seconds felt like hours as she waited for him to give up, but he kept plodding along.  She began to assess her situation, looking for anything she could use as a weapon to protect herself in case he stumbled upon her hiding place.  That's when she noticed the wilted carnations on the grave next to her.  Even in the sallow moonlight, she recognized the flowers.  It was the same grave Otis had cried over when they had visited a few days ago. Slowly reaching her hand from the shadow, she gently cleared the tombstone to reveal the inscription.

It was simple, but profound. It read: Jessica Pérez, aged 20 years.

# ☽ 23 ☾

"I know you're in here," Fen cooed into the darkness. "Come out and play, little hare." His voice teasing like one tricking a toddler. Having searched the other half of the cemetery, he turned toward her hiding place, strolling the headstones like a retriever about to flush out a pheasant.

Calle heard his words, but she couldn't ignore the puzzle that was piecing together in her mind. Was this Jessica Lisa Jill's mother? It all seemed to fit. Otis' gesture at the grave and the uncanny resemblance between his dead true love and his daughter Lisa Jill. With the all the pieces falling into place, Calle began to contemplate the ramifications. Jessica was a Pérez, that meant, by blood, Lisa Jill was too. In turn, that made her an heir to the estate.

She was startled out of her rumination as Fen strode within a few feet of her. A creepy dampness swept the night air as he stopped, stared through the dimness directly at her. He massaged his bloody hand and broke his scowl to speak.

"There you are, you meddlesome little tramp," he said with even confidence. He held out his wounded hand into the moonlight and continued, "See this? This is going to cost you." His tone as cold as frozen blood.

Calle was shaken, but not stirred. She grabbed the

wilted carnations from Jessica's grave and vaulted to her feet to face the behemoth bully.

"You see this," she shook the dead flowers at him in defiance. "This is the evidence that will put you away for the rest of your life." Her voice mimicking a furious Della Street delivering a conviction.

She knew full well that her statement made little to no sense, but it was the delivery she was counting on to buy her some precious seconds to think. Baffle them with bullshit was the strategy, but she knew her reprieve would only last a moment, so she pressed on, trying to tie the flowers to the situation.

"You killed Jessica Pérez," she spat like a politician fabricating the truth.

Sometimes when truth surrounds you, but you can't seem to put your finger on it, if you go with your first thought, fate will give you the correct words to hit the nail right on the head. When she uttered the statement, she thought she was concocting more bullshit, but the look on Fen's face told her she had touched the matter with a needle. He had indeed killed Lisa Jill's mother.

"That's enough out of you, you little bitch!" He advanced on her, but she leapt aside to place a tall tombstone between them.

They began the dance of death around the headstone. As he moved left, she pivoted in time, effectively keeping the grave marker between them. Then he feigned a step right, but lunged left. It was a tricky move he must have mastered playing rugby or some other brutal sport, because her hesitation gave him just enough leverage to grab her arm.

He jerked her from behind the grave marker and as she slapped his face with the flowers, a rock flew from the darkness and clocked him on the back of the head. He released her, shook his head and fluttered his eyelids trying to clear the cob webs. As Calle backed away, a Valkyrie voice spilt the night.

"Hey tough guy, you like beating on women? I'm standing right here. Come on, I'll dance with you," Lucy commanded as she reared back and launched another stone like a major league pitcher hurling a no-hitter. The rock bounced off Fen's chin with a mighty thud and the beleaguered man reeled backward.

"What the hell?!" He staggered further away as Lucy picked up another rock. As she wound up for another strike, the besieged cutthroat bolted over the cemetery wall and into the forest, the rock whizzing inches by his head as he disappeared into the relative safety of the trees.

Calle stood in astonishment as she watched the whole thing unfold. She angled her head to get a better view of his escape and then back at her grinning friend.

"Holy crap! You're one Hella good shot! That was amazing!"

"I grew up with a bunch of mean brothers, what can I say?" Lucy laughed as she stepped under the wrought iron arches and into the cemetery. "You alright?"

Before Calle could respond, a sinister voice leached from the shadows. Drenched in malice, it chilled the darkness.

"Too bad he didn't rip your head off, you filthy murderer."

Lucy stopped dead in her tracks as Old Purply followed by Jamaica entered a small clearing adjacent to the opposite wall. Calle backed up until her hip was against the wall from where Fen had made his escape and Lucy watched as the pair approached. A shiver of recognition sucked the oxygen from graveyard as the friends realized with whom they were dealing.

Clarita stepped through the crumbled side gate like a reincarnated Persian goddess and raised her hands into the air, one of them handling a crooked branch about the length of a ruler. Jamaica sidled along behind as the witch mumbled some ancient language, her words drifting aloft like steamy breath in the wintertime.

A bruised purple glow trickled down her arm from the branch and into the dirt in front of her like blood spilling from a severed head. Where it pooled, the earth began to boil and from the molten soil rose a form that bubbled, then grew into the shape of a large bull. With another hiss from its conjuror, the earthen bull became animated and with a flick of her magic wand, Clarita commanded her creation to attack Calle.

As the elemental gaged its quarry, Clarita leveled a promise to Calle, "I don't know how you avoided Cuün, but you will not escape tonight."

The earthen beast having gained its bearings, sank its massive hooves into the ground and moved to corner Calle. She ran to zig zag around the headstones, but the bull plowed them over like blades of grass. Lucy, seeing Calle's plight and having picked up a broken, discarded shovel handle, ran to intercept the soulless bovine.

The automaton's focus was on Calle, so he hardly noticed when Lucy sprang onto his back and began to beat him about the head.

Having grown up in a ranching family, Lucy was an ace rider, but her attacks went unnoticed as the earthen beast mercilessly chased its prey. As Calle, jumped the wall and veered into the forest, Lucy upped her ferocity and leveraged her entire weight forward to stab the handle deep into the base of the bull's skull, right behind its ear.

The maneuver finally got the attention of the beast as he planted his front hooves in the dirt and began to buck and spin violently, attempting to dislodge the annoying woman from his back.

Like a champion bull rider at the Ty Murray Invitational, Lucy clamped her heels tightly into his flanks and grabbed for the wrinkled skin on the bull's back. But only handfuls of muddy soil filled her palms as her handhold gave way and she was flung high into the air, cartwheeling ass over hairdo to the ground. The wind was throttled from her lungs as she landed in a heap against the base of another headstone. Cradling her ribcage and gasping for breath, Lucy struggled to right herself as the bull lowered his head and pawed the ground, preparing to charge.

Just as the earthen monstrosity snorted a blast of dust from his nostrils and scratched the dirt one last time before attacking, another solemn voice echoed over the arena of the dead.

"That is enough Clarita. Your reign of terror is over, it ends here," Samantha challenged from the faintly lit path in front of the graveyard. With her long blonde hair streaming in her wake, she strode majestically through the moonlight like a queen meeting her destiny, Fiona trailing a few feet behind. Clarita raised a wicked eyebrow, flicked a command from her enchanted stick to halt the bull, and turned to face her bitter rival.

"Samantha," she spit the name from her mouth like

lukewarm cod liver oil. "This is none of your affair, go home to your crayons and your infantile finger paintings before you get hurt." Clarita's open contempt broiled like smelted slag between them.

"No, it is you that has gone too far. You've sealed your fate. My back is not turned this time and I will show you no mercy," Samantha steeled her threat.

An immortal silence engulfed the cemetery as the two witches squared off. The sweet scent of destruction began to crackle from all corners of the universe causing the moon to stop like a spotlight from the sky. As the tension began to boil over, Fiona stared wide-eyed near the graveyard entrance, Lucy pulled her battered self to her feet, and the sleepy dead sat up in their graves to witness the festering firestorm.

Clarita pursed her lips then spit in Samantha's direction. Samantha angled sideways to minimize her profile and slipped her hand inside her shawl as Clarita began to mumble arcane syllables under her breath. The air began to bristle as Clarita swung her wand in a circle over her head then whipped it downward like an invisible hammer onto her enemy. Samantha crouched to a defensive stance and countered with a fistful of sparks flung from her exposed hand.

The cemetery lit up like a fireworks display gone wrong only feet above their heads as the two spells collided. As the hammer blow slowed to compress the atmosphere around Samantha, the sparks blew its edges into spits of fire like a blowtorch cuts metal, sending shards of deadly melted magic aloft like lava spewing from a volcano.

Samantha pirouetted and slashed a festooned backhand to the massive magical deadlock, her rings sparkling under the unseen friction as she dodged the resulting shockwave. Clarita's eyes glowed a glittering crimson as she levitated slightly and weathered the blast like a surfer riding the Big Kahuna. Under her, a mound of earth began to rise into a pedestal on which she planted her feet as she conjured a small, lurid ball of orangey energy into the palm of her open hand. Then simultaneously with her magic stick in her other hand, she redirected the elemental to assault her foe.

A glint of nervous recognition passed Samantha's continence as she quickly pulled her hand from inside her shawl. In its grasp clung a root that contorted to her hand like brass knuckles with a slight protrusion near her pinky finger. Her eyes rolled back into her head leaving only the whites visible as her skin color and texture turned to that of an aging avocado and a riot of bright blue morning glories sprouted from her hair. A serpentine vine grew rapidly from the protrusion of Samantha's wand, its dainty flowers dancing hungrily as the creeper ensnared the elemental only inches from its intended victim.

The liana rooted itself deeply in the ground, spiraled up cloven legs, and bound the elemental to the earth from which it was summoned. The spells struggled for supremacy, but the elemental's strength proved to be its weakness. All plants thrive on soil and the mighty earth elemental was no match for the voracious flowering vine. In a scant few seconds, the vine had consumed the bull, leaving only a pile parched tailings behind as it swiftly grew up the pedestal and emmeshed the confounded sorceress on top. Clarita fought for control as her orb of orange energy sailed toward her nemesis, but her effort collapsed in a fizzle as Samantha commanded the climbing morning glory to constrict and consume.

As Samantha's physique ebbed back toward normal, the two enchantresses locked eyes for the last time. The balance of power avalanched against her as Clarita's life force began to wane. Fiona thought she saw a flicker of remorse cross Samantha's face as her spell choked the soul from her one-time close friend.

Fiona stood helpless watching the heart wrenching scene. She was still very inexperienced and her sympathy had overwhelmed her, but Jamaica was as calloused as an old tortoise shell and was not going sit idly by and watch her accomplice get strangled to death.

With the dexterity of a practiced killer, she pulled what looked to be a thin walking stick up to her mouth and blew a ferocious breath into the thing. But it was not a walking stick, it was a cleverly disguised blowgun. And it was all business.

The dart flew like a bolt from a crossbow and buried itself deeply into Samantha's shoulder. The poison it delivered was fast acting and within seconds, Samantha's spell faltered and Clarita gasped a new lease on life. Samantha realizing what was happening, immediately refocused her attention and began to chant an antidote charm as she fell to her knees. With the words sputtering from her lips, she pulled a vial of pinkish liquid from her pocket and sloshed it into her mouth.

Lucy was already halfway to Jamaica when the dart flew from the blowgun and by the time it had hit its mark, she had one punched the leather skinned vagrant into unconsciousness. With the cataleptic trespasser laying at their feet and the witch subdued, Lucy and

Fiona exchanged glances.

They looked from Clarita to Jamaica, then Fiona asked unsteadily, "What now?"

"Will Sam be alright?" Lucy gestured toward Samantha.

Fiona shrugged her shoulders as if to say, "I don't know," when "I will survive," crumbled like asphalt from Samantha's mouth.

Lucy quickly glanced around and sized up the situation. Fiona was in minor shock, Clarita was still bound by the thicketed vines, Jamaica was out cold, and Samantha looked bad, but like she was going to live. Lucy fetched some rusty baling wire that was hanging from the fence and instructed Fiona to bind Jamaica's hands and feet. When she was confident Fiona was safe, she directed her young friend, "You watch these two, I'm going for Calle. See if you can get cell service and call 911."

Having been given direction, Fiona's nerves began to settle and she leapt into action.

As Lucy grabbed Jamaica's blowgun and blazed off into the forest, Fiona hogtied Jamaica then went to Samantha's side. Samantha was nodding in and out of consciousness every few minutes until she finally passed out completely.

Fiona wandered the graveyard, even clambered up on the stone wall, but she couldn't get service. Climbing down, she was mumbling to herself as she heard the cracking of branches like an animal crunching through a bramble. Turning to face the racket, she saw that Clarita had fully regained her faculties and had freed herself from the crumbled shrubbery. An angry vengeance swept the witch's face as she stepped from the pedestal toward Fiona. With phone still in hand, Fiona retreated until her back was against a mossy gravestone as the sorceress advanced and pinned the teenager with a malevolent stare.

"So, you're the talented apprentice I've heard so much about," Clarita said dourly. "Not much more than a stupid girl if you ask me." Fiona's eyes grew wide and she dropped her phone as she shrank against the tombstone.

"I hope Samantha is still coherent enough to hear you beg for mercy," the witch sizzled. "But it really doesn't matter who dies first," she added just for spite. "Does it?"

Terror streaked up Fiona's spine as the witch began to twirl her magic stick. But grappling for courage, the young woman leaned forward, back to her feet, and away from the headstone to face the danger in a final act of defiance. Feigning poise, she did not possess, Fiona said the only thing that came to mind.

"You have branches in your hair... Just there." She grimaced a scowl, cocked her head, and gestured to her own hair.

She knew her attempt at trash talk sounded ridiculous, but at least there were words coming out of her mouth. She was never good at arguing anyway and knew it was no use trying to match insults. She needed to jump start her mind and shed her intimidation and though the nonsense was a feeble volley, at least she was fighting back.

"That's it? That's all you have to say?" Clarita intoned with disgust. "Why, you're not only spineless, but you're stupid as well."

Stupid?! That was the second time in as many

minutes the hateful, old toad had called her stupid and it was the one thing Fiona detested more than anything. Her blood began to boil and her resolve hardened. The shit was about to hit the fan; come hell or high water, she'd show this hatchet-faced bitch stupid.

Fiona stepped closer to Clarita like a prize fighter at the weigh in. She matched Clarita's contempt as she unclipped Festus from the silver chain around her neck. She placed the trinket on her outstretched palm and channeled the voice of a powerful sorceress from one of her fantasy novels, then nobly commanded, "Scala Libre!"

The tiny figurine shuddered to life and shook like it was shaking off miniscule fleas then buzzed into flight above her palm. As the teeny dragon hovered unevenly between the combatants, the women shared a look of surprise. Clarita at Fiona's puny attempt at magic and Fiona at the paltry scale of her defense. She was obviously expecting something more sensational, something spectacular, but there was Festus, fliting erratically like a mosquito in the wind.

"By all that is unholy, is that what Samantha gave you? A gnat?! I should have brought a flyswatter!" Clarita roared with derision. "She has betrayed you, just like she betrayed me." The witch reached into her battered cloak and produced a crystal ball about the size of a golf ball and held it aloft in one hand and her wand in the other. "Now watch as I show you the power of real magic."

A cloud of translucent mist began to coalesce between her upstretched hands and she drew a deep breath as if to push the magic from her body. Disheveled and terrified, Fiona stumbled back as Festus buzzed forward.

The witch was calling upon all that was evil as the tiny reptile began to lumines a bright neon, cherry red. He festered up to the size of an over ripe pomegranate and before his opponent had time to react, a tsunami of pale cyanotic, smoldering mucus exploded from his maw like napalm blasting from the nozzle of a flame thrower. The discharge was of a phenomenal scale, hundreds of times larger than that of the teensy wyrm's body and it wholly engulfed Clarita, clinging acidly to every inch of her body.

Fiona stood in awe as the dragonfire incinerated the witch's clothing then blistered through her skin and muscle tissue, exposing her skeleton, internal organs, and still beating heart. Her flaming wand shot from her bony hand like a misguided bottle-rocket careening through the canopy of the surrounding glade. The doomed woman teetered in place for a second before her bladder burst and her carcass began to convulse. As her eyes evaporated from her skull, and her soul sifted from her corpse, her body's ashes began to float downward like cindered snowflakes. But before her remains hit the ground, an almighty tremor shook the earth beneath her.

Like a scalded bat out of hell, Cuün breeched from the depths like a blue whale feeding on krill, encompassing Clarita's soul and devouring every astral atom. The action thundered like a real-life horror film as Isla catapulted into view behind the raging demon, grasping frantically to the golden chain still noosed around his neck like an expert parasailer battling a tremendous gale.

Cuün, having consumed Clarita's soul, paused to

hover overhead with Rey's holy artifact jutting from his back. He flashed an angry, naked eyeball at Fiona, who stood petrified under the living nightmare. They shared a paralyzing moment, then Isla yanked the demon back into submission like an ill-behaved dog, but his hungry gaze never strayed from Fiona until he was dragged from the physical plane and back into astral captivity.

In the eerie calm that remained, amid the stench of burnt human flesh and the scorched ozone of freshly spent magic, Fiona leaned against the grave marker stupefied. The dragonfire had completely reduced Clarita to a rapidly dissolving smudge, only the crystal ball remained intact.

Gathering her wits, she pulled a scarf from Jamaica's clothing and used it to pick up the magic crystal which appeared clean and unscathed. Even through the cloth, she could feel the coolness of the polished gemstone. She wrapped the orb in the scarf and pocketed it, then went to Samantha as the again tiny Festus winged haphazardly about in the settling haze.

Samantha was leaning crookedly on one elbow like a woman who had just suffered a stroke as Festus flitted in between the two women. He drifted near to Fiona's face then playfully nipped her on the lip. She gasped in surprise as he spiraled to a landing on the tip of her nose making her eyes cross like a hypnotized toddler. As she worked to regain focus, he kneaded her skin like a tiny kitten, then purred off into the night sky like a honeybee in search of a beautiful flower.

Feeling like someone had just stolen her favorite new toy, Fiona watched as her savior disappeared into the midnight sky. Astonished and exhilarated, she stood rubbing her slightly bloodied lip and scratching her tickled nose when Samantha pulled on her pant leg to get her attention.

"Well done my girl, well done!" she preened. "I think he likes you."

Fiona, popping out of her stupor, looked down to her smiling, but battered mentor.

"You think? But he flew away," she dejected as she fingered her silver necklace.

Samantha choked out a laugh, "My innocent child, don't you worry, he's been resting for a long time. He wants to stretch his wings a bit, but he'll be back." She pushed herself upright and grinned, "Besides, you're in his debt now, you owe him."

# ☉ 24 ☾

Calle's thoughts were a jumble as she hurtled through the thickening underbrush. She desperately needed a place to hide, but could she really hide from a raging magic bull? Or would she run headlong into the murderous brute that was trying to kill her? Trapped between the hammer and the anvil, she wished she could fly like she did in her dreams, but that, ironically, wasn't even a dreamy possibility. If it were, she wouldn't be so vulnerable.

She pushed the thought out of her head, she needed to think practically. Slowing and keeping her head down, so not to poke an eye out, her flight had led her through a grove of spindly and spiky pines. Her blouse was torn and scratches seeped droplets of blood from her skin as she stopped to rest near a small clearing.

The forest was holding its breath like a spectator on the edge of its seat. It was way too quiet. The bull should be crashing through the trees like a bulldozer, but there wasn't a sound coming from behind her. Maybe Lucy had disabled the clay-clad conjurant, but Calle doubted that even as capable as she was, Lucy could have subdued the bewitched beast. Even if she had somehow, what about Clarita and Jamaica? Calle realized Lucy was outnumbered. She had to return to the cemetery.

Spinning on her heel, she parted the branches and began to head back. She knew she couldn't have come very far because the brush was so thick, but if she was as close to the cemetery as she thought she was, she should be able to hear something. Stopping again to get her bearings, she heard nothing. Not good, not good at all. Fear began to stalk her every thought.

Maybe she had gone farther than she realized. Looking around, she tried to recall any landmark, but in the darkness, all the trees looked the same. There was no sense plodding along aimlessly, so she found an open area nearby and gazed at the moon. Beautiful as it was, it offered no assistance. She was lost, but she knew she couldn't be too far off track. Like anyone lost in a wilderness, she had to either sit and wait for help or bravely venture forth and hope her sense of direction proved reliable.

Calle measured her pace and kept her ear to the wind. She was not the type of person to sit and wait. She remembered going down a hill and then up over another, so she set out down a nearby slope. If she reached the bottom and started back up, she thought that would most likely be the way back. With her plan laid out, sketchy as it was, she gradually started to regain her calm.

At the bottom of the hill, she thought she recognized a ponderosa pine and the swell in the landscape that led back up another hill. It looked familiar; her confidence was building with each step. With luck, she would come over the rise and the cemetery would come into view.

As any gambler will tell you, luck is a very fickle mistress. Everyone is lucky, but what's lucky for one is usually unlucky for another. And with every stride, Calle's luck was running out.

She passed the towering ponderosa and glanced down to make sure she didn't trip on the many branches lying in the shadows underneath. When she looked up again, a slab of human flesh with painted fingertips shot from the shade and latched onto her hair and nearly snatched her bald headed. The vicious attack jerked her from her feet and in an instant, she was slammed on her back with Fen's full body weight on top of her.

A gnarly branch dug into her back as the man began to blather maniacally.

"Don't fight and this won't hurt as much," he said benevolently like a demented dentist pulling teeth.

Her mind was racing, but her body was trapped beneath the huge murderer. He had her right arm pinned under his left knee, so it was her left hand against both of his. God, he weighed a ton! In a desperate act of defiance, she managed a piercing jab to his groin, but it wasn't enough to dislodge the monster.

"I hate it when you fight back," he gritted. "Then I have to do this..."

He slapped her face so hard her teeth clattered in her skull. With crossed, lazy eyes, she grappled to remain conscious as the man continued to yammer.

"See there, isn't that better?" he cooed like a madman then locked his beefy hand around her throat.

She tried to pry open his grip, but he was too strong. With her breath cut off, she knew she was a goner. It would only be a few seconds and it would be over.

One would think that when facing such a violent death, fear would consume your being, but for Calle, her mind went sideways.

What kind of man paints his fingernails? Ironically, she found the thought amusing. The dash of solace her humor provided slid past like a newsreel on fast forward. In fact, everything was on fast forward. With only a few heartbeats left to live, she expected to see her life flash before her eyes, but it was only the precious moments of love that glimmered.

A vision of her late husband's charming laugh, Matthew's wholesome face, her mother's uncompromising affection... Her arm lost all its strength. Isla's angelic devotion, Lucy's unwavering loyalty, the unborn child she never got to nurture... Her lips had gone numb and her vision blackened. And Ethan. Oh God, her heart cried out in agony for Ethan.

As her spirit started to leave her body, the sensation was nothing like astral projection. It was more like a straining muscle ripping from the bone. She did not want to die. Fearing it might be too late and with every remaining iota of energy, she thrust her soul backward. It was her last grasp at life and her final hope for salvation.

# ☽ 25 ☾

Following a guttural squeal and the sound of crazed snorting like that of a pig in warm mud, Lucy shambled wildly through the trees upon a scene right out of a psycho-thriller.

"See, I told you it wouldn't hurt," Fen's psychotic grunts turning to primitive words in her ears. The bulk of his frame was angled downward, his attention focused on the limp body of her best friend pinned beneath his girth.

With the agility of an incensed timber elf, Lucy leveled the blowgun mid stride and launched a dart deep into Fen's exposed neck. The dart had hardly delivered its poisonous dose when she skidded up next to the startled lunatic and wrapped the blowgun around the bridge of his nose. It contorted to the shape of his facial profile as he rolled off of Calle and feebly lunged for his attacker, the deadly poison already taking effect. Lucy sidestepped the move and landed a front kick savagely to his chin. Defeated and dying, writhing in anguish, Fen bowled over into the darkness to face his fate.

Even in the dappled lunar glow, Lucy could see Calle's face was ashen and a pale blue ring had darkened her blood-stained lips. She knew, that by all rights, Calle was dead, but she could not accept what she was seeing. Fending off hysteria, she knelt next to the wilted body, tilted its head back, and pressed her lips to Calle's. Through teary desperation, she started mouth to mouth resuscitation. She couldn't remember if CPR was two breaths, then eighteen chest compressions or the other way around, but she knew one thing for certain, Calle needed air. Though her heart was crushed and her thoughts were whirling out of control, Lucy tried to remain focused.

She placed her palm on Calle's forehead and pinched her nostrils shut. Calle's chest expanded and contracted with every breath blown into her lungs, but she remained unresponsive, her body lifeless under the exertion. Lucy could feel the grim reaper peering over her shoulder, but persisted frantically until she began to hyperventilate. And even though she was dizzy and on the verge of blacking out, she didn't give up. She couldn't, she wouldn't. *Come on girl, I know you're still there, come back to me.... Oh, dear God, come back to me...*

Calle's consciousness moved to the astral as the dream displaced her death. She felt the warmth of a kiss on her lips. She returned the kiss and moved her soul toward the taste of genuine, absolute love. She deepened the kiss and as their tongues caressed, she felt her soul wrenching back into her body. With a liberating gasp, the dream of death dissolved into a fresh breath of life and her spirit settled back to where it belonged.

She choked out a cough, then tried to swallow, but her throat felt like barbed wire drenched in blood. Deliberately, but unsteadily, she opened her bleary eyes to meet the tear-stained expression of utter despair.

Blinking back her own tears, she recognized the source of unconditional love and the muddy, heart-wrenched face of her closest friend.

"Luce?"

Lucy brushed the hair from Calle's face, then leaned back and with the same finger, pulled her own matted hair behind her ear. As Calle sat up, clarity replaced desperation. They locked eyes and their sixth sense ignited. Before the next breath, a million thoughts passed between them.

Sometimes words are more confusing than silence. It brought them close, but not as close as they just were. An awkward moment passed as Calle began to comprehend what had transpired. Lucy had just saved her life and she had just French-kissed her best friend. Though they couldn't deny the passion they had just shared, they muddled through the unexpected sexual tension.

"I didn't mean, I just reacted…"

"It's okay," Calle stumbled. The stillness that followed hung as thick as chilled molasses and twice as sweet.

"Thank you." She took Lucy's hand in hers.

"I can't afford to lose you," Lucy's voice now a strained whisper. "You're my best friend." Her heart raw. "But I didn't mean…"

"I know, I didn't either," Calle faltered. She started to say, "I love you too," but the words lodged in her chest. She cleared her throat and confessed, "I thought you were Ethan. I thought I was dead."

"I thought you were too."

The heartrending release racked them both to the core. Lucy pulled Calle into a comforting hug and as the tension eased, they found their emotional footing. With their friendship intact, they broke their embrace.

"Will you two shut up already!" Fen moaned. "I'm dying here. It's all that old woman's fault, I loved her..." His suffering effectively disrupted the spell between them and they went to him as he lay in the throes of death. There was nothing they could do for him. It was a sure-acting poison, but before he died, he admitted to killing Jessica those many years ago in Pennsylvania and Gloria's subsequent abandonment of her newborn granddaughter into adoption.

# ☽ 26 ☾

What a mess.  The pavilion looked like a Delta House toga party had just blown through and Calle wasn't anywhere near in the mood for the clean-up.  The side of her face still ached from the slap Fen had delivered and she was on duty only in body, her mind, a thousand miles away.  Ezra, Verna, and Lisa Jill along with a few mansion employees toiled away in the morning sunshine as she sat in the shade and supervised.

Last night, after the police showed up and the subsequent questioning, Calle and Lucy were checked out by the paramedics and sent home.  Samantha avoided any contact with the authorities and had Fiona whisk her away while Isabella took care of her artwork.  With the arrival of the police, the party came to screeching halt, leaving the constituents of Sister Cities International with a night to remember and a tale to tell for years.

Calle was texting Alby her resignation notice, effective right after the clean-up, when her phone jingled an incoming call.  It was Fiona.  Not having had the chance to touch base the night before, they had a lot to talk about.

"Calle, how are you?" Fiona's concern saturating her voice.

"Getting along.  Alright, all things considered.  How

is Samantha?"

"Better, but still nauseous. She's nursing something she cooked up from her spice rack. Smells worse than boiling roof tar, but she says it will do the trick. How's Lucy?"

"She's okay. She's at home with Polkadot. You know, puppy therapy."

"Sounds better than what Samantha is doing."

"So, what happened? How did you guys know to come to the cemetery?" Calle asked the burning question.

"Well, when Samantha saw Lucy tear off up the mountain after you had disappeared, we figured something was wrong. Samantha somehow knew Clarita was involved, so there we went. We left Phillip in charge."

"Ah... Yeah, she was involved alright, but it was that gorilla, Fen, that damn near killed me."

"I heard."

"If it wasn't for Lucy, I'd be dead." Calle leaned back and twirled a leaf between her fingertips.

"She's pretty tough, she knocked Jamaica out with one punch."

"She told me she took care of her, but not like that. Sheesh! What happened to Clarita? I heard there was no trace of her. Wasn't she trapped in vines or something?" Calle asked.

"She was, but she escaped after Lucy went for you."

"Oh? But Samantha was poisoned. What happened?"

"That's right, she was," Fiona answered hesitantly. "Clarita cornered me and called me stupid."

Calle knew that for Fiona, an insult to her intellect

was worse than spit in the face. "Uh oh. So, then what?"

Fiona went on to summarize the rest of the events, but their conversation was cut short when Calle interrupted.

"Fiona, I gotta go. Here comes the detective. Let's all get together later and compare notes."

"Sounds good." Fiona rang off.

"Ms. Roslyn, good morning. I'm surprised to see you here today," Shawn Ramirez said lightly. "You look much better in the morning sun." He removed his sunglasses and flashed a full-faced grin.

"Thank you," Calle said as she instinctively caressed her bruised cheek. She slipped her phone in her pocket. "I feel better."

"Quite a party you threw here last night."

"Mmm hmm." Was he flirting with her? If so, she wasn't amused and made her irritation was easy to read. She resented his making light of her near-death ordeal.

"You might be glad to know we verified your claim that Fen Kilter was responsible for the murder of Jessica Pérez," he offered as an olive branch for his faux pas.

She eyed him suspiciously.

"We questioned Gloria Pérez and she confessed to everything."

"Hmm, is that so?"

"I guess she didn't count on the advent and accuracy of DNA testing."

"It hardly makes sense. Why would she want to kill her own granddaughter?" Calle puzzled.

"Because Jessica was not her granddaughter. She was the result of her husband's affair with an employee," the detective asserted smartly, then continued.

"Having banished the girl's mother from the estate and back to Costa Rica, she always held a grudge against her step daughter. Years later, when Jessica became pregnant, Gloria saw her chance to remove the illegitimate heir from the bloodline. So, under the guise of an education, she sent Jessica to Pennsylvania to have her baby in secret, but really planned to have Fen kill her before the baby was born."

"So, Lisa Jill was born before Fen killed her mother?"

"Precisely. When Jessica died in the 'accident', Gloria became the baby's legal guardian. As such, she immediately gave the baby up for adoption."

"She didn't know about DNA testing," Call repeated the crux of Gloria's mistake.

"And when Lisa Jill showed up here looking for Otis, her father, Gloria called Fen to finish what they thought had been dealt with twenty years prior."

"Unbelievable. Didn't Otis know Jessica was pregnant with his child?"

"Apparently not, there's no indication he was aware. I don't think any of the family knew. Gloria acted quickly, not wanting to bring anymore shame on the family name and Jessica trusted her."

"Thinking she was her mother, she probably did," Calle said. "Who doesn't trust their mother?"

"You might be surprised," Shawn said with a shake of his head. "At least she's going to spend the rest of her life in prison," he perked up.

It was the typical law enforcement's cliché response that implied justice well served, but it rankled Calle like poison sumac in one's underwear.

Here was an affluent, entitled woman, who

commissioned the murder of an innocent girl that trusted her implicitly and after the crime, went on to live a full and complete privileged life of her own. Then later, she conspired to murder of the rest of the girl's family, not to mention the near success at killing an innocent caterer along the way. Gloria was rotten to the core, and by all accounts, a raging bitch to boot.

There was no telling what other treachery the woman had been a part of and gotten away with over the years. It was enough to make an angel spit. And now, in her decrepitude, she was supposedly being punished by essentially spending the rest of her sorry existence in luxury at a convalescent home for the rich. There was nothing just about it, it was a travesty.

The disgust on Calle's face was unmistakable and her attitude began to sour. She didn't want to crucify the messenger, but the detective was one strike away from dismissal. One more curt or callous comment and the conversation would be over.

Blind self-importance and the desire to impress drove the man onward.

"We made a few other arrests as well," Shawn added self-assuredly.

"Oh?"

"We arrested Jamaica Spinner for repeated trespass and attempted murder, but we haven't tied her to Gloria Pérez. She claims to have killed a witch, but her dart was found in the man who tried to strangle you. We think she's insane, she keeps rambling about magic and the devil. Do you know anything about her?"

"Not really, she didn't like Otis and she's Native American, but I already told you what I know. I don't remember anything else."

"She's not native.  At least she can't prove any affiliation with any tribe.  We've checked before."

"Hmm.  Then I guess I won't be any help.  I thought she was native."

"Did you notice anything unusual, paranormal maybe?  You know, out of the ordinary?" Shawn asked trying to catch her off guard.

Calle laughed inwardly.  Paranormal, to most people meant out of the ordinary, but to her it was as ordinary as cereal for breakfast.

"No, nothing unusual," she said truthfully.

It was his turn for suspicion.  He met her eyes searching for any sign of deceit, but finding none, he smiled and nodded in concession, then continued on with his ulterior motive.

"So, I was thinking maybe we could get together someday for a drink," he segued smoothly like a TV cop on the make.

Strike three, Bozo.

"No, thank you.  I'm seeing someone," she politely declined.  "Sorry, but I really need to get back to work.  Good-bye," she dismissed as she slipped away toward the kitchen, leaving the cop alone with the person she was sure he loved the most.

The conversation with detective Shawn Ramirez proved to be a mixed blessing of sorts.  He had cleared up a few things about the Pérez family and he had shown his true colors as to his interest in her, but of equal importance, he had riled her off her butt and back to work.

Sometimes the best medicine for life's little knuckle balls is to keep busy.  Easy to say and easy to suggest to others, but often times, one needs a little outside motivation to get their blood pumping and their feet moving. With her attitude properly adjusted, Calle joined her crew in the thankless task of the final clean-up.

Calle and Lisa Jill were folding and stacking chairs over by the fountain when one of Jill's prayer cap strings got caught in one of the chairs. It was a good time for a break anyway, so they shuffled into the shade as she removed the lacey head covering and brushed out her long hair while Calle sipped a glass of iced tea.

In her simple, youthful manner, Jill looked like an airbrushed model from a shampoo commercial. It was one of those serendipitous moments where the timing of the universe is in perfect sync. As she silked her slender fingers through her hair, Michael and his mother appeared from behind the fountain and met the young woman face to face. Lisa Jill wasn't accustomed to being seen with her head uncovered and her hair down in public and her innocent embarrassment only made her all the more appealing.

Calle expected the gasp that slipped from Michael's lips, but the astonished reaction by his mother, completely caught her by surprise.

The woman jilted to a halt and her face went ashen as if she was looking at a ghost. Calle thought she might be having a heart attack as Teresa locked eyes with Lisa Jill.

"Holy Mother of Jesus..." she whispered to herself. "Jessica? No, no, I'm sorry..." Teresa was clearly befuddled by the near perfect resemblance Lisa Jill had to her mother, Teresa's half-sister. It was the first time she had ever laid eyes on her niece and the emotion was overwhelming.

"I so sorry," Teresa wailed as she pulled Jill in close for a hug. Never minding her hair or the fact that they had just met, Lisa Jill returned the embrace with tears of her own. For Teresa, it was as if her sister had returned and for Jill, it was as if her mother was alive again. But for both of them, it was a love they both had been denied and needed desperately.

The reunion had drawn the attention of all who were working under the pavilion. Everyone paused to witness the small miracle unfolding before them. Teresa had clearly accepted Lisa Jill into the family and had apologized for her mother's behavior, explaining she had no idea what had happened. Jill could hardly contain her enthusiasm and had a million questions.

As their conversation deepened, Calle ran interference, urging everyone back to work in an effort to give the two some privacy. Teresa suggested going to visit Otis and Jill looked to her boss for permission. Calle smiled and shooed them off with a wave.

As the two chattered and walked away, everyone felt a sense of joy. Everyone except maybe Michael, whose elation was flattened by the realization that the girl he was trying to impress, was actually his cousin. But to Calle's amusement, his disappointment was offset by Verna's delight in the fact that her main competition was finally out of the way. Life and love are funny like that.

# ☽ 27 ☾

Calle bookmarked her latest M.C. Beaton mystery and picked up her phone. She answered and after a few minutes of back and forth, she rang off, satisfied she had done the right thing. Too exhausted to continue reading, she clicked off the light, snuggled Beely a quick good night, then closed her eyes in sleepy contemplation.

The late-night call from Alby begging her to rethink her resignation was the only speedbump she had to hurdle in the days following the Sister Cities International gala at Pérez Mansion. It wasn't that big a deal for her because her mind was made up, but for him, it was an apparent disaster. She had always told him she was just temporary, but he had gotten it in his mind that she was committed to Kokopelli. Having to sternly rebuff his offer of more money and more authority was difficult, but he had to realize she couldn't be there for him anymore. It was over, there was only so much she could do for him.

The conversation reminded her of one of her high school suitors who had refused to accept her rejection of him. He continued to call and bother her for a while, but his childish behavior was to be expected, he was young and immature. She imagined Lucy's long list of men who behaved the same way. Sheesh! Glad she didn't have that extensive of a problem, Calle couldn't help but notice a similarity between all these people.

They all had a problem. A serious issue for themselves that could easily be solved by someone else, so they thought. But they were only thinking of themselves. They completely ignored the needs of those they supposedly cared about. Pretty shallow and selfish actually, but she had to admit, she had once or twice behaved in a similar fashion. She realized it was a common condition brought on by the unavoidable act of being human. The solution? Grow up and face your own problems.

She was feeling very wise for the moment, but as all newly gained wisdom does, it opened the door to more questions. Particularly, what about problems people couldn't solve for themselves? What about the weak or oppressed? What about those that are abused or neglected? What about justice unserved? Wouldn't it be nice if these people had a hero to stand up for them?

Calle thought about Ab Pistola. She was definitely heroic, but even in comic books, heroes can't possibly solve all the world's problems. There are just too damn many. She realized sadly that in order to have the greatest effect, a heroine must choose her battles wisely. One person could only do so much.

As usual, when she thought about Ab Pistola, her thinking naturally swiveled toward herself. What battles would she choose to fight? Instantly, the image of Gloria Pérez popped into her mind.

Maybe an astral visit to that old carp's dreams might be the punishment she deserved. Calle relished the torture she would impose on the woman. If she could find her, she was sure she could repay some of the injustice the woman had dealt out over her lifetime.

It was a delicious thought, but the idea of repaying pain with pain didn't sit well with her. On the other hand, who was going to protect those that can't protect themselves? That quandary dissolved into the ether as she fell into a deep sleep and let fate choose her next battle.

He struggled for escape, but pent-up frustration drove Calle's fingernails deeper into his neck like the talons of a pitiless eagle. She shook him mercilessly, forcing his attention back to her face. Snotty tears smeared his cheeks as he whimpered into submission. She parasitically tapped his evil essence and channeled it back to him as her eyes became crocodilian and her skin scaled into that of a toothy carnivore. Rancid breath tarnished his lips as he recognized his own hatred inches from his soul. A bully is a coward and Howard Lewis was terrified.

"I'm your personal nightmare," Calle sliced a whisper. "Every time you see your nephew, you will think of me. It will be my pleasure to torture you every second of your sleep. I don't care how drunk you get or if you pass out, I will wake you in your sleep and I will delight in your anguish."

Calle couldn't believe her venom, but her disgust of the creature before her unleashed something maternal and fierce within her.

She continued as sure as the Angel of Death himself, "Give Mona full custody and leave Spencer alone. This is my last warning."

Howard was a drunken abuser, but he wasn't a complete fool. When she released him, he stumbled backward, his gaze never leaving her face. It took a second for him to realize he was free. The disconcerted parting look he gave her was enough to convince her that Spencer would be safe from now on, but just in case, she would stop by occasionally to make sure.

She had done what she thought was right, but had she gone too far? That thought catapulted her back into consciousness. Now awake, she lay in the silent darkness of her bedroom and weighed her astral actions.

It was a heady feeling, having that much power over another person. She could see how someone could get addicted to it, but it also felt wrong somehow. People should be able to rationalize things out. Solve their problems by talking, right? But if someone has no respect for others and brutalizes them, harsher measures must be taken. Where does one draw the line?

Had she been too vindictive? Was that justice? Wasn't judgment God's job?

Feeling more like Freddy Krueger than Ab Pistola, she slid from her bed, questioning the morality of what she had just done in her dream.

# ☽ 28 ☾

The next few days were a blessed curse or maybe a cursed blessing, Calle couldn't decide. Three nights of unadulterated, blissful sleep. It is a fact that lucid dreamers often know they are dreaming and for a precious few, those dreams can move out of body, allowing the dreamer amazing abilities. It is also a fact that lucid dreamers need regenerative rest as much as any other living person. In the realm of lucid dreaming and out of body experience, just like most situations in life, when a person desires one thing, they often get another.

So, it was for Calle. After her Ab-like assault on Howard Lewis' dream, she had hit a lull in her supernatural dreamcapades. Working on her daytime meditation in an effort to reach a transcendental state proved to be good practice, but she hadn't achieved her goal. Patience was not her strong suit and her inability to reach Ethan was beginning to irk her to the bone. It was like having her internet service on the blink with no other option and after three nights of astral isolation, frustration was creeping in like a softball player in a hitting slump.

Lucid dreams are a natural phenomenon for many, but the act of exiting your body to roam the astral plane is an extreme rarity. First, it requires an innate natural ability, a little luck, then a great deal of relaxed concentration. The notion sounds contradictory, but it is actually a fine line, like being awake and asleep at the same time. Success requires exceptional balance made available only through excessive mental self-discipline.

One might recognize the pull of an out of body experience when they are asleep and dreaming then feel an urgent need to awaken, but they cannot. It is a terrifying feeling, but if the dreamer can relax and embrace the sensation, they can consciously enter the astral realm and interact there until they lose their balance or awaken, which by the way, produces the same result.

In the course of modern history, extraordinarily few people have ever had that ability and Calle Roslyn was one of them. So, it was natural for her to suspect her recent failures were due to a lack of concentration because that was the one thing that was the most difficult to maintain. She knew frustration would only cloud her focus, so that night, she went to bed knowing the only way out of her slump was to relax, trust her instinct, and keep stepping into the batter's box.

She fell asleep with no expectations and was pleasantly surprised when she went lucid and out of body with hardly any effort. Maybe that was the trick or maybe her spirit and body just needed to rest as one for a while. Whatever the case, she was glad to be free in the astral world again and wasted no time going in search of her mentor.

But who was looking for whom? It was like opening your front door first thing in the morning and there, standing on the porch, was your favorite rock star.

Before she could rise into flight, Ethan's essence

surrounded her as if she were his last breath. He coalesced into his handsome elfin form behind her, wrapping his arms around her waist and pulling her close, teasing her bellybutton with his thumb. Instinctively, she arched her lower back and thrust her pelvis backward, spooning her hips comfortably into the crook of his lap. She softly moaned with pleasure as he kissed and nuzzled his lips up the base of her neck to nibble behind her earlobe.

"I've been waiting for you," he whispered as a tingle tickled down her spine. She waited a second for the sensation to settle in her abdomen then slowly spun to face him. She kissed him full on the mouth and sighed inwardly as he returned her passion. Their spirits began to mingle and her desire mounted. She spread open her soul as their eyes met and he entered tenderly, caressing her like a mother in awe of her newborn child. His sturdy affection kneaded into her steadily like waves on a lonely beach, each growing in strength and intensity until her essence ached with delight. She drew him deeper and matched his rhythm, milking him greedily until her thighs began to spasm and her body quivered. He joined her in climax, suckling to her breast as they swirled together in sweet, creamy ecstasy.

They spent an eternity in delicious rediscovery of each other. Making love with Ethan was beyond anything she had ever experienced on the physical plane. It was a connection so primitive and transparent; she couldn't quite tell where she began and he ended. But she didn't care, it was like their DNA were welded into a single strand. Like an embryo receiving life's basic instructions from its parents. Nothing to hide, nothing unshared, just complete and utter harmony.

As they unwound themselves from each other, it was this connection that made her aware he had something he was burning to reveal. Something important, something serious. Not really a secret, because a secret is impossible to hide between lovers like these. No, it was something he had been avoiding, something essential to their relationship, a truth he wished he didn't have to share. She knew he expected her to ask him about it. So, she did.

"I have something to show you," he replied somberly as he took her by the hand and teleported them inside a dimly lit room by a window opened to overlook a steep canyon. On the bed across the room, tucked beneath a blanket, with his head reclined on pillows, lay a sleeping old man. She could tell he was once quite handsome, but age had taken its toll. Even so, he still had strong features and thick, healthy hair, but he was unwell.

Calle stepped closer into the light to get a better view. Something about him was familiar, but she knew she had never laid eyes on the man before. She felt an instinctive pull and moved to his bedside. Admiring his peaceful expression, she saw laugh lines wrinkled into the corners of his eyes and a grin permanently creased around his lips. *A man in love with life*, she thought as she turned to Ethan for an explanation.

When their eyes met, it all came together like a thunderclap and her heart sank.

"I hoped I would have recovered..." Ethan said heavily.

Calle's eyes bored into his as she grappled to avoid what she had already surmised.

"I wanted you to see me as I truly am before I die,"

he said. "This is what I looked like when I was your age," he gestured to his astral presence. "But this is me as I am now." Her eyes followed his as he glanced to the sleeping old man in the bed.

"I knew you were my soul mate the minute you stepped into my dreams," Ethan emoted. "Age means nothing to the spirit and true love can appear in many forms. When it does, it usually doesn't look like what we thought it would, I think you know that now. I didn't plan to deceive you, but I've been fighting this illness for a long time..."

That's why you avoided meeting me in person, she finished his confession in her head.

"My reading to you was a way for me to leave thoughts in the back of your mind, wisdom that you can use later when I'm gone," he continued like an executor reading a will. "I hope the amulet will help you contact me, but I don't know for sure if it will work. It's all new to me."

His astral aura began to shimmer as he struggled to stave off the inevitable.

"I only restrained you hoping to protect you from the demon, I would never imprison you," he said choosing his last words carefully. "I visited Mathew trying to open his mind to your astral abilities, but I don't think he was convinced. I'm sorry, I want you to be happy..."

Her heart in tatters, she stepped toward him, caressing his cheek with the back of her fingers.

"Good-bye Sweetleaf," he whispered, the words wisping across her spirit like purified droplets of absolute devotion. The unspoken 'I love you' shining urgently from his gorgeous green eyes, his last act as a living human being.

They stared at each other as his spirit dissipated down along a silvery cord attached to the back of his head. His threadlike essence glistened like dew on a spider's web as it drained into the forehead of the sleeping man, uniting Ethan's soul with his body briefly before his eyes opened and a tear spilled down his cheek.

Calle stood alone on the astral plane and watched as Ethan's body seized then fell limp, his eyelids still partially open as if to see death's arrival face to face. Her heart completely shattered, she waited in numb observation as Ethan's ghost emerged from his body like a gypsy moth molting from its chrysalis. As time lost its influence, age rinsed from his features like dust in a drizzle.

She hovered by the handsome young man she fell in love with and followed him as he began to ascend into the ether.

"Come back to me," she pleaded through her tears.

He paused to share a smile of reassurance then glanced an impish grin to her like Huckleberry Finn going to meet Tom Sawyer. An image and final lesson she would cherish for the rest of her life.

Returning his face upward, he then resumed his journey into the afterlife, fading gently into the deep, dark matter of all that is intangible.

She lingered by herself a moment in the room with Ethan's body. It was odd, her living spirit and the physical shell of the man she loved. She pondered the irony for another moment, then caught up in deep introspection, she walked to the window and without looking back, glided off into the night.

As she floated aimlessly above the steep mesas and rocky canyons under the moonlight, she recalled the death of her husband. That dreadful incident sent her into a severe depression that ironically led her to Ethan and her uncanny ability to dream trek in the first place. Ethan's departure from earth was similar to Mark's, but its effect was very different for her. Sure, it stabbed like a mortal wound and would leave a scar, but she was stronger now; she had learned so much from Ethan and she was wiser. It would be difficult, but she would survive.

The silence of her dream trek became crushing. Her sadness and heartbreak began to compress around her and the realization that she was truly alone for the first time on the astral plane hung like an albatross around her neck. She knew she wouldn't relapse into depression, but she was adrift, like a lone survivor orphaned into a sea of uncertainty. She closed her eyes and sailed without purpose into the clouds, thankful no one could see her.

She awoke like dry and crumbled leaves blown to the curb. Her spirit was parched and she knew there wouldn't be any relief in the near future. Life can be harsh that way. She shifted her emotions into low gear and idled forward a second at a time. It was the best she could manage under the circumstances.

A certain calm understanding seeped into her as she contemplated what is and what could never be. It wasn't necessarily good or bad, it simply was. She had to admit she had been lucky. In a world where everything is temporary, she had met and loved her soul mate. For that she was grateful, but the wound was so fresh and so deep, she couldn't help herself.

Everywhere she went and everything she did reminded her of Ethan.

In an effort to escape herself, she called for her cat and they went for a walk under the few remaining stars still twinkling before dawn. He was a perceptive and protective companion, never leaving her the entire day. With him by her side, she began to sort out bits of her future. Later that morning, when she called Matthew to end their relationship, Beely remained within earshot.

She couldn't pretend any longer. She explained that she couldn't handle a distant relationship and that she didn't love him like she thought she should, but fell short in admitting that she couldn't be completely honest with him. Matthew tried to convince her that it could work, but the more he talked, the more she thought of Ethan. The voice over the phone began to grow distant until it became a dull droning in the background.

She had learned a lot about true love and wasn't going to settle for anything less. Mourning Ethan felt better than trying to love Matthew. When she hung up, she was so far over Matthew she couldn't remember if she even said goodbye.

# ☽ 29 ☾

It was hard to imagine thousands of faithful pilgrims walking, sometimes crawling, the wind swept and dusty roads to the Sanctuary, but Calle knew they came in droves each Spring during Holy Week. She'd witnessed the spectacle first hand more than once. But now, she motored serenely along the High Road to Taos by herself admiring the natural towering hoodoos and chiseled landscape on a pilgrimage of her own.

Santuario de Chimayo is a Catholic mission nestled sweetly in the Sangre de Cristos north of Santa Fe. Built at the turn of the nineteenth century, the church is famous for its miraculous healing power, but the legend goes back centuries into Native culture. The holy dirt is said to be able heal any ailment or malady a person of faith might have. Calle was not Catholic, but she was faithful and she knew from prior visits to the property, there was a very real magic about the place.

She wasn't expecting a miracle, she only needed a special place to mourn and meditate. Kissing her fingertips then touching them to the holy inscription on the polished granite stone that greeted parishioners as they entered the Sanctuary, Calle made peace with her ancient past, then found a quiet pew in the back corner and knelt in prayer.

Her prayers started with Ethan, asking for grace

while dealing with her loss, but as all holy places do, the Sanctuary moved her self-pity toward gratitude. Before long, her spirit felt bandaged, not completely healed mind you, but like a soothing salve had been applied to her soul. After several minutes of introspection, she went to the tiny room beside the altar where she filled a small container of holy dirt, then exited to stroll beside the river along the Stations of the Cross.

As she wandered in solitude beneath the cool shade of the cottonwoods, she spun a long blade of grass between her fingertips and contemplated the value of love.

If a person is loves someone, when they die there will be heartbreak. Even if a couple spend a lifetime together, in the end, one of them will mourn the loss of the other. If a couple breaks up, there is always one who suffers. Love by nature, always ends in pain. So, why waste our time pursuing something that will hurt us in the end?

Her reasoning was sound, but what of the virtue of love?

Yes, there is always pain and difficulty, but it is the act of genuine care and concern that makes us better people, we learn about ourselves, we grow. She was sure that true love was transcendent of time and space. Wasn't that the simple truth that anchored the cornerstone of the universe? It's so much grander than one can fully comprehend solely from a physical point of view. Her thoughts rang in her head like a well-polished sermon from a tele-evangelist, but she felt a certain truth to the notion, so she let her train of thought clatter down the rails.

When we hold on too tightly, isn't that when love is

the most painful? It only hurts when we try to contain it. By letting the one we love go free, we can see that love is the most excellent way. In her mind, her thought stream reverberated like a Bible verse.

Love always protects, always trusts, always hopes. It always perseveres and never fades. It is perfection and it lasts forever. Convinced the oracle of the Sanctuary had spoken, Calle struggled to digest the insight and after watching her hand spun grass boat sail down the creek, she hopped in her truck and pointed it homeward.

All the way back to Santa Fe, Calle kept replaying her newly acquired wisdom in her head, but she felt little solace. The logic seemed hollow, just words expressing a lovely sentiment, a consolation prize. She wondered if her love for Ethan would ever feel the way it once did. She seriously doubted it, honestly, how could it possibly? She resigned herself to rely on faith, let her inner guide percolate, and trust that, in time, she would figure it out.

All the wisdom in the world cannot mend a broken heart. Wisdom is a seed that when planted requires time to grow. In the meantime, until its roots take hold and the knowledge becomes steadfast, personal anguish is a constant companion and each day is a trial. Emotional equilibrium is like a gyroscope and once out of balance, it demands time and commitment to regain stability.

So, Calle's personal struggle continued. One moment, pity party deluxe, then a dash of acceptance. She seesawed back and forth like a flag whipping in a dust devil. Each time her grief would swell, her inner guide would remind her of the bigger picture and she would metaphorically spray pesticide on her sorrow hoping to extinguish the pain but not to kill her precious memories. After a few days in a manic stupor, simple peace of mind would be miracle enough.

The day to day with Beely was difficult, but in her dreams was where she felt the pang of sadness the most. Dream trekking had become a lonely endeavor since Ethan died. In fact, without the hope of his company, she felt crippled in the astral realm. She spent most of her dream treks sitting atop the south spire of the cathedral wallowing in her unhappiness, replaying memories of him until her heartache bled. What once was a grand kaleidoscope of adventure had become a pale landscape. Alone is an ugly color and Calle wore it like a wedding dress.

"You know you're scaring those poor people half to death, don't you?" the angelic voice chimed, coming from out of nowhere.

"What?" Calle cast a double take as a beautiful young blonde girl holding a book and a lantern materialized beside her.

"Your moaning and groaning, it's scaring everyone that walks by the church," Isla pointed to a few tourists scurrying nervously away to the other side of the street. "And that last Midnight Mass, well, nobody's going to forget that," she continued with a chuckle. "You're a mess."

Calle downcast her eyes and shrugged a sigh that screamed dejection.

"I'm sorry, I didn't know they could hear me," she said. "I just can't seem to get over Ethan."

"Hmm, I see, maybe you could hang out somewhere else? Like deep in the Pecos wilderness or on the moon,"

Isla smiled.

Was she joking? Calle looked to her guardian angel like she was mad.

"Seriously?"

"Yeah, sure, I suppose..." Isla's cheery face met Calle's dismay. "Or maybe you could try to see things as they really are."

Calle's expression went blank.

"What are you talking about?"

"Ethan isn't gone, he's just dead."

"What?"

"I've got to go check on Cuün," Isla's childish appearance belied the fact she was a very wise and powerful angel. "You think about it."

"What?" Calle was beginning to sound like a broken record.

"What's what? He's been moved to a safer place," Isla playfully redirected. "We couldn't leave a demon chained up to a mausoleum in downtown Santa Fe, could we?"

"I guess not," Calle replied trying to keep up as Isla disappeared as mysteriously as she had appeared.

Calle sat in confusion for a second then glanced down at a man on the sidewalk wearing a sous chef uniform who was pointing a camera in her direction. She knew he couldn't possibly see her, but most probably had heard her. In that instant, she realized Isla was right. She had a new perspective and a lot to think about. Heeding her cherubic guardian's advice, she eased into flight and zipped up over the mountain into the wilderness to watch moonlit brook trout swirl lazily in the river, shucking her mourning dress along the way because it just didn't seem to fit anymore.

# ☽ EPILOGUE ☾

Calle approached her mailbox like the bomb squad investigating a suspicious backpack at the shopping mall. It had been a couple weeks since Clarita's death, but she wasn't taking any chances.

Standing to the side, worried about the potential lingering effects of a hex, she prodded the latch open with a juniper branch. Cautiously, she snuck a peek inside.

"Looks good Beeler," she said in relief as her cat sat and sniffed tiny white flowers blossoming nearby. He looked to her with nonchalant body language that implied, "I never had a doubt."

"Hey, I got a package from an attorney," she said, her spirits rising as she flipped the mailbox closed and trotted off to her casita, leaving Beely to sit unmoved, seemingly fascinated by the aroma of the flowers.

She plopped herself on the couch and dug into the package like a kid on Christmas Day. The package contained a stuffed manilla envelope and a small cedar box. Inside the envelope was a copy of Ethan's will. Most of his estate was given to charity, but he had bequeathed to her a sizable tract of raw land near the Valle Grande caldera. In the correspondence, it was indicated that she already had the keys and could claim ownership immediately.

Keys? What keys? She picked up the simple cedar box and spun it in her hands like a Rubric's cube trying to figure out how to open it. She needed a key for that too. She held the box to her ear and shook it hoping the noise would give her a clue about what was inside. Not a chance, it sounded empty.

She leaned back, closed her eyes, and tried to remember any keys, but there had been so much that had happened as of late, she couldn't remember any keys. Her mind spun through the events. The Sister Cities convention, Pérez mansion, Otis, Lisa Jill, Lucy's dream, the trip to Portales, the break in, dead rats, magic, demons, Ethan's death, it was all a jumble, but no idea as the whereabouts of any keys. Maybe 'keys' was a metaphor for something else, a secret puzzle to be solved. *Hmm...*

She chuckled under her breath as a vision of her elderly self dottering around merrily in senility, looking for lost or nonexistent items, crossed her mind. *Already well on my way*, she thought as she placed the box on the coffee table next to the will. *I wonder if Isla will still be looking out for me when I'm old and dim?*

That thought accompanied her into the bedroom where she picked up her medallion. Isla had returned and there, etched in the face of fine porcelain talisman, she stood holding out her lantern, gazing over the peaceful horizon indicating that all was well. Calle took solace knowing her guardian angel was on duty and placed the pendant back into her wicker basket of treasures right on top of the keys Barrow had given her a month ago.

So caught up in her thoughts about Isla, she almost overlooked the obvious. Like her uncle used to say, "If it had been a snake, it would have bit you." Overjoyed, she hustled back to the cedar box and using one of the keys, opened it with a click.

Inside, wrapped in tissue paper, was the amulet Ethan had shown her when he was reading to her in her dreams and a handwritten note that read, "Come visit me."

Elated, she slipped the amulet around her neck and went to admire it in the mirror. It was a beautiful faceted garnet baled onto a soft leather lanyard and it looked wonderful, but if it was magic, she felt nothing. Disappointed, she went back to the note and contemplated its message. Seconds later, she was on the phone with Lucy, they had to go to the Jemez Mountains.

"I don't know where he is actually," Calle replied early the next morning as they motored north past Camel Rock Casino. "But I think the answer is at Ethan's property."

"Your property, you mean," Lucy corrected.

"Yeah, I guess so." Calle glanced to her friend then into her side mirror as they passed a lumbering motorhome towing a compact car. "But it hardly sounds real yet," she added as they sped toward her inheritance.

"I hope we find the right forest road; I'd hate to drive around all day looking for it."

"Isn't Barrow supposed to be there?"

"That's what the note said, but he doesn't know when we're coming," Calle said doubtfully.

"I wouldn't worry about that. He seems to find you anywhere you go."

"That's true. He's kind of weird that way."

"Even if, by some chance, we miss him, we still have a picnic lunch and it's always good to get out into nature. If nothing else, it will be a fun day trip, right?" Lucy encouraged.

The conversation waned then briefly picked up again as they passed Bandelier National Monument. It was impossible to drive by the ancient landscape without talking about the cliff dwellings and the one hundred forty feet of death-defying ladders scaling the cliff face on the way to the Ceremonial Cave. Besides, it was a pleasant distraction from the errand they were on, but after that, the rest of the drive was quiet except for the *Urban Cowboy* soundtrack playing softly in the background. When they turned into a thicketed forest road and crossed a cattleguard, Calle broke the silence.

"I think this is it."

"Now what?" Lucy asked.

"I don't know," Calle said as they pulled into a small clearing about fifty yards from the highway. "Let's get out and stretch our legs."

After a few minutes and a visit to the bushes, the women sat on the tail gate and waited as the animals of the forest relaxed back into their routine. The stillness was interrupted by a squirrel bustling in the pine canopy and the rat-ta-tat-tat of a flicker banging on the bark of a piñon snag looking for beetles. A flutter of violet butterflies stopped to drink from the mud puddled in the rut of the road as a pair of hummingbirds zinged by in a jubilant frenzy. The breeze picked up slightly as the forest accepted the visitors, welcoming their company.

Lucy laid back in the bed of the truck, swinging her feet off the tailgate until she had nearly fallen asleep as Calle began to second guess herself. She wondered if Barrow would be able to find them or maybe she had been too impulsive, leading her friend on a fool's errand. Just as she was about to suggest they move on, Barrow swooped to a silent landing on her shoulder.

His stealthy arrival startled her, but the excitement of their reunion made her laugh out loud.

"You scared the crap out of me, you little bugger," Calle giggled as she fished a peanut from her pocket. Barrow took the peanut and flitted to a nearby tree stump to crack it open as Lucy sat up to join the conversation.

"That's amazing," Lucy said.

"What?"

"The bird," she nodded Barrow's direction. "There's never a dull moment around you."

"What can I say? Sorry."

"No, I mean it's totally cool," Lucy smiled. "You're the most interesting person I've ever met."

"Most people think I'm weird."

"Well, yeah, there is that, but you're my kinda weird, so, I guess I'll let you stick around a little longer," Lucy laughed.

"Thanks? I guess, sheesh."

When Lucy hopped off the back of the truck, Barrow jumped into flight, landing in a scrub oak a short distance down the road. He fluffed out his feathers briefly and scrunched his topknot on end then relaxed it back. He fluttered his wings then cast his emerald gaze to the women and back down the road again.

"I think that's our cue," Calle said as they loaded into the cab and idled down the path following the blue jay deep into the forest.

After several miles of narrow undulating two track road, the trail petered out into a rough rut with jagged rocks jutting up from the ground. Barrow flew to the knoll at the top of the severe rocky stretch and waited for them to follow. He squawked impatiently when Calle slowed the truck to a stop at the bottom to choose a line up the treacherous trail.

"Hang on a minute!" she hollered out her window. "Pushy little tyrant, isn't he?"

"Yeah, but it's easy for him, he doesn't have to worry about popping a tire or poking a hole in the oil pan," Lucy said.

"I know, right?" Calle added as she shifted her truck into four low. "Thank goodness for skid plates. Here we go."

"Good thing you've got four-wheel drive," Lucy chuckled as she hung on for dear life as the truck muscled up the bumpy trail.

"Yahroo!" Calle's yell was accompanied by Lucy's "Yeehaw!" as they crested the rocky hill and began a descent into an overgrown, jaw breaking, and forgotten path. Like a dam beginning to crack, their childish enthusiasm loosened the icy underlying sorrow, that for days, had been building. Every jarring bounce and each silly joke that followed inched them away from their loss and further down the road to recovery.

It was hard to gauge distance as they idled along after Barrow. Him flitting ahead a few yards amongst the branches, them slowly picking their way through dense underbrush and small boulders. After about an hour, the forest had grown impenetrable as the Steller's jay led them to a small meadow just large enough to park the truck.

"Looks like it's the end of the road," Calle observed as she turned off the ignition.

"Thank god, I think I bruised a kidney," Lucy clowned as they piled out of the truck.

Solid, unmoving ground felt good beneath their feet as they stretched and found their land legs again.

"I bet there hasn't been anyone here in decades," Lucy said. "If ever."

"I know, it looks like a place where you might run into Indiana Jones."

"Well, I didn't bring a whip, so I hope it's not as dangerous as that."

"Wait, I've got bear spray in the truck," Calle said as she went to shuffle things around in the extended cab. "Here we go," she added just as Barrow called from a lopsided blue spruce.

"I guess we're on foot from here," Lucy said as they grabbed their backpacks and hiked after their bossy feathered guide.

Several twists, turns, and nettles later, they came upon a cattle gate hung in a rusty barbed wire fence. It was very old, strangled in ivy, and chained shut with a locked padlock. Calle pulled out the keys Barrow had given her and slipped one inside the mechanism and turned. She thought it a minor miracle when the lock sprung open easily. It proved harder to dislodge the partially buried gate and shove it back enough for them to enter, but after a minute of finagling, it tilted ajar a bit and they squeezed through.

"Welcome home," Lucy jibed as the two trudged up and over a rise to come to a clearing on the edge of a cliff. The view was magnificent and sprawled northward with a majestic towering volcanic neck projecting from the earth and a crystalline lake nestled in the valley behind and below. The multi-faceted desert landscape stretched on for miles and miles until it melded into a light blue skyline.

The kindred companions stood in awe of the scene as Barrow hopped off into the aspen canopy, his job seemingly finished for now.

Lucy sidled up to Calle and pointed across the fantastic expanse spread out in front of them.

"That's El Pedernal," she said gesturing to the volcanic neck. "And that's Abiquiu lake, see the dam right there? That's Colorado on the horizon and there's Ghost Ranch where Georgia O'Keefe used to hang out."

"Wow," Calle mouthed.

"The natives gather flint and obsidian from El Pedernal and knap it into arrowheads. It's a sacred place," Lucy added sagely, drawing from her extensive New Mexican heritage. "Much like I think this place is too," she continued as she directed Calle's attention to the long spacious ledge along the cliff on which they were standing. The cry of a bald eagle soaring overhead drew their gaze back out over the open space yawning endlessly before them.

"So, this is my inheritance," Calle said. "It's spectacular, but it's pretty primitive and inaccessible for the most part."

"Unless you can fly," Lucy teased as she watched another eagle catch a thermal and sail upward.

The jibe went unheeded because Calle suddenly understood the meaning and magnitude of Ethan's gift. A wave of sadness washed over her as her heart cried out for her deceased astral lover and mentor. She loved to fly and he knew it. The place was perfect for an astral dreamer and she realized it must have been special for him as well. It instantly became precious to her and over time, it would become her favorite refuge.

Lucy noticed Calle's change of spirit and went to stand close to her. She wiped a tear from Calle's cheek, took her by the hand, and suggested, "Let's go see the rest of it, okay?"

Calle followed like a child who just fell off the swing set, but her melancholy retreated as they entered an ancient makeshift graveyard. The burial ground was set away from the edge of the precipice, tucked unevenly into the shimmering aspens, but close enough to feel the wind bluster up the face of the crag.

There were a number of indistinct graves spread about, some unscripted, some plain stone markers, and a few decaying wooden crosses. The space was littered with interesting artifacts stationed haphazardly about the area. If the items were related to the inhabitants of the cemetery, the women were unable to make the connection. Amongst other things, some of the objects they noticed were a dented WWI army helmet, an ancient spyglass with a cracked lens, a worn leather quiver of three handmade arrows, a pair of red, weathered women's dress shoes, and a rusted tin coffee can full of tarnished pennies.

They shared a look of wonder as they wandered further inward.

"We sure spend a lot of time in cemeteries," Lucy ventured.

"Seems that way, doesn't it?" Calle countered, as their words dissolved into the forest.

Lucy moved deeper into the graveyard while Calle searched nearer to the footpath along the edge of the cliff as the cool breeze purred through the leaves.

"Was he buried or cremated?"

"Good question. I don't know," Calle replied.

"I mean, there's no freshly turned dirt or footprints. It doesn't look like anyone's been here recently. It's completely undisturbed. How did he get up here anyway?"

"I have no idea, but then again, there's a lot about him I didn't know."

"Ah, so... Okay," Lucy replied, learning to accept the illogical things that seemed to follow her friend everywhere she went.

On the periphery of the cemetery, with a clear view of the horizon, Calle found the grave she was looking for. It was a simple trapezoidal flagstone lying flat on the earth with the words 'Ethan Lent' etched into the grain. She thought it fitting the epitaph was open ended, no beginning, no end.

She froze when she spied an envelope on the ground next to the grave held down by a smooth river stone. It was addressed to 'Sweetleaf'. Her thoughts began to flutter as she reached to pick up the note, but she was startled out of her musings when a long millipede uncurled from under the stationary and came to life. Like an armored sentinel delivering a salute, it circled once, then marched off into the mossy undergrowth.

Having noticed her friend's movements, Lucy joined her side as Calle opened the envelope. Inside, a single page with a single line, written in slightly slanted, handprinted prose read the words: *The key is here.*

Lucy didn't understand the statement, but she didn't pry, instead she let the moment pass as private. Standing close in emotional support, she watched as

Calle placidly folded the note and returned it to the envelope which she tucked into her pocket. Calle's eyes lost focus on the physical as her thoughts spun through her treasured memories. Lucy knew it was a secret between lovers and if one day Calle decided to share the meaning, she would be waiting.

"I'm so sorry about Ethan," she whispered.

The comment didn't register for a moment, but a second later Calle responded.

"Oh, my..." Calle said as she popped out of her revelry and stumbled back to the moment. "And I'm sorry about Rey," she said as she took Lucy's hand and empathy swelled between them.

The situation hung heavy, but the tender exchange reminded them that they were not alone in their grief. Instead, there they stood, two astral widows facing heartbreak and uncertainty together as best friends with a special love all their own. They would endure, together they would be alright.

It was Lucy who busted from the gloom with her characteristic sarcasm.

"Well, if we're done feeling sorry for ourselves, let's have lunch," she said as her fingers slid from Calle's grasp.

And with that, they shed their sorrow and spent the rest of the afternoon eagerly exploring Calle's new property and gossiping over a splendid picnic banquet.

Intrinsically, she knew what he meant. And since she had spent all day there with her dearest friend, she would never have a problem returning. But going there for the first time in spirit only was like going on her first date. She was nervous about everything.

She checked her teeth and hair twice before slipping on her comfy Arizona State t-shirt and slipping into bed. She wanted everything just right. Not that her physical appearance would matter all that much to a ghost, but a girl has to be ready.

Anticipation is often more thrilling than the actual event and the anxious energy it creates is like a ball of static electricity crackling in one's tummy. Like a toddler trying to wait patiently for Santa Claus, Calle tossed and turned until Beely had to abandon ship for a calmer place to rest. He watched from the dresser as his human grappled with herself until she finally wore herself to a frazzle and fell asleep. Satisfied the coast was clear, he returned to her side with a reassuring nuzzle to her cheek and a soft purr in his throat. He snuggled to her breast on watch as she floated aloft in her dream.

She tried to take her time, but in an astral instant, she was standing over Ethan's grave. Her essence shimmered beneath the enchanted New Mexico moonbeams as she reached down to pick up the spectral skeleton key lying where she had found the note earlier. With the key in hand, she knew what she had to do.

Hovering over her sleeping body was always surreal. It was downright creepy actually, but seeing Beely curled up next to herself comforted her. Turning her attention to the cedar box, she slid the astral key into the lock. She felt like Pandora as she turned the mechanism and the lid opened without a sound. Not knowing what to expect, she was pleasantly surprised when inside what was an empty box on the physical plane, lay the astral twin of the amulet hanging around her neck.

As she reached for the treasure, she spied the silver feathered ring she wore on her astral thumb, another cherished gift from her beloved. Irony washed over her as she picked up Ethan's most recent incorporeal gift and placed over her head and around her neck. With the halves of the talisman in place, they connected.

She wasn't sure what, but something on the astral plane shifted. A door opened. Like an elevator coming to rest on another floor, the environment was different, fresher maybe, but subtle, yet powerful. Before she could put her finger on just what had changed, she felt his presence.

"I always thought it was a lovely necklace, but on you, it's magnificent. The heavens pale next to your beauty."

"Oh, Ethan," she said as she spun into his arms.

He met her desire as tears flowed freely down her cheeks. Their spirits joined in flight as they sped through the night sharing thoughts and feelings as effortlessly as if they were one. Their love making deepened as he shared newly learned truths about the afterlife.

The sentiment filled her with an eternal righteousness that sweetened her soul, but was too timeless for her to fully comprehend, but not so secret it didn't tease her imagination. She didn't have to know; she didn't even care to know. She could feel. Lost in each other, they wove a delicate, lacy fabric of exotic bliss that bound them beyond what mere words can describe. A love so pure, it transcended space and time.

But alas, Calle was only human. Her lover might not have been a slave to time any longer, but she still bore the shackles. And as with anything related to the living, there is always a beginning and there is always an end. So, it was with her dream and her ecstasy with Ethan.

He explained that the amulet would only grant them this time together once. It was temporary. So, when her dream ended, so would his visit. He would be returned to the ether permanently and she to her physical life. But he assured her that in the future, the amulet would allow her to access the lessons and wisdom he shared when he had read to her. And if they were lucky, it might serve as a portal for him to visit sometime in her dreams. Of that, he wasn't certain, but strangely enough, only time would tell.

They spent the rest of their time together as one might expect. Afraid of the finality of the moment, they intermingled and touched each other's soul in ways that defied ordinary imagination. Desperate to show each other the full extent of their love, they risked everything, readily submitting to fantasies that in the flesh would certainly cause cardiac arrest. Reckless in lust and madly in love, nothing was taboo. They laughed like drunken gypsies and loved like there was no tomorrow until they were emotionally exhausted, then collapsed peacefully into each other's arms.

Thoroughly satisfied and spiritually spent, they relaxed at his grave until Calle began to nod out. Like a drowning sailor bobbing in the ocean, she fought to remain afloat, but their time was over, her dream had come to an end. Ethan coiled around her as her spirit dissipated from his grasp and she drifted back to her body. His heartbreak was so severe, it shook the earth beneath the Valle Grande caldera causing windows to rattle and drinks to spill in nearby villages as the magic of the amulet ushered him from the astral plane.

Waking up is a lot like falling asleep. You fall asleep in your dream and wake up in your bed. It happens so naturally and so comfortably; you hardly notice you have shifted planes.

Calle didn't need to open her eyes to know the dream was over. She intentionally kept them shut savoring the lingering elation of Ethan's company. Lying there in the warmth of her comfy bed, she wrapped an arm around her cat and basked in the brief clarity that a sweet dream affords the newly awakened dreamer.

Something was different though, her miraculous time with Ethan had changed her somehow. She could feel it in her soul. A secure calmness engulfed her being, a certain understanding grew inside her. The sensation was so strange and unique, she thought she could feel it tickle just below her belly button like jovial butterflies trying to well up from within her.

The feeling was a welcome relief from the heavyweight grief that had been suffocating her. Ethan was gone for good, but his love remained. Where there is love, there is a way. Granted, it would most likely manifest itself as something unexpected, but it would persevere.

Beely stretched, then repositioned himself with his head on her shoulder, his fervent sapphire gaze watching every expression that crossed her face as she pondered love once again.

Her thoughts began to cascade. True love might be difficult and sometimes painful, but its effect is irreversible. It is a cumulative gift passed between people that steadily grows and improves humanity with each passing generation.

She knew she was on to something as her thinking moved to a tangent. Love is often confused with sex. Both are very powerful, but they are entirely different. Sex is primal, physically essential. It can be used to express love, but more often, it is used to satisfy a carnal desire, a means to an end. Love, on the other hand, is transcendent. It is spiritually driven and comes from the soul. It lingers and its effect is felt long after the physical has decayed. That, she knew for a fact, she was a living example.

She considered the many different and sometimes unpredictable ways love could be displayed. Recent events came to mind. Rey's sacrifice for Lucy, Mona's commitment to Spencer, Fen's loyalty to Gloria. Her thoughts then began to snowball around her own personal interaction with the virtue. Ethan's unconditional acceptance of her, Lucy saving her life, her mother's unflappable devotion, and even her offer to trade herself to Cuün for Lucy's safety.

She realized some form of love could be found in just about everyone and everything. It is many things to many people. It comes in large bouquets and tiny unspoken promises, but there is no greater love than when someone risks their own life for the sake of another.

Her introspection began to ease as she got out of bed and considered her future. She accepted that things were different, but she was confident she could handle the change. Afterall, wasn't change the only true constant in life? As she started her morning routine, she wondered if she would ever share love again with another on this plane. It was a possibility, but if not, so be it. It wasn't a priority and she was already way ahead of the game.

Beely had returned from his sunrise patrol and was currently spread eagle on the grass in the backyard soaking up the sun when she fired up her tablet. *What a weird cat*, she thought as she opened her email. With so much going on lately, she hadn't checked her messages in a while. She took a healthy quaff of coffee as she deleted the spam that overpopulated her inbox.

There was a reason she didn't check her email very often. She rarely got anything interesting. She used to have friends who would send funny jokes from time to time, but she hadn't received anything worth reading in months. She was about to give up when a message from *Dreamy1* via Ancestry.com caught her eye. When she opened the file, her heart stumbled midbeat.

She had a DNA match. A 99.9 % accurate DNA match. She had a sister.

# ACKNOWLEDGEMENT

A special thanks goes out to the City of Santa Fe, the oldest and highest state capital in the United States. The City Different and the surrounding area is the backdrop for this story and plays an important role in its telling. I especially would like to express my appreciation to the many wonderful restaurants, galleries, historic places, and events that operate daily with exemplary class and professionalism. Most importantly, a sincere shout out to the colorful and entertaining locals of town. It is you folks that make Santa Fe the gem we all love and cherish.

My utmost appreciation goes out to frenta, Binkski, Somail, justdd, and hannadarzy at CanStockPhoto.com for the spectacular original photos used on the cover.

Many thanks to Lara Harrison. If there is such a thing as a book angel, it has to be you.

Also, I would like to thank all the family, friends, and colleagues, past and present, that have supported and enlightened me over the years. It's been my honor to have shared your company and learned from you. Any historical inconsistencies that may appear in this story are all on me and my imagination.

Finally, many thanks to those who like to read. I hope you enjoy this book. You're an inspiration to people like me. You are the reason we authors write in the first place.

# ABOUT THE AUTHOR

## Jacob Janey

As an ex-math teacher born and raised in New Mexico, I came into this world on Abraham Lincoln's birthday. Unlike Honest Abe, I come from a long line of embellishers and exaggerators. One might call them liars and there might be some truth  to all that, but one thing is for certain, they were excellent story weavers. Especially on the fly and in a pinch. So, it's safe to say fiction is in my blood.

JacobJaney@gmail,com

Please leave a review at Amazon.com or Goodreads.com

Thank you!

# BOOKS BY THIS AUTHOR

## Little Big Dreams

Mayhem erupts in this paranormal thriller when lucid dreamer Calle Roslyn finds a man murdered in her closet and sexy new lover in her dreams.

Made in the USA
Columbia, SC
05 August 2022

64374355R10207